FREEGIFT

Also by James R. Benn

Billy Boyle World War II Mystery Series

Billy Boyle
The First Wave
Evil for Evil
Rag and Bone
A Mortal Terror
Death's Door
A Blind Goddess
The Rest is Silence
The White Ghost
Blue Madonna
The Devouring
Solemn Graves
When Hell Struck Twelve
The Red Horse
Road of Bones
From the Shadows

Stand Alone Novels

On Desperate Ground
Souvenir
Shard

FREEGIFT

by

James R. Benn

Ranger Publications
Bradenton, FL

Ranger Publications

First Printing, 2022

ISBN: 978-1-7379472-2-6 Print Paperback
ISBN: 978-1-7379472-3-3 E-Book EPUB

Dedicated to my wife, Deborah Mandel.

As always and forever.

FREEGIFT

· One ·

⊢——⊣

Your mother is dying, lad."

"I know she is, Mr. Stoddard," I say, setting another log on the stump. I swing the heavy maul and split the oak neatly. One piece bounces toward Mr. Stoddard, and he jumps aside, nimble enough for a man with pale wrinkled skin and patchy white hair.

"Sorry, sir," I say, apologizing for the length of firewood that nearly took him in the shin. For as he owns me, I must be careful of my actions and of any accident he might think malicious. Ira Stoddard is a good enough man, I believe, but I do labor to give him no reason to prove himself otherwise. As for my mother, she has been dying for weeks now. Mr. Stoddard is a man of few words, and I am surprised he used this handful for something so obvious.

"No, I mean now," he says. Gently phrased, as is the hand on my shoulder gently placed. I wish to turn away from his touch, but as I said, he owns me, and can do what he wishes with his property. Gentle, firm, or vicious. "Go to her."

I obey. I pass the pigs, snuffling through the mud behind the split-rail fence I made last year. Before Maame took sick. Bilious fever is the name they gave it. Near as I can tell, that's what they call what they don't know. All I know is that she's wasting away, fever sweating the life out of her.

I fear her death.

I open the rooms where we live, built off the back of the house, space enough for two narrow bedrooms and a spot to sit by the fire. Maame sat in that old rocker by the hearth, shivering in the heat and sweltering in the cold, until one morning she couldn't rise from her bed.

Eight days ago. Eight days abed, hardly able to eat.

I am afraid to enter her bedroom, but I know I must. She is all I care for in the world, the only person close to my heart, and I cannot bear that she may depart it alone. My hand trembles as I push open the door, and my senses rebel against the stench. Maria, a Mohegan servant girl of eight or nine years, darts out of the room with a basket of soiled clothes.

"Freegift," Maame whispers. She tries to raise her thin, bony arms to greet me, but they fall back, defeated, onto the worn quilt she'd made from scraps when I was a little boy.

"Maame," I say, kneeling at her bedside and grasping her hand. I try to smile as I feel the bones beneath skin like brittle paper. "I'm here."

"My time has come, son. I'm sorry to leave you, but the spirits are calling me home. I can feel them now," she says, her other hand over her heart as if to still it at the joy of seeing her ancestors. Her eyelids flutter, and I wonder, is this the moment?

"Home to Akan," I say, thinking of all the stories she has told me. Stories of our African homeland her father had handed down to her and her brother on these strange shores.

"Yes, Kwasi," she whispers, using my secret name. No one else knows it, and I wonder if I'll ever hear it spoken again. Her breath is ragged, and her eyelids give up their dance and close.

"Tell me about our people," I say, caressing her hand, willing her to stay. I am unsure about spirits, gods, or ancestors, but I know she loves these stories.

"No, there is something else," she says, her voice so very faint. "Help me sit up. I must tell you a new story."

"Maame, you should rest."

"No, help me, Freegift, now." I hear the old iron in her voice, and it is not to be denied. I lift her shoulders and get her sitting against the headboard, the pillow cushioning her head. She has the weight of a sparrow.

"What story?" I ask, pulling a stool next to the bed and leaning in, our faces inches apart.

"The story of your name and how you came to have it," she says, a heavy sigh escaping her throat.

"Kwasi is my day name, I know that, Maame," I say. The Akan have many names, and one is based on the day of the week you are born. I am Monday's child, Kwasi, and my destiny is to protect my family. But there is nothing I can do to protect Maame, and no family left at all after her.

"No, I mean Freegift. Have you not wondered about it?"

"It is just a name. Not a common one, but I've heard stranger," I say, mystified. "Why?"

"It has to do with your father."

"You never spoke of him," I stammer, confused and surprised. "About who he was." Maame always refused every question I ever asked. So much so that I had given up. Besides, one look at her dark black skin and my lighter brown color told me all I needed to know.

"I should have, Kwasi. But there would have been no reason to. Now, there is."

"I don't care about him, I care about you," I mutter, turning away so she won't see the tears welling in my eyes. I am eighteen years of age as of a month ago, and it is unseemly for a man to weep.

"I must tell you about your father. Before it is too late," she says.

"What does it matter?" I ask, trying to keep the anger from my voice. "When you're gone, I'll still be a slave. What can I do?" Many times I thought about taking my vengeance upon the man who abused Maame, but it was nothing more than a daydream, a child's fantasy. I know that if I raise my hand against a white man, flogging is the least I would get.

"It does matter, please trust me, Kwasi," she says, smiling with a grace evident even through her suffering.

"Yes, Maame," I say, willing myself to be silent and listen, if it gives her peace.

"Freegift is an unusual name," she says. "But not to your father. It was his great-grandfather's given name." She coughs and leans forward, gasping for air. Her lungs draw it in, and she falls back, exhausted, her hand covering her mouth.

"Then why give it to me?" I want to know and cannot wait for her to regain control.

"So he might take notice when you tell him your name. He held his great-granddaddy in high esteem, and the name will not go unremarked." Her hand comes away from her mouth, and she rubs a stain of red from her palm.

"It is nothing but a name, Maame. Anyone might have it," I say, pretending I did not see.

"Some might, yes, but those gray eyes of yours, those are his as well. And your long nose, too." She lifts a hand to stroke my face, as if I were still a babe.

"Who is this man?" I hold back the rage I feel at the back of my throat. Rage at what he'd done, and how powerless I am to avenge it.

"He is a famous man," she says, her voice weaker now. "Or once was."

"Who?" I ask, leaning forward with my hands clasped, as if I might pray. Which I never do.

"He's a general. By the name of Benedict Arnold."

"What?" I laugh, in spite of myself. With my mother on her deathbed, I laugh in disbelief, and am ashamed at my unseemly display. But still, I ask, "Why tell me this?"

"Because it is the truth. I want you to find your father and make yourself known to him," she says. "Promise me."

"Maame," I whisper, glancing to the door, making sure no one might hear. "I can't run away. You know that." I am horrified. Maame lies dying and tells me to run off and risk the agonies of the lash, if not death itself. It makes no sense. They'll hunt me down, whip me hard, and Mr. Stoddard will sell me off to the Indies where they work runaways to death.

"Don't you worry about that, Kwasi," she says, handing me a folded piece of paper. "Take this. It's part of the story. Show it to Benedict."

I pull back, startled at her use of his given name, as if they were familiar, and she had leave to call him anything but master. I hesitate to read it, but curiosity wins out and I unfold the paper. Within is a torn bit of newsprint. From the New London Summary, dated July 17, 1763.

To be sold, for no fault but being saucy. Likely Negro man and his sister, with her two-month old child. The fellow able-bodied and good with farm work. The wench good at kitchen work.

Inquire of the Printer.

"Is that me?" I ask. "The child?"

"Yes. And the man is my brother Akú. They called him Cato. Bury me next to him, do you promise?"

"Yes, Maame. I promise. But I cannot go to General Arnold. It is impossible, even for a free man. He's with the British in New York, a hundred and fifty miles distant. Redcoats and Continental militia stop anyone from crossing the lines, they say."

"You must find your way to him, Kwasi. Otherwise you will be adrift in this place, so far from home, with no kinfolk," Maame says, both her hands gripping mine. She pulls herself up and stares me square in the eyes. "It is your destiny to seek him, this much I know, no matter how many miles there are between you, no matter how many obstacles.

When you find him, show him the paper. And tell him Sally remembers the shade of the locust tree behind the barn. No one else knows of that."

"Maame, what happened with Arnold? Everyone hates him and calls him a scoundrel. Did he force himself on you?" Blood rushes to my face. I am angry to think of what passed beneath that tree, and embarrassed that we speak of it so openly.

"I was a slave. He was the master, and he knew what he wanted. He was not mean, not violent, but I had little choice in the matter. If I rebuffed him, things would have gone badly for me, sooner or later. But, I came away with something valuable. You, my son." She drops back onto the pillow, a loving smile lighting her face.

"Maame," is all I can say. Tears course down my cheeks, and there is little I can do about it. I let them fall on her hand.

"If that message of what I remember allows him to see his past deeds in a better light, it may do you some good, Kwasi. Remember, we must use what we can to gain what we want in this world of slave and master, African and Englishman. Appeal to his vanity as the kindly lord of the manor. He was no lord, but at times he did show kindness."

"But then he sold you. Us."

"His father did. The family fell on hard times. His mother died, and his father turned to drink. He became a useless drunkard and squandered much of what they had, finally sending us to auction. Benedict never knew you were his child."

"Why, Maame? He might have kept us."

"Why? Because I was afraid he would keep only you, Kwasi. That you would never know your mother and uncle, never hear the stories of your people. Now the stories are here," she says, tapping at my heart with her hand, which falls lazily at her side.

"Maame?" I shake her, unwilling to let her go at the very moment she reveals the greatest mystery of my life, setting out great truths before me, then leaving them forever unknowable. I am a starving man, brought before a banquet table in chains. I want so much. I have nothing.

"Kwasi," she murmurs, her eyes half open.

"I am here, Maame," I say, clasping both of her bony hands in mine.

"Make your way to New London town," she whispers, her voice raspy and faint. "In the North Parish. Hardwick Farm. Topheny. Find Topheny. She will help you."

Her eyes open wide, looking at me, then beyond. I turn to see who came into the room. There is no one.

No one I can see.

A gasp of breath escapes her lungs. Nothing is drawn back in.

Maame is still.

Maame is dead. I place her hands across her heart, and brush my fingers over her eyelids, as I have seen her do, surprised at how easily they are moved. I hope she finds her ancestors, not that they have been of any help to us. But I know she will find comfort with her father, who meant so much to her. I almost laugh once more, thinking it will be easier for her to seek her agya in the spirit world than it will be for me to seek mine in New York.

But the mirth sticks in my throat, and I despair.

I am abandoned, left alone with tales of my famous English father and the unknown name Topheny. And me enslaved, in the northeastern fields of Connecticut, so far from Akan.

· Two ·

⊢——⊣

I tell Mr. Stoddard Maame has died. Sally, I call her, the English name he knows her by.

"I'm sorry, Freegift," he says. "She was a good woman." He sits back on his shaving horse, wiping his brow, and surveys the stave he'd been working on. It looks perfect to me, ready to join its mates in the making of a barrel. Still, he puts it down and works his heading knife on it a few more times. It's a fine spring day, warm even in the shade of the lean-to where most of the wood work is done.

"Yes sir, she was," I say, knowing that such a compliment must be acknowledged. But of course he thinks of her as a good woman, a good servant. Such is a slave's daily bread—the content master.

"You'll want her buried soon," he says. "I've set aside some planks for a coffin." He nods in the direction of a pile of yellow pine near the barn.

"Are you sure, Mr. Stoddard? Those are fine pieces."

"Good pine for a good woman. Best get to it, Freegift. Tomorrow's the Sabbath. Much work to be done today."

"Yes sir," I say, heading for the toolshed. I stop and turn, watching him begin another stave. "Thank you, Mr. Stoddard, for the kindness."

He nods, not looking up from his work. His knives are sharp, and an experienced cooper doesn't take his eyes off the blade as he pulls it towards him. There was that, or perhaps he knows something I don't.

Most people do. I know little beyond this wooded corner of Plainfield, up against the banks of the Quinebaug River. I know white oak, chestnut, and yellow pine. I can find trees with the densest grains, which Mr. Stoddard prefers for building his best barrels and casks. I can work all day and into the evening. I can hammer together bits of wood, but I have none of the cooper's skills, other than what I learn by watching.

I am a slave, meant for heavy labor, cutting and hauling trees. But there is one skill I have, which many coopers, carpenters, and the like cannot boast of.

I can read.

It came easily to me. I recall tracing letters with my small finger in *Guthrie's Geography*, a book of maps and pictures which Mr. Stoddard left open on a table. When he caught me at it, I expected to be thrashed. Instead, he taught me how to sound out a few words. How to write my name. From then on, I read every printed word that came into the house.

I have read the Bible, entire. It convinced me that if there is a God, he's a silly fool to have wasted a perfectly good world with wars, disease, slavery, and general meanness. That fellow Jesus was nice enough when it came to poor fisherman, whores, the hungry and the lame, but none of his preachers around here give any thought to such folks, much less African slaves. But I go to church as is expected and bow my head. As expected.

Mr. Stoddard has *The Iliad*, and one volume of Shakespeare. All the Greeks fighting at Troy confuse me, but one of the Bard's plays is *The Merchant of Venice*. I like it.

I dreamt of taking a pound of flesh.

Poor Shylock. I root for him every time I read the play.

The villainy you teach me, I will execute, and it shall go hard.

Yes, I want much in this world. But as with Shylock, the powers are against me. Even Mr. Stoddard's yellow pine conspires against my rage. It is an unexpected gift, and I wonder what lies behind it. The goodness of his Christian heart? He keeps a decent cemetery for slaves and servants, but the last bondsman who'd gone into the ground had nothing but a shroud, worn cloth good for nothing else.

If he is a decent man, how can he own slaves? I find no answer, and it vexes me.

So I hammer nails, seeing Maame's coffin take shape. A place for her head, a width for her shoulders, the sawed planks tapering to where her feet will rest.

"Good work, Freegift," Mr. Stoddard says, standing with his arms folded, studying the nail holes, his head bobbing as he counts them. I can see he appreciates my thrift. I'm not one to waste metal. "You're a smart lad."

"Thank you, sir." I nod in half agreement, half bow to the master. He looks like he wants to say something else. Instead, he turns away, starting on another stave. I work the wood of my mother's coffin. Another hour, and I am done. I set the lid on top, along with the hammer and six nails. I do not speak, afraid Mr. Stoddard will want me to place Maame's body in the box. That is one thing I think I cannot do. So I fetch a shovel and head to the cemetery.

The Stoddard family cemetery sits on a small hill behind the house. It has a fine view, which Mr. Stoddard enjoys when he visits his wife. Maame told me that is silly, it is only her bones up there, and that her spirit is everywhere. Maybe it is foolish, but it gives Mr. Stoddard a pleasant view and a moment of rest on a log bench.

On the other side of the hill is the slave's cemetery. Lower than the English folk, of course. Not much of a view. But roomy, in a fine meadow up against a stand of balsam firs, which are of no value to the cooper's trade.

I mark out a rectangle next to my uncle's grave. I begin to dig. In spite of my doubts about the spirit world, gods, and heaven, I apologize to Akú for disturbing the ground around his bones. I think it is because I am a little afraid, but I don't tell him that. His grave is marked by a wooden cross, with the name Cato carved on it. It amuses the English to give their slaves names of famous Romans. Never Greeks, only Romans, as if that makes the joke even jollier.

It hardly matters. On the back of the cross, carved in even larger letters, is his true name, Akú. Wednesday's child, he was always ready with a story. I remember his laugh, deep and throaty, but little else.

I dig. There are more stones than soil, and I try not to curse since Maame was never pleased when I did. Perhaps someday I will utter oaths and curses as I've heard other men do, but right now, her spirit is too close. Or her memory, since I do not believe in spirits, of course.

I pry out a large, flat stone, and set it aside as a marker. Mr. Stoddard makes the wooden crosses, but I think the granite will set well at the head of the grave. Perhaps I will carve her name, if he will let me use his chisel. I am a foot deep now, the stones stacked, and the dirt to the side.

Yes, her name in stone. Like the English do. It will not be perfect, but it will last, longer than the crosses already weathered and rotting here. Nucquitty, a Mohegan fellow, who pledged his labor for ten years and died a month before his bond was up. Mingo, an African man who was bought in Newport, straight off the boat from Africa, and died of smallpox. Esther, another Indian, was Mrs. Stoddard's maid, an indentured servant, who had nowhere else to go when her mistress died. She cooked and cleaned, indifferently, from what I heard. Then we arrived. Maame was a good cook, and that earned her a place as mistress of the kitchen. Mr. Stoddard could have sold Esther's bond, but he kept her on, since he fancies himself a kind man.

Other crosses are rotted, fallen to the earth to become one with the bones beneath. The Stoddards have been here three generations worth. The oldest grave is nothing but a depression in the ground, marking a forgotten servant. Perhaps an Indian slave from the Pequot War.

Three feet deep now.

I shudder as I think about shoveling this soil back into the grave, covering Maame's coffin. I try not to think, at least not about that. I think about Mr. Stoddard, and wonder what he'll do with me. I know he won't sell me, not now anyway. I am too young, strong, and useful. He has no sons to train in his craft, his children being all daughters. Two are buried up the hill, taken by the same pox that claimed Mingo. Three others are married and live up and down the river. When they visit with their husbands and children, Mr. Stoddard is happy. When they leave, he spends more time than usual sitting on his bench and talking to his wife's bones.

He never visits his daughters. Perhaps he doesn't like leaving his property in the hands of slaves and servants. Or maybe he likes being the lord of his manor. Like Benedict Arnold.

Five feet deep and I hit a rock. Very big, perhaps part of a ledge. Five feet will do.

I climb out and spread the dirt away from the open grave, making sure there is room to carry the coffin and let it down. I sit on the slab of granite and say those words in my head once more.

Benedict Arnold.

My father, Benedict Arnold.

Maame is dead.

I have lost her and gained the faint notion of a father. But he is no more than a ghost to me, a man who took advantage of my mother, no matter how sweet the words he might have whispered to her. If he even did. A slave can say many things to a master, but *no* is seldom heard.

True, he is a man of this state, Connecticut, but it is not my state. I labor within it, but feel no loyalty, no joy at a famous neighbor. For Benedict Arnold was famous, when these English began their war against the other English. He took Fort Ticonderoga and sent cannon to General Washington at Boston. He fought the British when they raided this state and sent them back across the Devil's Belt, the sea between Connecticut and Long Island.

I read all this in the newspapers and broadsheets that made their way here from Norwich, Arnold's town of birth. And mine, now that I think of it. He won other battles and was renowned for his bravery under fire. Wounded twice in the same leg, they say he walks with a limp, having lost two inches of height in that limb. I don't understand how that can happen, so perhaps it's a story told since he's become a traitor.

I admit, I swell with a bit of pride for my brave father, if that he be. Perhaps I will be brave one day. But I tremble at the thought of musket balls in my leg, and the great effusion of blood that must bring. No, I am scared enough of the lash. I need not add sword, lead, and grapeshot to what may tear my flesh.

How can I be a soldier anyway? To make it all the way to New York, I'd have to evade militia patrols, magistrates, and suspicious citizens. A slave may not venture outside his master's property at night without a pass. I did hear from Pompey, another Roman-named slave, that an English general in the Carolinas was granting freedom to any slave who ran away to join the Redcoats. But the Carolinas may as well be on the moon.

Pompey, who'd come with his master to take delivery of a wagon's worth of casks and barrels, also whispered to me that in Rhode Island, the Continental Army had formed a so-called Black regiment, inviting slaves to join the rebellion in exchange for their freedom. Owners were paid for their loss of property, but the Rhode Island English did not appreciate the scene of ex-slaves marching with musket and bayonet. A few hundred former slaves and freedman marched off to war, and that was the end of it.

So I will not be a soldier.

"Freegift," Mr. Stoddard says, softly, as if aware he disturbs my thoughts. I jump, not wishing him to think me lazy.

"I've finished, sir. Just now."

"A fine job of it, too. Now clean up, and we'll bring the coffin along. I've left a waistcoat for you in your lodging. You've outgrown yours, and you should look proper as we commend Sally to the Lord," he says.

"Thank you, Mr. Stoddard. I am much obliged," I say, as I set the shovel into the dirt. As is he, for he must clothe me, carrying the obligation of the master. Sometimes I feel the wit in my brain wishes to claw its way out and say things that are obvious, but most people are blind to. I am a slave, but I must not be one to my tongue, so I stare at the ground, hoping he sees this as sorrow.

We are silent as we walk back, past the graves of his ancestors, wife, and little girls. I glance up, and there do I see real sorrow, as he casts his eye across their gravestones. In his own English way, he is not a bad man.

I wash off the soil and sweat at the well, dousing my torso with cold water and brushing off the worst of the dirt from my breeches. In our lodging—no, I must say my lodging—I find the waistcoat Mr. Stoddard has given me. It is buff in color, worn at the seams, but sturdy enough. I think it may have been his own at some time, before age began to shrink him. I put on a clean linen shirt and button the waistcoat. Clean stockings as well. I look through Maame's sewing basket and find a length of blue ribbon, which I use to tie back my hair in the style the English affect.

My dark hair is curly, but long, and Mr. Stoddard jokes that it looks like the slow match cannoneers use to ignite their fuses. I admit, it does bear a similarity to twisted lengths of rope, so I do not mind laughing along with him. Once, I caught a hint of reprimand in his voice, but laughed even harder to distract him from the thought of telling me to cut it off. It is the only outward thing which proclaims who I am, and I cling to it, much as Sampson clung to his hair. Until Delilah, of course.

I am wary of Delilah, but so far in my life there has been no enchantress to cut my locks.

I might trade them for the experience. But I must not think of the flesh as I go out to bury my mother.

The coffin is outside, set on two blocks of wood. I am relieved Maame's body is already within.

There are often visitors to Stoddard's farm, but none today. There is Indian Jack, a day laborer who tends the sheep, and has a good way with them. He, Mr. Stoddard, and I hoist the coffin on our shoulders and trudge up the hill. Maria and the other serving girls follow. Lucy, a mulatto woman of some forty years, brings up the rear, heaving her bulk along the trail. Born of a Nipmuc mother and an African slave, she is a free woman. Mr. Stoddard brought her in for kitchen work when Maame took ill. Everyone likes her cooking. I am afraid Mr. Stoddard will move her out of the barn and into Maame's room.

I will be happy in the barn, I decide. Then I think of winter and am less certain.

We descend to the slave's cemetery, careful of our footing. I expect the coffin to press into my shoulder, but it is so light I hardly feel the burden.

We set the coffin down on ropes Mr. Stoddard must have laid out. We use them to lower the coffin into the grave, then pull them out. I stand at the foot of the grave and wonder how it will be to live a life without Maame. I look at Lucy, her mouth open as she gasps for breath after her exertions. I know it is not what I should be thinking right now, but I don't want her in Maame's room. I don't want to share our lodgings, no matter how small, cramped, and drafty they may be.

Mr. Stoddard reads from the Bible. I cannot hear him for all the voices of desperate rage inside my brain. I wish only to return to my room, light a candle, and think about what will become of me. I don't worry about Maame at all. She is with the ancestors.

I am here with an English man and his sweating mulatto cook, a scattering of serving girls, and Indian Jack the shepherd. I care about none of them.

I hate all of them.

I bow my head so I will not have to look at them. The droning of Mr. Stoddard ceases, and I feel a shovel placed in my hand. It is time to fill the grave. I toss in a shovelful, the sound of pebbles dancing on the plain wood like hail on the roof. I look to Mr. Stoddard, wondering if he will take a turn.

All I see is his back. He and the others retrace their steps, back up the hill to where his people's bones lay. I am alone in the fading light as it filters through the top branches of the pines. I dig in with the spade ferociously, sending dirt in great arcing sprays to hide the coffin from my eyes. Then I place the stones in a layer, protecting Maame from the beasts of the forest. Wolves and bobcat, cougar and bear. None of them will disturb her rest.

I cover the stones, setting the flat granite piece at her head. I tamp down the earth and apologize again to my uncle for stepping over his bones. I tell him to watch out for Maame and to tell her I am fine.

Why do I tell him and not Maame? Because she knows when I lie.

· Three ·

⊢—

Everyone is at table when I return to the house. Lucy serves out Indian pudding, along with brown bread from breakfast and butter. She cooks it often for supper, but complaints are few as she makes it well.

Mr. Stoddard sits above the salt, the rest of us beneath, as is the custom of the English. Enslaved, I am at the farthest end from the master of the house. I have seen the salt pot move north on the table over the years, as daughters move out. When his wife was alive, it must have been in the center, dividing the family from servants and slaves. Did he fear its progress? What would happen when he died? Would it sit at his place, with all of us south of it?

Perhaps I should consider this more seriously. Mr. Stoddard is not a young man. Healthy and strong, but old and gray, it must be said. Who would take his place at the table? If not a cooper, what would they want with me?

No one speaks as I take my seat. It is not out of respect, but because their mouths are full. I do not blame them. The burial has taken time from their day and delayed the final meal. Hunger gnaws at me as well, but I make a show of reluctance, until Lucy tells me I must eat.

I do so. Maame always said to eat when you can, you never know when the wind's going to blow. I never really understood what she meant, but as long as I got to eat, it was fine with me. I butter my bread, going about it slowly, so I will not embarrass myself with gluttony while in mourning.

I think upon the wind. Maybe it will blow me away from here. To where? It matters little. I decide to wait for the wind and let it blow at my back when it comes. Or so I say to myself now. It seems easy to be brave in my thoughts, where none can see. But to do the deed? To take my destiny into my hands. To risk all? I remind myself that the risk involves the lash, and I shudder at the thought.

Mr. Stoddard looks at me, perhaps thinking I am about to burst into tears. I drink down my cider and give him a polite nod. All is well.

But it is not. I look around this table and cannot imagine a year, not even a month, in the company of these people. Mr. Stoddard with his measured kindnesses: Lucy with her damp brow and heavy step. The silent Indian Jack, who comes and goes, not that it makes any difference in his conversation. The sniggering servant girls.

Maame in the ground.

I wait until dinner is over, and Mr. Stoddard rises from the table.

"Sir, may I read a while?" I always ask, and never do when he might say no. Darkness is settling in, and it will mean a candle lit, but he will not begrudge me at the end of this day.

"Aye, go ahead. It will ease your mind, I'm sure," he says, heading out to the cooperage to clean up before the Sabbath day dawns. Mr. Stoddard likes everything put away, just so. With the burial, he hadn't gotten that done before supper, but the setting sun gives enough light for him to finish and keep his hands from hard labor on the day of rest.

I light a candle at the hearth and take it to Mr. Stoddard's study. Once it was a bedroom, but no daughters remain. It is not a proper place for servants or slaves, so my master uses it for his papers and accounts. What I crave is the shelf of books, set against the outer wall, and the chair with its back to the south-facing casement window.

It is a pleasant room, I do admit. Mr. Stoddard's pipe and tobacco await him at his desk, along with quill pens and sheets of writing paper at the ready. I set the candle on the table and survey the books. Newly added is a *Dictionary of the Bible*. Mr. Stoddard likes his Bible.

I don't care much for it, except for the battles. The Hebrews smite the Amalekites and Canaanites, among many others, and I imagine the Holy Land knee deep in blood. In one fight against Judah, their Lord God gives Israel victory, and they take many slaves. As they lead them away, God tells the Israelites to free those slaves, even to clothe and feed them, which they promptly do.

I wait for that God to reveal his glory at the Congregational Church, but so far, he has not shown himself.

So I return to *Guthrie's Geography*, my first friend from these shelves. I do not linger over the South Sea Islands, or the strange names scattered across the maps of Asia. I flip the pages to the Americas and find New York City.

Thirty thousand people live there. I cannot imagine so many people on one small island. Perhaps many more now, with the Redcoats and Loyalists flooding in. I may not wish the company of those on this farm, but at least I can turn a corner without running into hundreds of strangers.

I move on to Connecticut. The map shows a few hills and mountains, but none along the shore. The coastline itself is jagged with inlets, rivers, and jutting peninsulas. It would be a long walk, of necessity inland. If I followed the setting sun to the Hudson River, I could eventually find New York. But they would find me first. With worries about Redcoat raids into the state, militias would be on the lookout for any traveler. And my skin marks me as the strangest of strangers.

I search for Long Island. South of where I sit, at the mouth of the Thames River, is New London, where Maame bade me go. And south of that, across the waters of the Devil's Belt, is Long Island, the eastern tip reaching out as if to touch its northern neighbor.

The coast is smooth, as if it is a long, sandy beach. Perhaps this is the path to New York City.

I cannot look at the map any longer. The prospect of the journey frightens me. Seeing the course laid out on paper makes it real, and I fear I may leave this house and start walking tonight. I turn the pages, looking for a part of the world to calm my thoughts. I find England, hoping to discover some clue as to my captor's weaknesses, a secret hidden amongst the rivers and villages that dot the map. Their cities are even larger than New York, and this dismays me. Could they not have taken their own teeming masses for slaves? Why journey to Africa and take my grandfather?

I gaze at west Africa next, wondering where the village of my ancestors is on this map. Maame would know, I think, almost ready to go and ask her.

I shut the Geography and place it carefully on the shelf. No, there are questions that I can never ask her, things I will never know. Calm washes over me. It is not a bad thing. It means from this day forward, all I know and do will come from myself, no one else. Someday a child will ask me a question, and I will speak the truth of my life in return.

If I were not another man's chattel, I would leave and make my own way. But I am, and I lay my hand on Mr. Stoddard's chair and stare at his desk and the many papers strewn about. His account books, open to a page of figures I cannot understand. I know my numbers, but what all this means is not anything I care to decipher. Names, materials, pounds and shillings going out and coming in, like the tide. Except the incoming tide of Mr. Stoddard is at a high water indeed. He knows wood and coopering, and business as well, it seems.

I turn away, weary. But an image from among the papers lodges in my brain, and I take a step before I realize what word has jumped out at me.

Emancipation.

Or at least most of it, written in a bold hand on a sheet held under the account book. The rest of the writing is smaller, but as I lift the cover of the ledger, I see the title of the document, spread out across the top. Words which mean freedom.

Certificate of Emancipation.

I, Ira Stoddard, hereby grant emancipation to Freegift Cooper, son of Sally Cooper, upon his eighteenth birthday.

What? That was weeks ago.

I read the rest. He says that as a believer in the rights of man and the cause of liberty for an independent United States of America, he can no longer abide holding another human being in bondage.

I applaud the sentiment, but as the day of my birth has come and gone, I find it hollow at best. The space for Ira Stoddard to sign his name is empty, as is the space for a witness and a mark where my name should go.

I replace the paper carefully, exactly as it was, and leave the room, listening for footsteps and making sure no one has spied upon me. I go to my room and fall upon my bed, my mind alive with questions, my heart beating as if it might burst.

Mr. Stoddard does support the patriot cause, quite strongly. I never expected the rights of man and the cause of liberty he spoke of so often might come my way, but they have now veered close. What has stopped him from signing and granting my freedom?

Maame. She fell sick, and perhaps he held off to keep me here until she died.

Did he think I would run away and leave her?

There is no mention of Maame's freedom in the document. In Mr. Stoddard's view, it might have been the proper thing to do, to keep an old woman and care for her in her last years. Even so, I would have remained, perhaps laboring for wages, doing the same work I do now, but as a free man.

The thought did not sit well. Knowing I was free but unable to leave Maame would have wrenched my soul. And she would have wanted me to go, while the wind was at my back. So yes, Mr. Stoddard had acted wisely. A good Connecticut patriot and man of reason, he had weighed every course of action and decided upon this one. It must be so.

Tomorrow, then, he must free me.

No, tomorrow is the Sabbath. Not a day for legalities and business. I hope that on Monday morning, that beautiful piece of parchment will be graced with his name, and perhaps mine.

Freegift Cooper, Freedman.

· Four ·

├────┤

I give the horses a light snap of the whip, not that I am eager to hear the preacher this morning, but because I am impatient to get on with this business of freedom and at a loss to know why Mr. Stoddard will not speak of it.

He sits next to me on the cart as our two sorrels pull us to town. Lucy and the servant girls sit in the back. Indian Joe is gone, off to observe the Christian Sabbath in whatever way he wishes after a night sleeping in the barn. He is free, but his is a miserable existence as far as I can tell. I am determined to do much more with my own freedom, even with my deficit of years enslaved.

Freegift Cooper, Freedman. I allow the phrase to roll around in my mind as I have nearly all the night. I like the sound of it and cannot wait to write it out as the opportunity presents itself. Cooper is the name Mr. Stoddard gave us, after his profession. He does not hold with the custom of giving slaves their owner's surname. Perhaps he does not wish a slave to be associated with his family. The feeling is quite mutual.

Cooper has always been my last name, and Maame's too. I never thought to wonder what it was before she was purchased by Mr. Stoddard. Sally Arnold? If so, I am glad he gave us a different name. I doubt anyone is hated more than Benedict Arnold, at least within my earshot. If I get to New York, perhaps there I will take on his name. The name taken from my mother and me.

Freegift Arnold.

It sounds strange, and I give it up for now. There are many miles between myself and my father. First I must get free, legal or not, and make my way across Long Island. Then I shall worry about what to call myself.

"My daughter Abigail will be here," Mr. Stoddard says as we descend from the cart. He has never discussed the comings and goings of his family with me, and I hardly know what to say.

"Yes, sir," I say as the girls scatter, and Lucy eases her bulk off the wagon bed. "Will she and Mr. Anderson come back to the house?"

"I doubt it," he says, brushing the dust from his coat and shaking his head. Maybe he is wondering why he shared this news with me. I follow him to the front of the church, its clapboards blindingly white in the morning sun.

I see Abigail and her husband John in the crowd, standing by the steps. She is the youngest of his daughters and smartly married. John Anderson owns a gristmill upriver and breeds horses as well. He is tall, his skin pale even for the English. His thin hair hangs like straw parched by the bright sun. I have heard Mr. Stoddard brag of his fine house, but I know he has not visited in some time.

So why are they here, at a church an hours' ride away?

It is not my concern. I give them a polite nod as I pass, but Abigail looks past me. She is four or five years older than I am, and I remember her days as a young child. We played together, but at what or for how long I do not recall. She was friendly then, and I made believe she was my older sister. But such fancies do not last.

I see Pompey and Cato, Africans close to my age. They are not from Akan, but in the world of the English, this difference means little. We talk, grateful, like all the others, to exchange gossip and news as we wait for the service to begin. Everyone arrives early, not to show God how eager they are but to learn who knows what about whom.

The crowd begins to move up the steps, slowly. I ask Pompey to save me a seat and dash away around the back of the church to the necessary house. It was a long ride and will be a long sermon, agonizing enough without aching to empty my bladder.

I hurry back, thankful to catch a glimpse of people still heading in, as I near the corner of the church. It would not do to enter as the prelude is ending.

I stop, as I see the back of Mr. Stoddard and hear the voice of Abigail. She is angry.

"It is foolish, Father, to throw away such an investment," she says. Mr. Stoddard does not reply, but I see his shoulders rise and fall in a great sigh. I press my back against the wall, so as not to be seen. "If you will not keep him, John would profit from his labors. The boy is valuable, Father. He's strong and can read and write. He's worth far more than most slaves."

She's talking about me. Faint praise, to be called a valuable slave. So this is why the emancipation document is unsigned.

"I am uncertain about slavery, Abigail," Mr. Stoddard says. "It cannot be God's will, and I cannot preach liberty in the American cause and deprive another man of his."

"Do you think more of a slave boy than your own family, Father? Think of me and of your grand-children. Isn't that what Mother would want?"

I do not stay to hear his answer. Against the notion of caring for his own family and the wishes of his dead wife, there is little I can do or say. I clench my fists at my side and go around the other side, up the steps behind father and daughter, who apparently have settled things. To her satisfaction, from the look on her face.

I slide into the rear pew as they walk proudly to the front, taking a place of honor before God. I see Abigail lean her head to whisper to her husband, who nods approvingly. My new master, if she has her way.

We rise and sit, sing hymns, and listen to the sermon. I take none of it in. I damn myself for looking at Mr. Stoddard's desk. It would be better to never have known freedom was so close. Legal freedom, that is. I am resolved to be rid of these people, with or without that slip of paper. They declared their independence from the King, so I shall do the same of them.

Pompey nudges me, and I come out of my day dream. The service is over. Mr. Stoddard, along with Abigail and her husband, pass by down the aisle. This time, she nods to me. There is no condolence in her expression, only calculation. Trained in obedience, I nod back. Her husband looks at me dispassionately, assessing the worth of this new live stock.

They will never have me, I vow. To my ancestors, and the sky father Nyame, not to this Sunday god of the English.

The ride back to the house is quiet. Mr. Stoddard is in no mood for chatter, nor the sharing of further news of his family. The girls doze in the back, scattered around Lucy, who must settle in the center, otherwise her bulk might tip the cart as we round a curve.

I do not speak to him. In less than a day, I have buried my mother, thought myself about to be freed, and now find I am more likely to be given to another household. I do not know what would come out of my mouth should I open it.

But open it I do as we come within sight of the house.

"It's Miss Rebecca!" I say, spying the oldest daughter of Mr. Stoddard. A thought flies through my brain that I am to be argued over by all three women in turn, and I cannot help feel a bit of pride, however misplaced it might be.

"Dear God, what has happened?" Mr. Stoddard says and leaps from the wagon, running toward her, making better time on foot. His shock is understandable, and I see that her appearance has nothing at all to do with me. She stands by her wagon, loaded with furniture. Her oldest boy, Daniel, is in a smaller cart piled high with chests and trunks. Young Samuel sits astride a packhorse weighed down with canvas sacks. Their faces are stricken, and I am certain a great calamity has befallen them.

Rebecca's husband, Jeremiah Moore, is not with them.

"Oh Papa," I hear Rebecca say, in great distress. "We have been burned out, and they've taken Jeremiah."

They embrace and her tears come, in such an effusion she cannot speak. Mr. Stoddard is a confusion of questions, neither of them making sense. I pull the wagon under the shade of the great oak tree in the yard and make for Daniel. He is close to my age, perhaps a bit younger, and we have had civil discussions on the occasions we've been together.

"What has happened, Dan? Where is your father?" I ask. The serving girls gather around, but Lucy shoos them into the house, knowing that food must be prepared in ample amounts.

"They came three nights ago," he says, clambering down from his perch. "Tories from Long Island. Made right for our house and took Papa. Revenge for his last raid. But this time they went too far." His hand quivers in rage, his mouth set in a firm line.

"What raid, Dan?" I ask. "Is he with General Washington?"

"No, he's a privateer. Hasn't Grandfather told you? Papa is famous, leastways along the Sound. He has an official letter of marque from the governor and an armed sloop."

"He took an English ship, Freegift," Samuel says, his voice full of a six-year-old's pride in his father's achievements. "It was loaded with muskets."

"Well," I say. "He must be very brave, Samuel. Like you. Why don't you go into the kitchen and see what Lucy is making. You can't miss her."

"Lucy and your mum, Freegift?" Samuel asks.

"No, Samuel. Maame died."

"Oh," he says and looks at the ground. "Sorry, Freegift."

I feel unaccountably sad as little Samuel runs off to the kitchen. The lad is the first person other than Mr. Stoddard to express himself concerning Maame's death. I press Daniel for details, knowing that his fury allows him to see little else but his family's loss of station.

"The last I heard, he was shipping goods up and down the coast," I say.

"Shipping is dangerous work, for little reward," Daniel says. "Papa turned his sloop into a privateer and took a number of Loyalist ships. One carried a load of muskets from Nova Scotia. That made him a rich man."

"And for that the Tories burned your house?" I ask. I am not privy to the rules of this war, but it seems an uneven exchange.

"It got their attention," Daniel says. "Last month Papa took two whaleboats across to Long Island. They raided the houses of known Tories and took plunder. But they didn't burn families out. Leave that to the King's men!"

"So they came to avenge themselves," I say.

"Aye. Someone must have recognized Papa. Likely a Tory who'd left Saybrook for safety on Long Island, which is full of Tory bastards and little else," Daniel says. "They came in the night and took Papa prisoner, stole what valuables we had and set the house afire. They ran off before they could do a proper job of it, and we got the flames under control. But we can't live there now, everything is scorched and blackened. My mother still trembles in fear. All she wanted to do was come here, to her father, far from the reach of whaleboats."

"And you, Daniel," I say. "What will you do?"

"See her settled in. Then get myself downriver and on a privateer. The only way to free father is to take an important Tory prisoner and exchange him. It's done often enough," he says, making it sound simple and straightforward.

"What about your father's sloop?" I ask.

"Burned at the dock. Papa thought we were safe enough a mile from the mouth of the Connecticut River, but they knew right where we lived. You can't trust a Tory, Freegift," Daniel says, and leaves me for his grandfather's embrace.

No, I expect not. Neither can I trust a patriot, it seems. So I must trust myself.

"Freegift, I am sorry to hear of the death of your mother," Rebecca says, standing before me with smudges of soot still on her garments. "Daniel will express his condolences once he collects himself. He is still upset from that horrible night." She brushes away a stray strand of hair, and I see in her face the young girl who used to play with me. Snowmen in the winter, when chores were done. Rolling hoops from the stack Mr. Stoddard kept in the barn for his barrels. She was determined in play as a young girl, and now as determined to salvage her family from the ruins of war.

"Understandable, Miss Rebecca," I say, delivering a bow. "And thank you. She spoke often of you and was glad of your good fortune." Often, perhaps not, but a soothing lie is a worthwhile lie, I think.

"Gone up in smoke, Freegift," she says. "But we will rebuild. The house is not a total loss, but it seems foolish to repair it now while the war continues and they may raid again."

"Your husband's sloop was also lost, Daniel tells me."

"That is being repaired. They meant to take it, but the militia came running as soon as the flames from our house lit the sky. So they started a fire and rowed off. The damage was considerable, but it should be seaworthy soon enough. The first mate is a part owner and will see to it ably. The governor still owes us for the last prize taken, and I must see to that payment now that we are safe and with a roof over our heads."

"Daniel seems determined to take to sea and obtain a Tory prisoner to exchange," I say. I am struck by the grim determination in Rebecca's plans. She has indeed fared well for herself and is no helpless damsel.

"And I am resolved to keep him from the sea," she whispers. "Which is one reason we've journeyed so far inland. I plan to put him to work with Father, to learn the cooper's trade. I'll not lose another across the Devil's Belt, mark my words. And you, Freegift, must not encourage him in any such plans. Instead, talk to him of the virtues of honest labor. Will you?"

"Yes, Miss Rebecca," I say. She is a smart woman, already laying plans to keep her oldest son safe and secure funds for the rebuilding of her husband's privateer sloop. But she is not smart enough to know I have my own plans to cut across the Devil's Belt, and not to rescue Jeremiah Moore, but rather myself. I tell her I will counsel Daniel to remain here, even as I wonder what he may know about crossing deep water.

After I have carried most of the chests inside I unhitch the horses, bring water, and brush them down in the barn. First Mr. Stoddard's, then Rebecca's horses and mule. The animals are unsettled, the new ones unused to these surroundings and Mr. Stoddard's unsure of the intrusion. In truth, I feel much the same.

Daniel walks into the barn. He looks down to the dirt at his feet.

"Sorry about your mother," he says. With as much sincerity as any boy forced to deliver a message.

"Kind of you to think of her, Dan," I say, as I finish brushing down the mule. "Tell me more about the men who took your father, if you're of a mind to. I've never seen a Tory, not that I know of. Folks around here are for the revolution, or at least claim to be."

"Big men," Daniel says. "Strong enough to row across the sound, ten miles at least each way."

"American Loyalists, not British sailors?"

"I guess so," Daniel says. "They must have been. The British wouldn't have recognized Papa over on Long Island. He's well known by anyone who sails up and down the coast."

"Yes, I know. He'll be fine, Daniel. They wouldn't dare harm a valuable prisoner."

"I'll free him," Daniel says, with the absolute certainty of a boy who knows nothing of what lies ahead of him. "Mother doesn't think so, but I will."

"Are there other privateers in Saybrook? Could you sign on with one of them?" I ask.

"No. And it will be ages before Papa's sloop is made ready," he says. "But in New London, I hear there are always ships coming in with rich prizes. I'll get on one of those, for certain. Captain Saltonstall is a friend of my father's, and when he visited last he talked of outfitting a brig in New London harbor. He'll take me on, I know."

Over Daniel's shoulder, I spy Rebecca listening at the barn door.

"You have to think about your young brother and your mother, Dan. Think about what your father would want you to do in his place. I'm sure he'd want you to keep them safe, wouldn't he?" I proclaim, the very voice of responsible youth.

"What do you know, Freegift? You're just a slave!"

"Daniel!" Rebecca says, striding over to him and delivering a sharp slap to his cheek. "Freegift is only trying to talk sense into you. He is a slave to your grandfather, but you must not be a slave to your tongue."

"I will join Captain Saltonstall, I will! And I'll save father, too!"

"You will remain here and work with Grandfather. You will learn his trade and make yourself ready in case the worst happens, Daniel. If your father does not return, you will need to know how to secure a place in this world. Better to learn from Grandfather than to be apprenticed to a stranger."

Daniel struggles to control himself, but his mouth quivers and his face crumbles into a red welt of tears. He is scared. Scared of the men who came in the night, scared that his father is dead, scared at his uncertain future of labor and loss. He runs away.

"I am sorry, Freegift," Rebecca says, laying a hand on my shoulder. Kindly, like her father. Not for the first time, I wonder at these people. They can show kindness and treat me well, even while holding me enslaved, the greatest unkindness of all.

"I understand," I say. And I do. He has been brought up the eldest son of a wealthy man. Perhaps not a man of great wealth, but a ship's captain, a man of prestige and standing, with a fine house. Now he is cast down, coming to live on his grandfather's charity and to learn a trade of calluses and cuts.

Daniel is unlucky, even though raised in freedom, and faces a life less than he hoped for. For myself, I can be cast down no further and have only hope to look forward to. And a father, as well. Though he may be scorned by every patriot between here and Philadelphia, and he may not even acknowledge me with the gray eyes which we share, I believe I have a greater chance of seeing him before Daniel sees his own dear plundering papa.

· Five ·

├───┤

It is the third day since Rebecca left to see Governor Trumbull, who is at the War Office in Lebanon, about twenty miles distant. She gave Daniel the job of driving the two-horse cart, which lifted his spirits some. It was an adventure and an honor to seek out such an important man and seek the payment due for his father's heroics. That it put off his apprenticeship for a few days was another blessing for him. She told him he'd be her protector, which appealed to his vanity and healed his wounded pride. I knew the road to Lebanon was safe enough, but wished him luck all the same, as if they were going through Iroquois territory. And as if his mother did not have a pistol in the pocket of her cloak.

The three days have been busy for Mr. Stoddard and myself. He is finishing up a large order of staves for the War Office. They are to be shipped to New London, where other coopers will make them into barrels and casks. From there, supplies will be loaded and shipped to New Haven, for French soldiers who have come to help General Washington's army.

I am glad for Mr. Stoddard. It is good business for him, and he swells with pride as he thinks of his staves going to help the cause of liberty. For myself, who hauls the white oak out of the forest, I wonder if my wood will help provision some Frenchman who might shoot my father before I can find him. Still, I bring out the best wood we have, possessing few knots and a fine grain.

I cut the wood and split it into quarter lengths. It is neatly stacked, tiers and tiers of oak aging in the open air. Two years are required for the best barrels, Mr. Stoddard says. I have brought in so much new wood that there is barely any room left, which serves us well as the seasoned oak is transformed by Mr. Stoddard's constant labor into tall stacks of staves. Which go into barrels he has made, of course. All of which will be billed to the War Office, at a fair price. But a goodly one, according to him. I think it must be a fine thing to supply an army, especially a French one, since they have a king who has the riches of his empire at his fingertips.

I carry a load of seasoned lumber to Mr. Stoddard, dumping it next to his shaving horse. We both look up at the sound of a wagon clattering along the lane.

"That's Rebecca, lad, it must be," he says, a smile lighting his face. "With good news, I hope."

I agree and follow him to tend to the horses. Her news is of no value to me, even though I do wish her well. Tomorrow there will be more white oak to haul in, so two years from now, Mr. Stoddard can make more staves. This vision of my future stretches out in front of me, and I wonder if the forests shall run out of white oak before I see that emancipation paper signed.

It is Rebecca and Daniel. By her smile, I see she has had success.

"Wonderful news, father," she says, giving Mr. Stoddard a kiss. "Governor Trumbull has paid us Jeremiah's share from his last prize and has promised to work out an exchange of prisoners."

"I met the Governor," Daniel says, as Samuel runs out into his mother's arms. "He shook my hand."

"Well done, Daniel," Mr. Stoddard says, pleased as he can be by the good news and their safe return. "Now help Freegift with the horses and then you can tell us everything."

"Why do I have to help a slave?" Daniel asks, as if having shook the governor's hand, he mustn't soil it with everyday labor. "Isn't that what he's for, to do chores?"

The joy vanishes from Mr. Stoddard's face. He glowers, and at first I fear he may strike his grandson. He shakes his head, as if more angry at himself than the boy. "If that's what I've taught you, Daniel, may God forgive me. Now help Freegift with the horses as I told you and do the best job you are capable of."

"Yes, Grandfather," Daniel says, subdued by the old man's reaction. I feel as if something broke inside Mr. Stoddard at the sound of Daniel's impertinence. Is he ashamed at selling me off to Abigail? Or at reneging on the promise he made himself to free me? Whatever deep emotion was stirred, it leaves me uneasy. A decent constancy is a slave's comfort, and this seems to signal disruption and despair.

We each take a horse by its driving line and guide them to the barn. I unhook the wagon and Daniel fetches water, a bucket for each horse. Without being bid to do so. Perhaps constancy is a boy's comfort too.

"Was the journey hard?" I ask, as we begin to remove the harnesses.

"No," he says, passing up the opportunity to impress me with his adventures on the road. "It was hot and dusty, mainly. But I did like the War Office and meeting the Governor. He really did shake my hand, you know."

"I believe you," I say. "A great honor. And good news about the exchange."

"It may take some time, the Governor told us. Months, perhaps."

"Which means you will be working with your grandfather. It's not a bad trade to learn, even if you don't need it later. A man who can work wood will be well prepared for life on sea or land."

"I suppose," he says, going quiet for a moment. Then, "I don't mind helping you, Freegift. I didn't mean to offend."

"I'm glad of it, Dan," I say, pausing to meet his eyes. He looks away, abashed at the sentiment. "You've had a lot to get used to lately. It is a different life here."

"I do miss my friends," he says, beginning to rub down his horse. "We catch quail in snares and fish for trout in the stream behind my house. It's great fun. I don't expect there's many families close by, are there?"

"No. None with lads your age, leastways. I think the Crawfords, about five miles down the road, have a pair of boys, maybe a bit younger than you," I tell him.

"I can see my friend John's house from my bedroom window," Daniel says. "It's different along the river, we're not stuck out in the middle of the forest."

"Well, your grandfather needs the forest. He does own land down to the river. Perhaps he'll take you fishing there."

"I hope so. Will you come, Freegift?"

"If he allows it. But now you have the governor looking to exchange your father. Perhaps before the snow flies, you'll be back in your house again, and among your friends," I say, offering hope, which costs little, except when later it turns false.

"Yes. And father home," he says, brushing his horse's mane, a smile on his face. "By first snow."

I gather up fresh hay for the horses, thinking of friends. In truth, I have no notion of what it means to have a friend. Mr. Stoddard is kind enough and cares for me in his way. Maame loved me, I know, but a fellow cannot rightly call his mother a friend.

There is no one else. No one but servants and Indians who hire out for the day and then vanish.

I have never fished, not in the way Daniel means. When the shad run in the spring, we go to the river and cast our nets, pulling in basketfuls of the silvery creatures. It is a break in the routine of our daily labors, enjoyable as the promise of warm weather and food on the table. But to sit on a river bank and dangle a line into the water, idling away the hours in hope of a trout or two, with an amiable companion, as free as I might be?

I have not had the pleasure.

I think to tell Daniel how lucky he is to have done so. But I know he only sees what he has lost, not the value of what he once had. I finish with the horses and return to my work, carrying more wood for Mr. Stoddard. For, is that not what I am meant to do?

The Reverend Cooke sits at table with us. He was last here when we buried Mrs. Stoddard. He acknowledges Maame's passing and tells me he has prayed for her. He makes no mention of doing so over her grave, which might have strained his spindly legs were he to walk there. But I thank him, as I wonder why he shares our dinner.

"Ira tells me you found good fortune with the governor," Reverend Cooke says to Rebecca as he butters his bread heavily.

"No more than the fortune earned by and owed to my husband," she answers. "But it is timely. It will help us rebuild and pay Father for teaching Daniel the cooper's skill."

Daniel looks sharply to his mother and then away. This is news. It means Daniel will be an apprentice to his grandfather, not simply a family member learning a trade. Such an apprentice is bound by contract for a term of years, and the master craftsman obligated to cloth, feed, and house him. What does this mean? I consider how it may alter the rhythm of my life.

Young Daniel will not be trapping quail in the fields of Saybrook with his friends, for one. And for another, he will not go off to sea privateering, nor to join General Washington's army. I see satisfaction in Rebecca's face, and I understand what she has done. If Jeremiah does not return, she has funds and a safe place for her oldest boy. Many women have fared worse in this rebellion, I am sure.

"I look forward to seeing you at Church," Reverend Cooke says to Daniel. "In your grandfather's pew."

"Yes sir," Daniel manages, mindful of his elders but showing little joy in it.

That is why the Reverend is here, to welcome the boy into his flock. Mr.

Stoddard looks pleased, as he should be. So does Rebecca. I wish if I am to be sold or given away to a daughter, it be to her. But she does not covet, so it shall not be.

Dinner is done, the table cleared and cleaned, and candles lit, even though there is still light in the summer sky.

"Freegift, come here please," Mr. Stoddard says, standing at the head of the table. Reverend Cooke is at his side.

The emancipation paper is in his hand. Pen and ink on the table, placed by the Reverend.

"Yes, Mr. Stoddard," I say, struggling to keep my knees from buckling. I pretend not to recognize the document and wonder if my face betrays me. Rebecca ushers her boys into the room as she smiles. Surely this is a good sign, but I try not to hope.

"Freegift Cooper, I have here a declaration," Mr. Stoddard begins. His voice cracks, and he coughs his way into clarity, beginning again. "A declaration to you as precious as our nation's declaration of independence, I am sure."

More so, I think, but I say nothing, as he has his words already planned, and I do not wish to delay them one more moment.

"You have served me well, as did your mother. Now, it is time for me to serve you, and to more properly align myself with the cause of liberty and the rights of all mankind," Mr. Stoddard says.

"And with the Lord God Almighty," Reverend Cooke says. I wish he would pray silently.

"Yes, in the eyes of God as well," Mr. Stoddard says. "Freegift, I can no longer own another human being. As I sign this, and Reverend Cooke witnesses it, you will be emancipated from your servitude. You will be a free man."

"No longer a slave?" I ask, since his words are buzzing inside my brain like bumblebees, and I want to be certain there is no mistake.

"No longer," says he, dipping a quill into the inkpot and signing his name with a flourish. "It is what you desire, is it not?"

"Yes," I whisper, barely able to speak. Reverend Cooke signs as a witness. As I watch the ink dry, I feel the chains fall from my heart.

The quill is placed in my hand, and I sign on the line Mr. Stoddard drew so carefully, days or perhaps weeks ago.

I am free.

I know not what to do.

· Six ·

⊢——⊣

I face the morning sun on the first day of my free life, standing over Maame's grave.

"Maame, it is me, Kwasi. You told me to find my way," I whisper. "The way to my destiny. It has begun. I now have my freedom."

I smile as I kneel at her grave, the soft earth yielding at my knees. I take the mallet and chisel from my sack and begin to hammer at the granite. I am no expert, but the letters begin to take shape.

Afua. Her Akan name, the name her ancestors now call her by.

Afua, my Maame.

I stand and survey my work. Wooden crosses shall rot and fall into the ground, but the granite will remain, guarding her bones, holding her name. I will never see her grave again, nor that of my uncle. But it matters not. They and all my ancestors are with me.

I return the tools to the shed and find Mr. Stoddard at work, the pile of new staves already growing at his feet.

"Sir," I say, approaching him. "I must take my leave of you today." It feels odd telling Mr. Stoddard what I am about to do. Without having asked permission to do so.

"Why so soon, Freegift?" he says, eyeing the curve and grain of the wood in his hand.

"You have no obligation to me anymore," I say. "I must make my own way in the world."

"Come, sit with me for a while," he says, rising stiffly from his shaving horse. He takes a drink from an oaken bucket, made by his own hands, and offers me the ladle. I take it and drink, the water cool against my throat. Still, it is not my water, or the water owed a slave for his labors, and it sits uneasy in my stomach. We take our places on a rough bench against the barn wall, the cooperage before us.

"You must be pleased to have Daniel as your apprentice," I say, if only to fill the silence.

"I am. For the next seven years. Then he'll be a cooper. Perhaps not such stuff as dreams are made on, eh? But a good, solid trade. Did you ever wonder why I never taught you, Freegift?"

"No, sir. I had my work, you had yours. It seemed enough."

"That's true, Freegift. You're a stout and strong lad, and you dove into heavy labors without complaint. You possess a keen eye for the right wood and know how to seek it out. That comes from observation and calculation. Using your mind. And that's why I never taught you."

"I don't understand, sir," I say, befuddled.

"You're intelligent, Freegift, more so than most. I knew it when I first found you paging through my geography. You wanted to learn, and you did so quickly. I never knew a child to take so readily to his letters."

"So, I was not taught to be a cooper because I was smart?" I say, trying to follow his logic.

"Not exactly. What I mean is, you are too smart. I needed you for the heavy work, to be sure. But I saw little reason to put you on the shaving horse and school you in the secrets of the cooper's art. I always knew I must free you one day, and when that day came, I didn't want you astride that horse for the rest of your life."

"You always knew?" I say, dumbstruck. Can this be true?

"Since you learned to read and absorbed every word in my poor library. My God, Freegift, there are few men who know the Bard's plays as you do. Those we have, that is. Are you not aware you have a sharp mind?"

"That is kind to say, sir. But I think it would be hard for any man to know if he is clever or no. How could I compare my mind to another's? I barely know my own."

He laughs. He laughs so hard he begins to slap his knees and weep. I worry he might be having a fit, but he soon gains control of himself. "That proves my point, lad. I doubt even Benjamin Franklin himself could improve upon that response."

"But I still do not understand, Mr. Stoddard. Why did you never tell me I would be freed?"

"I thought you might begin to resent being a slave, knowing freedom was coming. As you say, it is difficult to know another man's mind, but I sensed you were accustomed to this place and your work, as long as your mother was alive."

"Accustomed, yes," I say.

"You never would have left her."

"No, sir."

"So, knowing this day was coming, I set aside a small amount of money for you. Wages I would have paid a free man, minus lodging, food, and care. I have it for you when you decide to leave."

"Wages?" I do not believe what I hear.

"Since you were twelve years of age. In an amount appropriate each year to your ability. A man's wage, this past year. I take this business of liberty with great seriousness, Freegift. How can we Americans hold men enslaved while fighting to free ourselves? It makes no sense to me, and I felt I must act according to my principles. You've been a good worker, Freegift, and you'll have what's coming to you."

"Why did you not mention this last night, when we signed the paper, sir?"

"Because it's my business with you, and no one else's," he says, leaning in to whisper. "Remember that, Freegift. Think before you speak. Often enough, thinking will be enough, and you'll find it useful to follow with silence."

"That is wise advice, Mr. Stoddard," I say. I cannot tell him how often I have followed it myself, and likely every slave in New England. We choke on the words we wish to speak. But Mr. Stoddard does not deserve to hear that. He has spoken well of me, better words than I have ever heard except for those from Maame.

Wages.

"You'll do well to heed them," he says. "Now, tell me plain. You wish to leave and seek whatever your fortune may be?"

"I do, sir," I say. "With regrets." I obey my former master and do not speak a word about finding my father, with whom I do believe my fortune lies.

"Then let me make you a business proposition. Being a free man, all you owe me is a good listen. If it's not for you, take your leave as soon as you wish, with my blessing."

I give him a listen. The proposition is for me, and I accept it.

The order of staves is due soon at New London harbor. Mr. Stoddard has contracted with me. With me, Freegift Cooper, freedman. I will build a raft of suitable size and take twenty barrels filled with staves to New London. For that labor, I will receive a percentage of the payment. Not a large portion, but suitable for the work.

And I will be on the river, a free man, heading to a destination I require. It is most excellent.

For the next two days, I cut logs and lash them together. One layer across the other to give me height above the water. Flat planks on top so I may stand between the barrels, tied down on either side. I construct a crude rudder, set between the forks of a maple branch. Cut a long pole for pushing off and avoiding obstacles in the river. I have Maame's quilt to sleep upon, and a blanket to cover me.

It is nightfall. My last day on Mr. Stoddard's land. I am ready. He comes to sit with me, on a log by the door outside my room.

"Here, Freegift," he says, glancing about. He pulls a pouch from within his coat and gives it to me. "It's oilskin. Put your emancipation paper in and tie it tightly. Wear it next to your skin and let nothing happen to it. Do you understand?"

"I do, sir. Fully." I heft the pouch and hear the clink of coins. "My wages?"

"Yes. Silver shillings and some pennies. Nearly as valuable as that piece of paper. Trust no one to catch sight of all that coin, lad. Use the pennies as you must but keep the rest well apart."

"I have a question, Mr. Stoddard," I say, feeling hot in the face. I do not like my ignorance on display.

"Ask," he says, and I search for the words.

"Is the world an evil place? The world beyond this farm, the woods, the church, and the river, I mean."

"Freegift, I have enslaved you and your mother. Was that not evil? You have become a man here, or nearly so, and lived through bondage."

"Yes. I have been a slave all my life, and as you yourself said, it is a great evil, contrary to the cause of liberty. But now I am free, and I still must not trust anyone. How bad is it, beyond what I know?"

Mr. Stoddard leans back, a heavy sigh emptying his chest. "It is bad enough that you must work to know the very soul of a man before you trust him. And it is good enough that once you do, you should give all your trust with an open heart. Does that make sense?"

I think about his words, turning them over in my mind.

"Yes," I say, telling him the truth. "It does. Does that apply to women as well as men?"

"Oh, Freegift, you have much to learn," he says, breaking into laughter. "So very much, none of which I can explain with mere words."

It is not an answer, and yet it is. We spend the evening talking, almost as old friends. In these last hours with Mr. Stoddard, whom I have known all my days, I realize it is the first time I have let down my guard and spoken plainly with the man.

The conversation is delicious, and I savor the taste, my appetite whetted for new acquaintances. At the same time, I am wistful for the past, as I never thought I would be.

· Seven ·

⊢——⊣

I am on the river. By myself. I stand at the rudder, guiding the raft as best I can. The water is high, running strong but not too swiftly. The morning sun is already well overhead, the final loading and goodbyes taking longer than I wished they would.

Mr. Stoddard, Daniel, and I carried the barrels aboard from the wagons and tied them down securely. I am traveling on a raft of wood, with a cargo of wood. Surely this enterprise shall stay afloat.

Daniel was glum. This certainly must look to be a great adventure to him, compared to his seven years of apprenticeship. Samuel was excited, as any young boy in the vicinity of a raft and a river would be. Miss Rebecca wept, which nearly made me do so. Instead, I told her to be brave, at which she laughed and clapped her hands. I laughed too, at the absurd notion of a boy counseling a grown woman, who endured rampages against her family and property, on notions of bravery.

Mr. Stoddard entrusted me with his invoices, to be presented at Shaw's Warehouse on Water Street to a Mr. Owen Tinkham. He said to tie up the raft at the New London wharf and ask anyone nearby for the location of the warehouse. It would be easy to find, he said, Water Street being conveniently near the water. Mr. Stoddard's share would be held on account for him at the warehouse. My own percentage would be paid direct to me.

The arrangement was quite suitable. Although what would follow was less certain.

Find the Indian woman Topheny, in the North Parish of New London, at Hardwick Farm. What that acquaintance would gain me, I knew not. But I had to trust Maame and go where the wind she had set at my back took me.

For now, I must concentrate on the river. It meanders, curving one way and then the other, requiring my attention at the rudder. It finally straightens, and I pass Jewett's Mill, keeping away from the rocks along the riverbank where the water is channeled to turn the gears and the massive millstones. Men wave from the mill, and I wave back.

Never have I felt such joy. I am my own man, conducting a freedman's business.

I see another river following into the Quinebaug ahead, and I know from Mr. Stoddard's description that I am near Norwich. The town where Maame was first a slave, owned by the Arnold family. Dark clouds move in, and I feel it right for a passage through the town where I was begotten.

I have little chance to think or to observe the buildings along the river. The water is rough, white splashes and foam marking rocks nearly hidden beneath the surface. I abandon the rudder and rush forward with the pole, pushing off against outcroppings of rock, working to avoid a collision which might threaten my cargo. Or my life, if my body is thrown into the current and dashed against stone.

As quickly as my raft entered rough and roaring waters, the flow abates. The river is quiet, broad, and dark as clouds gather. I pass wharves where small boats are tied up and where a sloop sits at anchor. People gaze at me, and I gaze back. I feel no desire to wave, perhaps because any one of them could be a relative. If any Arnolds are left to show their face in Norwich, that is.

Thunder rumbles in the distance, and rain patters into the river. The river turns south, and according to Mr. Stoddard, it now becomes the Thames River, named after a great English waterway. Just as New

London is named after a great city, neither of them living up to their old-world namesakes, according to him.

Norwich fades from view, as a sail appears behind me, perhaps the sloop making for New London, or beyond. It moves quickly, its elegant white sail filled with wind, the narrow bow slicing the waters. It is a beautiful sight, and I do wave, my greeting returned with enthusiasm.

I check the clearing sky, as I float slowly with the current. There is not much daylight left, and I do not wish to navigate in the dark into New London harbor, where every ship will be larger than mine, if ship it can be called. Ahead lies a cove, and I lean on the rudder to guide the raft in.

I tie the raft to a tree leaning out over the water. I secure a tattered piece of canvas across the barrels and rest beneath it, dry enough. I have a sack of food Lucy prepared for me, and I eat thick slices of buttered bread along with smoked shad. I drink from an earthenware jug of small beer, Mr. Stoddard having warned me against water from streams or the river itself. He hardly trusts water other than that from his own deep well.

I rejoice to find a gooseberry pie wrapped in cloth at the bottom of the sack. Lucy is an indifferent cook, but this is so good I tell myself Miss Rebecca made it for me herself. I cut a piece for the morning and clean my knife in the water. It is a bone-handled blade, much tarnished but kept sharp.

It is full dark now, and I settle in, wrapped in Maame's quilt and a blanket, under the canvas as a steady rain falls. The oilskin pouch is snug against my skin, the strap tight across my shoulder. The coins press hard against my side, but it is a delightful discomfort. Inside, I also have my emancipation paper, Mr. Stoddard's invoice, and the ancient advertisement from the newspaper, listing my mother and her brother for sale for no fault but that of being saucy.

I wonder, were they saucy? Or was that Arnold's way of disguising a need to raise money, masking his family's circumstances with a disparaging phrase. It was pitched perfectly, not too great a flaw, but one that would require any genteel family to sell off unappreciative slaves. To a sterner master, perhaps.

I grow drowsy as I wonder if it was Benedict Arnold himself who decided to sell them off, or was it his father. Perhaps the son desired otherwise. I shall ask him, someday, in the city of New York. I fall asleep, trying to conjure up the image of my father, an Englishman with gray eyes, a prominent nose, and pale skin.

I dream of him, I am sure. But it is all confusion, a distant figure in a red coat, always out of reach. Voices call out, but I do not understand them.

Voices. I am awake. Did I dream or hear them in truth?

The wind gusts, blowing rain in on me. A twig snaps. The wind?

I reach for the knife at my belt.

"Now what have we here?" This voice is rough and gravelly and ends in a spit of laughter. The raft rocks and tilts as the speaker steps aboard, a second man following.

I leap up, brushing aside the canvas that covers me. I can barely make out their faces, but their intent is clear enough. Robbery, or worse. The first man swats at the canvas with his club, a stout limb that he wields handily.

"I said, what have we here?" He squints his eyes at me and then at the barrels.

"A shipment of staves, sir, bound for New London and the Continental Army." I comply with his request, having little choice. At the moment.

"Staves? What do I want with staves, I ask you? What else do you have?" He steps closer, the rain plastering his hair to his face, which is fair ugly, matching his demeanor.

"Nothing, sir, other than slight provisions. Please, my master will be angry if anything happens to his staves." I decide to play the slave. After all, I have practiced my entire life.

"Tom, search those barrels," the big man says. Tom, stooped and thin, begins to poke around the barrels. Double lengths of rope hold them tight and he grows frustrated in his failed search. "Give us what valuables you have, slave, and we'll be on our way. Unless you're lying and got casks of whiskey aboard."

"Nothing but wood, sir," I say, eyeing Tom, who draws a knife to cut through the rope.

"Let me untie them, they're my knots," I say, moving to the closest barrel. "It will go faster."

Tom looks to his boss man, who nods. "Hurry," he says.

I kneel and busy myself with the rope. "Smart of you fellows," I say. "Coming out of the harbor on that sloop and getting ahead of me. They dropped you off just past the inlet, I'd wager."

"This isn't our first time to the dance, eh, Tom?" The big man turns to Tom and nudges him. They both laugh.

I cut the laughter short. I grasp the pole lying at the base of the barrels and give it a hard swing, slicing through the air and catching the big fellow at the temple. He crashes into Tom, pinning him against the barrels and I pull the pole back, giving Tom a sharp rap to his forehead.

There is a lot of blood, but I know cuts about the head bleed something horrible. Groans escape them, and I rejoice they are not dead. I hope never to kill a man, certainly not during my first days of freedom. And especially not a white man. Freedman or not, vengeance would be swift, with little regard for the paper I guard so carefully. With great effort, I drag them off the raft and deposit each on soggy ground. I return Tom's knife, sorry for the thump, necessary as it was.

Now glad of the rain, since it washes much of the blood away, I silently untie from my mooring and push off, the pole returned to its intended function. The cove is not deep, and I work my way north, so I can come out into the river as far away from the waiting sloop as I can. Their comrades expect to see the raft, but closer to them, not farther away. I feel the current take me and I pull hard on the rudder, sending me into the center of the river, where I float on in darkness, past the sloop, anchored in the shallows.

My first encounter has proven Mr. Stoddard wrong. The world—as much of it as I have seen—is indeed an evil place. Those two villains were ready to plunder me and my cargo, although they were sorely disappointed at the lack of anything more exotic than staves. Perhaps they would have let me go. Perhaps they would have searched me and stolen everything of value I own. And then gutted me, leaving my body food for the fishes.

I will give the world another chance, based on Mr. Stoddard's advice. But I will be much more careful and not so careless about where I sleep.

Shouts carry across the water. I think Tom and his large friend may have regained their senses. I hope they return upstream. Otherwise, they will follow me into New London, seeking revenge. Or perhaps they will take it philosophically. After all, a thief and brigand must expect the occasional failure and thrashing. And I could have rolled them into the water to drown. Although I doubt their thoughts are tending toward gratitude at this moment.

Only one day of freedom on the river, and I have already considered the drowning of two men. If not for my promise to Maame, I might think about returning to Mr. Stoddard once the cargo is delivered. There is a certain safety there. But even with the evil I have met, I am whole. Intact and free.

I drift with the current. I splash water on my face and taste salt.

Salt water from the Devil's Belt. Which I intend to cross, as soon as I find myself a decent craft. Then to New York and my father. I will tell him how I outsmarted and outfought the river pirates.

Yes, river pirates. Much better than common thieves.

I will endeavor not to brag.

· Eight ·

———

After an hour of drifting, I tied up last night along the riverbank, behind a fallen pine tree. To my back was a sheer granite wall. Hidden from intruders on all sides, I slept until dawn. Fortified with gooseberry pie, I push off on the last leg of my journey, watching for the sloop, fore and aft, as sailors say.

Daylight pries open the horizon and I see New London in the distance. A white church spire on high ground, and buildings close together, tumbling down a hillside in a jumble, ending in a row along the waterfront. More structures than Norwich. More roofs and chimneys than I have ever seen. Ships dot the harbor, masts one after the other.

Not being a sailor, and for that matter, having aught but a self-made raft, it is not easy to navigate amidst the ships in the harbor, coming and going even at this early hour. Finally, after some calls from men leaning on ship railings, which I hope is friendly encouragement, I tie up at a dock adjacent to a warehouse. The name *Shaw's* is painted in red letters over weathered wooden planks. A sturdy fellow in a green waistcoat and breeches stands watching me, puffing on his pipe. His sleeves are rolled up, like a working man, not a lord of leisure.

"Mr. Owen Tinkham?" I ask, as I ascend the ladder at the side of the dock.

"You've found him. What's your business?" He is as plainspoken as his dress. No wasted words for Mr. Tinkham. I respond in kind.

"A cargo of staves from Mr. Stoddard, as promised by him, sir."

"A day early, too." I believe this must be a compliment, since he nods his head. Once.

"Shall I leave them with you, Mr. Tinkham?" He puffs again on his pipe, studying the length and breadth of me.

"What's your name?"

"Freegift Cooper, sir. Freedman."

"That's an excellent type of man to be, Freegift Cooper. I've no laborers today. Last three went privateering, every man jack. Will you work for a day's wages?"

I agree. We set upon a fair exchange, at least I hope it is fair, not knowing what an Englishman might earn in such a city. I have no choice but to trust him, as a compatriot of Mr. Stoddard's. And the labor is not hard. I move the raft to a stretch of the rocky shore and set up planks to roll the barrels up and into the warehouse. I stack them inside, among sacks, casks, and numerous other barrels. In fact, there are more goods in this one place than I have ever laid eyes on.

Seeing I am alone, I draw the oilskin pouch out from beneath my clothes, and carefully unfold the invoice and instructions from Mr. Stoddard. I look for Mr. Tinkham to present him with the papers and see what other work he has for me. I walk to the front of the warehouse and find an office with a fine view of the busy street. Mr. Tinkham sits at a desk strewn with papers, quills, and ink at the ready. He studies a ledger book, his fingers tracing columns of tiny numbers. Profits, I think. Or losses. Why a man would calculate what he does not have, I cannot fathom.

"Mr. Tinkham?" I say, softly. He raises a finger, hushing me, intent upon his numbers.

I move to study a map, framed and set upon the wall. It is of Connecticut, divided into counties, and part of Long Island across the Sound. I still prefer to call it by the old-fashioned name, the Devil's Belt, since it bedevils me by separating a father from his son. I see Plainfield along the river, in Windham County. I trace my journey into New London County, past Norwich and the inlet where I defended my cargo. Trading Cove, it is called. Then to the harbor, where I now stand.

It is about as far over the wide water to Long Island as I have come downriver. But it will take more than idle drifting on a stout raft to get me there.

"All right, Freegift. What is it?"

"From Mr. Stoddard, sir," I say, handing him the papers. "The cargo is unloaded."

"Fast work, lad. You like the map, do you?" I nod, as I sense he is proud of it. The frame looks new, and it has a prominent place upon the wall. "This is our state of Connecticut. Here is where you came from," he says, tapping his finger on Plainfield. "Plainfield, with the capital P, do you see how it is made?"

"I do, sir," I say, and I understand he thinks I cannot read. Many English cannot, so why would he think an African capable? "Is this Connecticut as well?" I point to Long Island.

"No, that is New York state, and the land there is filled with Tories, enemies of the Revolution. Best to stay away from them, Freegift. Ah, it is a fine map, is it not? With this I could show you where most of the holdings in my warehouse come from, but I will not bore you."

"It is finely made, Mr. Tinkham," I say as he sits back at his desk, reading the papers. So far, I have encountered evil on the river, and see no reason to trust the first person I meet on land, even though Mr. Stoddard spoke well of him. So I do not correct him on my understanding of letters. "Do you have more work for me?"

"Shortly, lad. There's a schooner expected this afternoon and wagons due in with salt pork and hard tack. Now sit down and let me read."

I welcome the chance to sit in a chair, no matter how hard the wooden seat. I sigh and shift my weight.

"Worn out already, are you?" Mr. Tinkham says, without looking up from the papers.

"It was a difficult night," I say, straightening up. "But I can still do a full day's work, sir." I do not wish to forgo the wages we'd agreed upon, nor do I wish to seem lacking. Why, I wonder, do I care what this man thinks? Perhaps I am too used to pleasing an English master. Not possessing a father, I may put too much stock in how a man of standing sees me. All the more reason to move on, in the direction of New York City, where I might find the only man I should care to impress.

"Certainly," he says, waving my explanation away with a lazy flick of his hand. "I didn't mean to impugn your abilities. Tell me, Freegift, how long have you been a freedman?"

"Nearly a week, sir," I say, and catch him looking at me with narrowed eyes. "I have my emancipation paper, signed and witnessed."

"No need, I'm sure. I simply was not aware Ira Stoddard kept slaves."

"No more," I say. "He favors the struggle for independence strongly, and said slavery was at odds with liberty. So he freed me."

"And do you agree, Freegift?"

"I do find freedom agreeable," I say. "As well as a little troubling to be responsible for making my own way. But yes, I do favor independence, sir, for myself as well as our larger cause." True enough for myself, and I think it smart to align myself with these English who wish to be rid of their king.

"Well put," Mr. Tinkham says and reaches into a drawer to pull out a cashbox. He counts out a stack of coins and pushes them across the desk. "This is your payment, as instructed by Mr. Stoddard."

He has not cheated me. Actually, he has paid me more than my due. Not much, but still, I give him back one coin. "This is more than I am owed," I say.

"So you *can* read," he says and laughs, taking the penny. "I thought as much, from how you studied the map. You must be a smart fellow. I don't think I know of a slave who learned his letters."

"Few have the opportunity, sir. Mr. Stoddard was kind in that regard. It was he who first taught me how to understand letters and form words. He kept a small library and let me read in the evening."

"That accords with what I know of the man," Mr. Tinkham says. "Did he teach you to be cautious, or does that come naturally?"

"About reading, do you mean? I did not mean to deceive, sir."

"That is exactly what you meant to do. Tell me why."

"I apologize for offending you, Mr. Tinkham. I have spent all my life with Mr. Stoddard. I know few people beyond his family. I am unused to the ways of the world. I thought it best to watch and listen, before offering too much of myself."

"Hmm," he says, drumming his fingers on the desk. "Firstly, you have not given offense. I enjoy a man who is shrewd, while honest, in his business dealings. Secondly, continue to heed your own advice. Be sparse with your words and you'll not go wrong. Now, tell me, do you have any further use for that well-made raft of yours?"

"No, sir, I do not." If it would take me across to Long Island, I'd not part with it, but I think I would be swept out into the great Atlantic if I tried.

"Come, let's take a close look," he says, rising and leading me out through the warehouse. He glances at the barrels, stacked neatly to the side. By the way his eyes move, I see he is counting them. Again. Shrewd. We step outside, onto a deck which runs the length of the warehouse, steps leading down to the docks on either side.

I spy the schooner from Norwich, about to pass before us, its bow cutting through the choppy water. Men move about on deck, but I cannot discern them.

"Mr. Tinkham, do you know that schooner?" I ask, pointing to the sleek vessel.

"Aye, that's the *Badger*. Captained by John Cowburn. A man to stay away from, if you want my advice."

"Is he a large man? Bearded, with a big nose, and an unpleasant face?"

"No, that's his first mate, or at least your description fits him well. Titus Gill, a most disagreeable fellow. A pole-thin varmint they call Thin Tom always accompanies him. Now tell me why you ask, Freegift."

"I saw that schooner yesterday docked at Norwich. I planned to spend the night in a cove, just south of there. They passed me on the river and tied up downstream. Gill and another man ventured overland and tried to take my cargo. They were disappointed," I tell him.

"At the cargo?"

"Well, yes, but also at the thrashing I gave them. I left them on the shore, alive, but not in possession of all their wits," I say.

"Freegift, you have now surprised me twice in one day. You can read, and you are willing to defend yourself and your cargo. Your employer's cargo, to be precise. Why did you do so?" I think about his question, and his previous advice. I have several safe answers, aimed to please a man of property and standing. But I decide to offer up a bit of trust, spoken in a whisper.

"Because, Mr. Tinkham, I have been a slave. Now that I am free, I mean that no man should hinder my freedom. Not for a moment. Not for riches, nor for a raft of staves."

"Well, well," he says, leaning on the railing and gazing out at the water. The sloop slows, and eases close to a wharf farther down the bank. "That gives me something to think upon. Now, to the raft. I see it is well-built and can take some weight. I could make use of it, for the small barges that bring goods from across the river."

"Yes, it would be easier to carry cargo up the steps if it were stacked on the raft, I see. What will you offer?"

"Two things, Freegift. The first is a lesson. When selling, do not begin by telling the buyer you have no further use for the item. It lessens the value."

"I should have lied, then?"

"Not so much as a lie is required. You could have said you might use the raft to travel across the river, or further down to the Sound. Or said nothing at all. See?" He inclines his head, looking at me direct, to see if I have absorbed the lesson.

"I do, Mr. Tinkham. It is a useful lesson. Not as useful as the raft, though. What is the second thing?"

"Dinner. Let us go to the Red Lion Tavern and share a meal. You must be hungry after your travels and a morning's labors."

"For the raft?" I say.

"Yes. Do you think it too little?"

"It is best I do not say." Mr. Tinkham looks at me oddly, then bursts into laughter, understanding that I have taken his advice to speak little. For if I did, it would betray my excitement. I have never eaten in a tavern, and I am very hungry.

· Nine ·

ー

Hungry as I am, the first thing I take notice of as we enter the Red Lion is a serving girl. Dark-haired, with the high cheekbones of an Indian. But her skin is lighter than most, and her eyes a deep blue, different from the usual color of her race.

As are mine.

"Freegift," Mr. Tinkham says, taking me by the arm to a table. He seats himself by the window, where he can cast an eye toward the warehouse, as he is waiting for deliveries. Which suits me well, since my bench provides a clear view of the girl as she goes about her duties. Her skirt is blue and matches her eyes. I believe it is the first time I have ever taken note of such a thing. I know it is the first time I have ever seen such beauty.

"Freegift," he repeats himself, tapping the table to secure my attention. "Eyes on me, lad."

"I am sorry, sir," I say, but in truth I am not. Still, the smell of food is strong, and I am very hungry, so I keep my gaze fixed upon Mr. Tinkham.

"Now, listen to me about Captain Cowburn and the crew of the *Badger*. They are a mean and dangerous bunch. Mooncussers, all of them."

"Mooncussers?" I ask. I see a swirl of blue skirt from the corner of my eye. The girl sets down a tankard of cider before each of us.

"Two plates, Tink?" she says. Her voice is light and airy, and it has the echo of an accent I cannot place.

"Yes, Martine, thank you," he says, and she is gone before I can speak, or let my eyes linger over her face.

"Mooncussers? Tink? And her name is Martine?" I stammer, understanding little of what has passed.

"In reverse order, then. Yes, her name is Martine. Last name unknown or never given, perhaps. I am called Tink by many. It is the brief version of my surname and alludes to my trade when I first came to New London. A tinker, I was, before I went into the warehouse business. A tinker is a fine trade, but no man ever became rich at it."

"And what is a Mooncusser, Mr. Tinkham?"

"Those who cuss the moon, because it sheds light, even at night, on their thievery and worse. Cowburn, Gill, and their crew masquerade as privateers, but will take any ship they can. Or cargo on dry land as you well know. They're no better than pirates."

"Why are they still free?"

"Because they have brought in a British vessel or two, which the War Office values highly. And people are afraid of them. The last man to threaten charges against Cowburn had his barn burnt down, all over a stolen hog. So you see, they are very dangerous. Stay well clear."

"As they should as well," I say, taking a drink of the strong cider, my gaze darting over the rim for a sight of Martine.

"Don't mistake luck on one occasion for constancy on all others," Mr. Tinkham says. "Do you understand me?"

"I know what constancy means," I say, annoyed that he might think otherwise, ready to tell him it is an enduring faithfulness. But I am further distracted by Martine, who approaches with two wooden plates.

"Martine, this is Freegift," Mr. Tinkham says, as she sets the plates on the table. I am surprised but remember my manners and begin to stand.

It is a disaster. My head brushes against hers. In my rush to rise as a gentleman would, I do not give her space to move away. I feel her silky hair against my cheek and am overcome with embarrassment. I feel the blood rush to my face and stammer out an apology.

Martine holds her hand to her face, and I fear I have injured her. But I see it is only to cover her laughter as she walks away. I am the injured party, since I have shown myself to be a fool and a lout from the country.

"Sit down, lad. Martine is a fine girl and will not hold clumsiness against you," Mr. Tinkham says, taking a gulp of cider. Perhaps to disguise his own grinning at my expense.

"I am sure she is an upstanding female," I say. "But I care little if she thinks me clumsy over a trifling accident."

"Of course," Mr. Tinkham says, nodding his head sagely. "Now, I thought you hungry?"

"Yes, I am, sir," I say and begin to eat. The meal is smoked ham, green peas, and johnnycake. It is much better than anything Lucy ever cooked. I flatter myself that my slice of johnnycake is larger than Mr. Tinkham's, and then remember I do not care a whit about Martine's notice of me. Especially now that I have delivered her a blow to the head.

"Now tell me," Mr. Tinkham says, after I have eaten every crumb and morsel on my plate. "What are your plans? Do you look for work?"

"Yes, I do," I say, without lying. Of course my work will be in New York, at the behest of my father, but I eagerly follow Mr. Tinkham's advice and speak little.

"I told you I've lost my laborers, or at least until they come slinking back after another fruitless raid," he says. "I've seen you work, and you are as able as most. Come work for me, Freegift. There's a room by the office with a fairly comfortable bed. You can sleep there and keep an eye half open at night."

"For Mooncussers?" I say. "It sounds dangerous."

"Ah, you are using your brains. But no, those fellows aren't my worry, and I won't pay for a guard on the premises. But I'd sleep better at home knowing you were at the warehouse. In case of fire or any such emergency, like the Redcoats landing to rout out the privateers."

"Would they?" I ask, excited at the prospect of a boatload of Redcoat English.

"I didn't mean to worry you, lad," he says, mistaking the tremor in my voice for fear. "I don't think it likely. So what say you?"

"I say yes, Mr. Tinkham. But before we settle upon the wage, I must tell you I have an obligation to fulfill before I take on any duties. My mother died recently and had me promise to visit a friend of hers who resides here in New London."

"My condolences, lad. Certainly you must keep your promise. If you've been recently freed, I must think your mother was a slave as well. Is this person another in bondage?"

"I am not sure. She is an Indian woman who my mother knew in Norwich, where she was first kept. Topheny is her name. She lives in the North Parish at Hardwick Farm. Other than that, I do not know her current circumstances."

Martine comes to the table and stands at Mr. Tinkham's side. I wait for her to clear the plates.

"What do you want with my mother?" Her voice is no longer light and airy.

I cannot speak.

"Just to deliver a message, Martine," Mr. Tinkham says, patting her arm. "Freegift's mother and Topheny were evidently acquainted, and she charged Freegift with delivering the sad news of her recent death."

"Are you a slave?" Martine asks. I expected the courtesy of regret at Maame's passing, but instead she asks a question which can only demean me.

"No longer," I say. "As for my duty to my late mother, I intend to visit Topheny and carry the news to her. You would not hold a son's obligation against me, I hope." I struggle to keep my voice even and force myself to be quiet. Speak less.

"No, I shall not," Martine says. She glances at Mr. Tinkham, who gives a slight nod. What has passed between them? "I will fetch you at five o'clock."

She turns and bustles off to the kitchen.

"Mr. Tinkham, why does Martine speak so cruelly to me? I hardly know her." This I whisper, to be sure she does not overhear.

"Life is hard, as you well know. Especially for an African lad and an Indian girl. You've got a prickly demeanor yourself, Freegift. Or guarded, I might say. Why should Martine act differently? I daresay you are of half-blood, as is she. Both of you are part of two worlds. I mean no offense, it is a simple fact, plain as day."

"That is true enough," I say. Wishing to dwell no more upon the fact of my heritage, we commence to talk of wages. Mr. Tinkham being a fair man, and myself planning on staying only a short time, we settle quickly.

He bade me call him Tink. I say I will, but the word does not come easily. The fear of offending an Englishman will take some time to discard. Perhaps it best that I never do.

· Ten ·

├────┤

Mr. Tinkham—Tink, if I can manage such familiarity—and I walk back to the warehouse. The wagons have arrived, and I begin working to unload and stack their cargo. The work goes quickly, and I have time to retrieve my quilt and meager belongings from the raft as I reposition it, anticipating the barge we expect from across the river.

We. It is odd to say. I am part of an enterprise, entered into of my own free will. The journey downriver was at Mr. Stoddard's request, and given our long association, no matter how forced, I could not have turned down that employment. But here, I may quit and walk away as I please.

But Martine is a friend of Tink's, and I do not wish to anger her. Although what I do wish for in my acquaintance of her is a jumble of confused thoughts and rapid heartbeats. So I lay out Maame's quilt over the thick straw mattress and survey my lodgings. The bed is low and narrow, but as Maame always said, hard work makes for the softest mattress. I have a window, a table, a candle, and a chair. An empty chest sits on the floor next to a washbasin. The door opens into the warehouse. A privy in the alleyway is not far.

It will do until I can find my way across the water to Loyalist ground in Long Island. Until then? Work. Pay my respects to Topheny. Linger in the company of Martine, if I may.

I walk out onto the wharf and see a flat-bottomed craft being rowed across the river. I turn to go inside and inform Tink, but the heavy tromp of feet on the wharf draws my attention. It is Gill, and he glares at me with one fine eye while the other remains hidden behind swollen and discolored skin.

"You!" he bellows, jabbing a finger my direction. The thin, stooped fellow name of Tom is with him, and they are trailed by two lads close to my own age. The boys look frightened, hanging back from the angry Gill. Tom stares at me, his eyes black with hate.

"What do you want, Mr. Titus Gill?" I say, my legs apart for an even stance and my hands on my hips. It is a stern position to take up before angry men, telling them I am not afraid, although I do tremble. My main purpose is to keep my hand close to my bone-handled knife.

"Why your hide, boy, for giving me this," he growls, gesturing to his bruised face.

"You tried to steal from me," I say. "I could not allow it. And take note of where you found yourselves, dry on shore. I could have rolled you off the raft and let you drift off, face down."

"Now, Tom, what do you think of that?" Gill says, elbowing his partner. "He thinks we'll take his kindness at not killing us into account. Ha!"

"No one crosses the crew of the *Badger*, right boys?" Thin Tom says, grabbing the two laggard boys by their collars and thrusting them forward. "Grab 'im!"

We are less than six feet apart. The two young boys are rooted to the ground, despite Tom's pushing. One of them has blond hair falling in his face, his cheeks grimy and sunken. The other's head has been shaven indifferently. Lice.

"If you don't take him down, there'll be a whipping tonight," Gill says, now more put out with the boys than with me. I feel sorry for them. They have the look of captives, treated cruelly.

As slaves may be.

I draw my knife.

"Titus Gill, you are a soft and dull-eyed fool," I say. From *The Merchant of Venice*, but I see little need to explain. It has the desired effect. Gill goes wide-eyed, as far as he can manage, and roars forward, his arms wide, seeking my throat.

I sheath my knife and back up to the railing at the end of the wharf. They have me blockaded, my back against the rough wood. Gill grins, and the shaven boy leaps at my legs, missing as I vault over the rail and grip the floor with my hands, dangling above the stony shore. It is only a few feet below my feet, and I let go as a foot slams down where my fingers were a second ago.

"After him!" Gill yells, kicking at the boys and sending them slithering under the rails after me. I race up the ledge, gaining the flat ground which leads to the alleyway between the warehouse and the neighboring structure. The boys are hard upon my heels, and I am certain Gill and Thin Tom are racing around the building to trap me on Bank Street.

I run, squeezing past the privy which juts out into the alley. I skid to a halt, as I spy a bucket and shovel. Someone has dug out the night soil, and the container is full and ready to be collected. I have a better use than fertilizing crops.

I heave the bucket at the shaven headed boy, who is in the lead and looks as mean as Gill might have been at a more tender age. His meanness turns to wails and caterwauling as the stinking muck splatters him. He careens off the side of the warehouse, seeking the water below for a needed bath. The blond boy flattens himself against the wall, avoiding contact, quite wisely.

"Help me," he utters in a low voice. I am stunned, but glad he makes no move against me. I say nothing, but speed up and sprint out onto Bank Street, where he collides against my back. There he hides, one hand gripping my waistcoat. His head barely reaches my shoulder, and with a quick glance, I put his age at eleven, or less. A mere boy, no match for violent scoundrels. I mean to make for the warehouse office, but Tom is already past it, a knife in one bony hand. Gill trots close behind him, winded.

People pass us on the busy street. A gentleman and his lady take notice. At one glance from Gill, they take a sudden interest in a merchant's shop and enter in great haste. Others turn away, and I see the fear which these men use to exert their will. I pray that Tink does not come out into the street. It will not go well for him.

They advance. Gill snarls as he spots the blond boy to my rear. "I warned you, death to deserters!"

Out comes my knife again, but it is a small and puny blade compared to the cutlass Gill draws from his scabbard. I glance around, but there is no one about, not even a pair of eyes staring through a shop window.

"Don't hurt the boy," I say. "He can't be of much use anyway."

"Am too," a small voice says from behind me.

"Tom, go 'round and fetch the boy. I'll deal with this runaway slave myself," Gil says. Tom circles around, waving his knife in front of him, his grin revealing more gaps than teeth. I hear the clatter of wagon wheels from behind and wonder how long before the driver halts or turns about. I want to say I am not a runaway, but we are past mere words.

Gil steps forward as the boy darts off to my side, facing Tom. I see the lad cock his arm and throw something at Tom, nearly tumbling over as the velocity of his missile carries him forward. It is a stone, a smooth gray oval from the shore, which crashes into Tom's forehead with a crack that is sure to addle his senses, if he has any remaining when he awakes. Tom collapses, insensible, blood streaming onto the cobblestones.

"Good throw," I say. "Have you another?"

"No. Shall we run?" he asks, moving once again behind me. "He's old. He'll never catch us."

Gill looks shocked at Tom's injury, and I hope he has not heard we have no more stones. I would rather he retreat and show the hidden onlookers for the coward he is. So we stand staring at one another, while Tom's gaze is fixed upon the blue sky and the boy huddles at my back. Gill swings the cutlass with menace and takes a long stride toward us.

A whip snaps behind me, and the wagon surges forward, drawn by a sorrel mare at a gallop, straight for Gill. His mouth goes agape, and he leaps aside as Martine pulls back on the reins. The mare stomps and whinnies, excited at the unexpected dash.

"You'll pay for this, you Pequot bitch!" Gill snarls, scurrying back from the horse's hooves like a crab.

"Freegift," Martine says. She nods her head slightly, all calmness, indicating I should board the wagon. I grab the boy, and we climb up onto the flatbed. She holds the reins in one hand and the whip in the other. "You, Titus Gill, would be wise to remember what my people's name means in our language."

With that, she cracks the whip in the air above Gill, driving him even lower to the ground. We canter down the street as the church bell rings five times. She is a prompt lass, brave, and good with a whip. Comely as well. I try to stand, since there is naught but a small seat for a driver, but she snaps the reins and I fall back as the mare picks up the pace. The boy laughs.

Then I do as well. I watch Martine for some clue as to her demeanor, but all I can see is her thick, flowing black hair.

"Who is your friend?" She asks, as we pass the church and the burying ground.

"I know not. He was with Gill and begged me help him," I say, holding on to the edge of the jolting cart. "What are you called, boy?"

"Wait," he says, pushing thick blond hair away from his eyes.

"Why wait?" I ask.

"No, my name is Wait. Wait Jenkins."

"Who gave you that name, Wait?" Martine asks, turning from her seat to study the boy.

"It was my father's name. He's dead," the boy says, his voice flat as if nothing matters.

"And your mother?" I ask. "Does she live?"

"I don't know," Wait says. "Maybe. She was on the ship." He bows his head, his eyes fixed to the buckboard.

"What ship?" I ask, and I catch sight of Martine shaking her head. Leave him be, is her message. If Wait was aboard a ship with his mother, it was likely the men of the *Badger* who took him. And did the unspeakable to his mother.

I look at Martine as she gives the reins a snap. Her black hair glistens in the sunlight, and I feel unaccountably happy that she and I shared an instant understanding of the boy's situation. And, I wonder if there will be other occasions where our minds will be as one.

I must admit she saw the wisdom in silence first. Speak less is still a lesson to be learned. I do regret my thoughtless query of the boy, and wish I had stabbed Gill full in the belly.

"Is this the North Parish?" I say to Martine, after a few minutes, hoping to distract Wait from his misery. The horse pulls the wagon slowly along a rutted path, cleared fields on both sides. Charred stumps mark the progress of turning forest to farmland.

"Yes. The Hardwick farm is not far. Only another mile. Are you hungry, Wait?"

"What's your name?" Wait asks her, as if the question itself were foolish. Of course a boy in the service of ruffians would never have enough to eat.

"Martine," she says. "And this is Freegift."

"I know," Wait says, staring at me. "Gill wants to cut out his heart." He says this as one might state a man wants to cut a piece of pie. Calmly, and with a certainty that chills.

"Well, he did not get it today," I say, patting my chest, and looking alarmed as I pull open my waistcoat. "No, it is still there, I can feel it!"

Wait goes wide-eyed and then laughs. He pulls at his own grimy shirt and mimics me. "Mine too!" We all laugh. I look to Martine and feel my face flush at the thought of her patting her own bosom.

"Martine!" Wait shouts, urging her to join the game.

"I have my heart safe, worry not on my account," she says, and shakes the reins so the sorrel breaks into a trot, knocking us about in the wagon.

Wait becomes a bit livelier now that we laugh on Gill's account. I believe it helps scatter some of the fear he holds of this brute. He hangs over the rail, gazing at the fields ahead. They are cultivated here, rows of young corn stretching to the distant woods. Farther on, plants and vines cover the ground. Squash and pumpkin, perhaps.

Ahead, I spy a farmer working his hoe between leafy rows. Martine waves, and he nods, hardly breaking his practiced stride, although I see his gaze follow the wagon carrying two strangers toward his home.

"Is that Mr. Hardwick?" I ask.

"It is. Look, see the farmhouse," Martine says, as we turn off the road and take a hard-packed lane with grass growing in the middle. The house is stoutly built, painted a deep red, two stories tall with a fine brick chimney. Three gable windows jut out from the cedar-shingle roof, and a few steps from the house a barn sits off to the side. I hear the squawk of chickens and see the kitchen garden bordered by flowers, the sure sign of a woman's hand.

"Your mother lives in a fine house," I say, as Martine brings the wagon to a halt by the barn.

"She does not live in the house. She has a wigwam down by the river," Martine tells me. "I will take you there."

"She's an Indian?" Wait asks, jumping down from the wagon.

"Yes," Martine says. "We are Pequot. Have you heard of our tribe?"

"No," Wait says. "I know Nemo. He's a Narragansett."

"Is he on the *Badger*?" I ask. Wait nods a yes. I think he knows no one other than that crew. Except for Martine and I, and I marvel at how sweet the linking of our names sounds, even in this small matter of Wait.

"Was Nemo kind to you?" Martine asks, unbuckling the girth and patting the horse gently. Her voice is gentle as well, and I see she is bringing Wait along slowly, coaxing small bits of his story from him. It will take time, but is better than my clumsy directness.

"He never hurt me," Wait mutters. Which may have passed for kindness.

I recall something Martine said. "You told Gill to remember what the name of your tribe means in your language."

"What does it mean, Martine?" Wait asks, moving close to help her with the traces. He seems eager to move on from talk of the *Badger's* crewmen.

"Destroyers, some say. So mind your manners, Wait Jenkins," Martine says, all mock sternness. Wait grins, lapping up the attention of a woman like a kitten at a saucer of milk. "Now help me bring Cricket in."

Martine and Wait lead the sorrel into the barn. She introduces him to the three other horses, as if they were people, speaking to each in turn. Once Cricket is in her stall, Wait brings her an armload of hay and is rewarded with a nuzzle. He is at ease around animals, unafraid. A farm boy, then, before he was forced into the pirate band.

"You've brought us visitors, Martine." The voice startles me. A young woman, no more than ten years older than I, stands by the open barn door, a child sitting on her hip. Her tone is civil, but wary. Intelligent then, with her husband some distance away and perhaps no one other than the ancient Topheny for company in the sparse North Parish.

"Come, Martine," a sharper voice snaps, and I find myself staring at an old fowling piece. Or rather it stares at me, the muzzle pointed directly at my heart, held by a woman wearing Indian garb. "Move away from that filthy scamp."

The young woman with the child stares at me, her eyes darting across my person, landing for a second on the knife at my belt. She has her child at hand and will think of the youngster first. So I make no movement, wishing not to be seen at a threat. Wishing not to be filled with buckshot.

"Nonôk!" Martine says, stepping forward while pushing Wait behind her. "Put that down. These are friends."

Nonôk does not look convinced, but lowers her weapon. She is dressed in a deerskin dress, a leather belt cinched tight at her stout waist. Her hair is black, her skin wrinkled. Tattoos climb and swirl around her neck and onto her cheek. She looks fearsome enough without her finger on the trigger.

"We wanted to be sure," the young woman says. "You've never brought anyone here, and it seemed suspicious. Topheny thought it best to make certain you hadn't been forced."

Topheny? Where is she? Who is Nonôk? And should I be honored that Martine brought me herself? She need not have. I could have walked and perhaps found my way. My thoughts are all ajumble, and I strain to hear the words thrown at me by this native apparition.

"You! I asked if you are a runaway!" Nonôk says, advancing upon me with the weapon gripped in both hands. I back up, hands raised. She speaks with a clipped, sing-song cadence.

"I am a free man," I say.

"And the boy?" She demands. "Why does he smell so bad? That is a bad white man smell." She wrinkles her nose, and I must concur. Wait has not seen soap and water for a long time. Some of the night soil I flung at his companion must have landed on his garments, which were so dirty it was hard to tell one stain from the other.

"This is Wait Jenkins," Martine says. "He made a daring escape today from a band of cutthroats in New London. Privateers on the *Badger*, who had taken him prisoner. And this young man, who Tink tells me is no slave, is Freegift Cooper."

"If you say so, Martine," Nonôk says, finally resting the butt of her gun on the ground. "The boy still smells."

"I am Ann Hardwick," the young woman says, stepping into the barn. My husband Edward will be in from the fields soon. This is our son Rufus. He is almost three years old."

"Freegift Cooper," I say, bowing in her direction, unsure of how free folks greet each other. "I have come here to see Topheny, if I may."

"What do you want with her?" Nonôk says, stiffening with suspicion.

Martine approaches me and lays a hand on my arm. I jump, as if burned by a hot coal. "Freegift," she says, in the same gentling voice she used with Wait and the horses, her accent leavened differently than Nonôk's, with something sweet and foreign. "Nonôk means mother in my language. This is Topheny, the woman you have come to see."

"Why?" Her mother demands, wary of the stranger who has come seeking her.

"Let us all go inside," Mrs. Hardwick says, as Rufus begins to squirm. I can wait no longer.

"My Maame—mother in my language—bade me see you. On her deathbed. You knew her in Norwich, when she and her brother were owned by the Arnold family."

Topheny squints and studies my face. Then she smiles.

"Sally's boy," she declares. "Freegift. I've been waiting for you."

· Eleven ·

⊢——⊣

Topheny takes me along a well-trod path, blackberry bushes on either side. Her wigwam sits near a swift-running stream, water gurgling over stones. It is pleasant here, light from the setting sun filtering through trees, and soft green grass growing along the waterway. But all I can think of is how Topheny knew to expect me. I'd only spoken of it today, in New London.

How did she know to expect Sally's boy?

Near the entrance to the wigwam is a wooden frame set over two logs. A deerskin is stretched out on it, in the process of being tanned and turned into a soft and supple garment. I wonder if Martine ever dresses in such Indian garb, and remind myself I must stay alert as I am here alone with Topheny. I have never considered witches to be real—leastways not the English style of witch—but Topheny may be one if she knows what the future holds.

Or, perhaps she is quick witted enough to claim she knew I was coming and take some advantage for herself. There is witchery enough in that.

She invites me to enter the wigwam. Made of saplings overlaid with elm bark, the roof is covered by woven reeds and is high enough that I may enter upright. Inside, the same reeds are threaded into a thick mat, laid over the soft needles of the white pine.

"Sit," Topheny says, motioning to a sleeping platform covered in blankets. It is set barely a foot off the floor, blocks of hickory holding the oaken frame in place. She has chosen the woods wisely. The bark of the elm comes off the tree in large, thick sheets, and her walls are strong. The hickory will resist rot. The oak is sturdy. Walking on the white pine boughs releases a pleasant odor of greenery.

My life has been about finding the right wood. I cannot avoid casting an eye upon her choices and finding them more than suitable. But that is not why I am here, so I sit and face her as she sits cross-legged on the platform opposite.

"You knew my mother," I say.

"Freegift. A fine name to give you," Topheny says, her eyes shutting for a moment, perhaps conjuring up a memory. "You were a gift to her. She was happy to be with child."

"Not all gifts are accepted freely," I say and wish I had not. I cannot bear to hear of Benedict Arnold forcing himself on Maame. Is that the story she sent me to Topheny to hear? I cannot believe that, so I breathe deep and collect myself. "My apologies. Maame bade me come see you, although I know not why."

"We were friends. Good friends," Topheny says. "What did she tell you of our days in Norwich town?"

"Nothing. As she lay dying, she told me Benedict Arnold was my father. And that I should seek him out in order to make my way in the world. But that first I should journey here and speak with you. She said you would help me. In what way, I know not."

"You were born a slave," Topheny says, avoiding the question of how she can help me.

"Yes. Maame died a slave. Mere days ago, I was given my freedom. The English man who owned me said he favored liberty from the British and was hard-pressed to keep a slave while seeking his own freedom. So now I am emancipated, and I have done the first thing Maame asked of me. Soon I must do the other."

"Tell me, Freegift," she says, leaning forward. "Did Sally follow the news of the war? That your father has gone over to the British?"

"No one need follow the news of the war to know that. It is on every man's lips, what the traitor Arnold has done. She knew he is now in the city of New York, where I must go." I want to know more about this man, the traitor I now call father, but I am embarrassed. It is best if I display little care about him. Speak less, I remind myself. I ask how she and Maame knew each other.

"I was a servant to the Lathrop family, who were close to Arnold's people. I signed a bond, to work seven years for them," she said. A sigh escapes her lips, and I see sadness.

"You were a slave?" I ask.

"No. But my people are gone, scattered. When the English and the other tribes attacked the Pequots, back in my grandfather's time, they killed many. Took others for slaves, while the rest took shelter in the woods and swamps. There was nothing else for me but to sell my labors."

It is a sad thing indeed. Still, it is the same future most men and women face. It is the future I face, but I know that means little to Topheny. She lost her people. As I have. Perhaps the fault is not hers for feeling grief, but rather mine for not. Therefore, I practice speaking less and nod my head.

"Ma'am," I say, aiming to be polite but also to draw out of her why I am here.

"I am no fancy madam, Freegift. Call me Topheny, it will do as well."

"Yes, Topheny," I say. It is easier to call her by a familiar name, since she is an Indian. The English prefer their slaves to address them as if they all were lords and ladies, even the least of them, and such obedience is a hard habit to break. "Do you know why my mother wanted me to see you? Was there a reason, other than to give you the news of her passing?"

"You know my daughter, Martine?"

"Yes. She offered to bring me here," I say. "Mr. Tinkham—Tink— introduced her to me at the tavern. When we had our dinner. She overheard me telling him I intended to visit you and asked what my business was." Speaking less does not come easily.

"No, Freegift, I do not mean that," Topheny says, slicing one hand through the air in what I take to be a menacing manner. But her voice is not harsh, and I think she laughs a bit at my expense. "I mean to say, Sally and I had our children close by. Martine in the spring, you in the summer. Martine's father was a Frenchman, a fur trader from up north. Maybe he's back up there, maybe he's dead. I can hardly remember him now, but he wasn't a bad man. At least he was not English."

"As was my father," I say, if only to fill the silence, as I wonder what Martine has to do with the answer to my question.

"Yes. Benedict was a dashing young man. He ran off to fight the French and the Iroquois and was a great hero when he returned. Or so he claimed. No one thought to question a young man's proud boasting. Then things turned bad for him. His mother died, and his father, who always loved his rum, fell into constant drunkenness. Benedict was very sad. All the time."

"Did his father threaten my mother? Did he—"

"No," Topheny says, with that same motion of her hand. "Old man Arnold drank in public, at the tavern. Benedict often had to fetch him home, drunk. It was during this time that he and Sally began to talk together. Benedict had been expected to go to college to become a man of learning. When his mother died, his father drank more than he earned and there was no money for him or his sister Hannah. He felt the world fall from beneath his feet, and sought what comfort he could find. Your mother thought kindly of him, Freegift. And he for her, as far as he could. This was not a slave-owner taking advantage of the flesh he owned. Sally said he was tender. And that he promised to free her when his father died. He would inherit all his property, of course, and Benedict would be able to keep his promise."

"Do you think he would have?" I ask. For Mr. Stoddard to emancipate me now, in recognition of the struggle for liberty he so believed in was one thing. For a slaveholder to do so before this revolution was another.

Few would understand why. Others might sense his reason, and gossip. Aspiring gentlemen do not like gossip.

"We will never know," Topheny says. "When he said it, I think he believed he would. Sally was a smart one, like you are. I can tell these things. She was happy to believe it to be true, Freegift, that much I know. And her happiness came from Benedict's promise."

"What happened?"

"The elder Arnold found out. He sold Sally and her dear brother. There was nothing Benedict could do. He was in a dark mood for weeks and spoke to no one."

Sold for being saucy. So that was the real reason.

"Did he know? About me?" I ask.

"No," Topheny says, a sigh escaping her lips.

"Did you?"

"Yes," she says. "Sally was certain she was with child. I already knew I was. She made me promise never to tell a soul."

"Why? Why did she not tell Benedict?"

"Because her baby would be the property of old man Arnold. He might keep her only long enough for her to wean the child. Then sell her off, or you, as punishment. It had to be a secret. To protect you and keep you both together. It was all for you, Freegift. To keep you safe."

"That is what she wanted me to know?"

"We made a vow, to help each other if we could. An indentured servant and a slave have little but for each other. I found out where she'd been sold to and managed to get my Frenchman to take a message to her about Martine. That was when the Lathrops sold my bond to Mr. Hardwick. The father of this Hardwick."

"Did you ever hear from her again?"

"Yes. A year after you were born. A merchant came downriver and attended services at the Congregational Church. The magistrate is a firm believer in attendance on their Sabbath, so I must sit through their silly songs every week. He approached me, after asking for Mr. Hardwick himself, so as to not raise suspicions. But it was a message from Sally that he brought me. It was that you were thriving, and your name was Freegift. She said by that name I would know what she intended."

"That one day I would seek out my father," I say. She had planned all along, waiting for the day that never came in her lifetime. She used her own death to impart that message so that I could do little but obey.

"And find your place in the world," Topheny says, with great force, her hand slashing the air again. "I know you will find him. I have seen visions."

"Is that how you knew I'd come here?" Maame had spoken often of our Akan religion, and the ancestor spirits which guide us. Perhaps they had spoken to Topheny.

"I have always known," Topheny says. "It is your destiny to find your father. Or he to find you."

"How?" I ask. "He does not know of me. You have said so."

"This is true. But in my vision, he comes to you. I knew it would happen once you became a man, as you now are. I made this for you, last year."

She reaches into a leather sack at her side.

A tomahawk appears in her hand. A steel head on a hickory shaft. She hands it to me.

I cannot speak.

Soft leather is wrapped around the shaft at the base, giving a firm grip. It is bound by rawhide strips adorned with two black-tipped eagle feathers. It fits my hand perfectly, balanced as if made for me.

Which it was.

"You made this?" I ask, unable to say more.

"The steel is from France. It was left to me when Martine's father disappeared, among some trade goods he left behind. I searched out the wood last year, knowing it had to be ready soon. It is fire polished. I tanned the leather and found the eagle feathers on the frozen river this winter."

"Did your vision show you how I should use it?" I ask, feeling the edge. Sharp.

"Not everything that is foretold is for you to know, Freegift Cooper," she says. Her hand arcs again through the air. We are done.

· Twelve ·

⊢——⊣

T hank you, Mr. Hardwick, but I must return tonight," I say, in answer to his invitation to supper and to spend the night.

"It will be dark before you get a mile down the road," he says. "It is unwise for a stranger to walk about at night. You might be mistaken for a Mooncusser, or a runaway. You know slaves are not allowed to wander after sunset."

I do know, but hold my tongue. He does not mean an insult, and I may sound ungrateful informing him I am not a slave nor have I ever wandered anywhere.

Mr. Hardwick strikes me as a sensible man. He—Edward—and his wife Ann are not quite thirty years of age, if I judge correctly. He has strong forearms from his work in the fields but is lanky otherwise, and his look is insightful. He strikes me as intelligent, or at least more intelligent than a farmer needs be, other than possessing a knowledge of crops, cattle, and feed. Of which I have none, so perhaps a man must be exceedingly smart to coax a living out of the land.

"I will take you back to New London in the morning," Martine says, brushing by me as she carries a dish to the table. "Unless you are afraid of facing Gill and his men." This she delivers with a glance across her shoulder, and I see the twinkle of mischief in her eyes.

"What?" Edward exclaims. He sets down the clay pipe he was about to light.

"Tis how this fellow came to us tonight," Ann says, ushering Wait into the room. He is not recognizable, without his layers of dirt and grime. His hair is brushed and gleams like wheat on a bright summer's day. His cheeks are red from being scrubbed, and although dirt still shows itself at his fingernails, he is nearly presentable. He wears breeches that reach to his ankles, and a linen shirt tied at the waist.

He looks frightened.

I glance at Martine, her hand covering her mouth. She has not intended her joke about Gill to be overheard by Wait, who is in terror of the man.

"I only tease you, Freegift," she says, recovering quickly. "I have seen nothing so brave, except for Wait throwing that stone. What perfect aim!"

"Will someone in this household tell me what has happened?" Edward says, taking Rufus into his lap and bouncing his leg, much to the child's pleasure. I thought he might be angry, but he exhibits more of an amused curiosity than displeasure at our appearance.

"I had an encounter with the crew of the *Badger*," I explain. "Once on the river and again on Water Street, when they came to take their revenge. This lad, Wait Jenkins, was a captive of theirs. He broke free and greatly assisted me."

"With a stone, Wait? Can you throw well?"

"Well enough to knock old Tom down," Wait says, his pride overcoming fear.

"Thin Tom? That beak-nosed fellow who always stays in Gill's shadow? That Tom?" Edward says, holding Rufus as he begins to squirm.

"Yes, sir," Wait says, drawing himself up straight, a process made difficult by the need to hold up his breeches. "But I ran out of stones, and we were saved by Miss Martine, and Cricket."

"Well, well," Edward says, studying the boy. He glances at his wife, and I see a glistening in her eyes. Deep waters run between them, but they say nothing. Edward turns his attention to me. "And you, Freegift, what did you do when these ruffians came?"

"No more than stand idly by, sir. Between Master Wait's throw and Martine riding to our rescue, there was little need." I see Topheny smile and am pleased with myself. As if my own mother took note of my modesty.

We share a supper of rabbit stew and bread baked in an outdoor oven. All courtesy of Topheny, who I learn is adept at snaring rabbits and other game. She also knows the healing herbs in the forests and fields, Ann tells me. She has cured fevers, healed cuts and broken bones, all common enough on a farm. We talk of the curative powers of the white pine and the slippery elm, which Maame knew, and I guess that much of her knowledge came from Topheny and her Pequot ancestors.

Wait eats more than seems possible for a lad his size. Ann dotes on him, and it is Topheny who scolds her not to burst the boy's belly, while Edward leans back and smiles. It is an easy-going household. Mr. Stoddard was not a mean man at all, but now I see that he was not happy either. His household was about work and business. With only slaves and servants for company, there was little place for levity. I hope his daughter and grandsons will bring some joy to his abode.

Edward invites me to sit with him after the meal. He lights his clay pipe, and we retire outside, taking up our places on a bench facing the barn. We listen to the soft, shuffling sounds of the animals in their stalls, and the crickets chirping in the fields. The night is pleasant, and I marvel at all the people I may meet now that I am emancipated. Some good like the Hardwick family. Some worse, certainly. Still, it seems a great adventure to be free.

"You've brought Topheny news, I understand," Edward says, after a silence. It is his household, and he is within his rights to ask.

"Yes, sir. Of my mother's death. They were friends in Norwich, years ago," I say.

"I am sorry to hear of it, Freegift. It was a decent thing to journey all this way."

"I came downriver from Plainfield, sir. New London was my destination. And thank you."

"Are you planning on staying?" Edward asks.

"No, I mean, I will leave at first light," I say, confused, since he has already issued his invitation.

"You mistake me, Freegift. I mean, will you stay on in New London?" He laughs, lightly, to show it is not at my expense and claps me on the shoulder.

"Yes, yes I do," I say. I tell him about my position with Tink at Shaw's Warehouse, as if I plan to stay for years. I do not want to lie to this man, so I avoid details, leaving the impression I can see no farther than Water Street.

"You said you were emancipated," Edward states. "Do you have papers?"

"Yes, I do," I say, beginning to reach for the oilskin bag around my neck. I am disappointed that he wishes to see proof. But he quickly places his hand on mine.

"No, you don't need to show me. But there are some who might ask. And others who might take it from you," he says.

"Then denounce me as a runaway," I say. "Others such as Gill and his men."

"Actually, I think Gill too stupid and mean to calculate such a plan. He will bash your head in quick enough, but for thinking things through, that would be John Cowburn, captain of the *Badger*."

"What should I do, then?"

"You will have to register with the magistrate anyway," Edward says. I do not understand, and he must see the look on my face. "All residents must register for the tax rolls and attend services as well. Was that not required in Plainfield?"

"If it is the custom here, it must have been there as well," I say. "But Mr. Stoddard took care of all things. It was not my place."

"Well, now it is. You'll have to attend the Congregational Church with the rest of us. I don't like being told what to do, but I find it's easier to show up and sing along with the hymns than receive a fine from the magistrate. I hope I haven't offended you, Freegift. Are you religious? I mean, in an enthusiastic manner."

"I am used to attending and lending my voice to the choir's efforts," I say. "As you are." There. I spoke the truth, but not enough of it to show my true disdain for the Christian's babble. As lighthearted as Edward may be, he was still born of that tribe.

"There's one other thing," he says. "You should join the militia."

"Really? I may do so?"

"Certainly. I will vouch for you myself. I serve as a lieutenant in the Third Connecticut Militia, charged by the governor to protect the town and harbor." Edward explains he went off with the militia at the beginning of the revolution to fight in Boston. He tells me stories of standing atop Bunker Hill and firing at ranks upon ranks of Redcoats as they advanced. Of retreating only when their ball and powder supplies were gone. He narrates the scene with such enthusiasm that I do not think of the British as my father's men. Indeed, at the time they were not. Caught up in thoughts of martial glory, I readily agree to his proposal.

"Excellent," Edward says, pumping my hand. "This will thwart any question of your suitability as a citizen. And the crew of the *Badger* will think twice once you're a member of my company."

"But I have no arms, sir," I say, the reality of my situation catching up with my new-found patriotism. "Save for my knife and tomahawk."

"We will remedy that in the morning," Edward says, knocking the ash from his pipe. "I have half a dozen muskets and supplies stored here, for issuing to new recruits. Know you how to load and fire? You must have hunted in the forests up north."

"Of course," I say, not wishing to appear inexperienced to such a soldier, nor to abuse him of his bucolic notion of a slave armed and hunting in the deep woods. No owner of flesh and steel would let both roam free, perhaps never to see musket and man again. Yes, I did roam among the towering oak and hickory, but still was tethered to Maame, and my life with hers.

In truth, I have never held a musket, much less pulled the trigger and sent lead flying. But how difficult can it be?

· Thirteen ·

⊢——⊣

Wait and I are put in a storeroom at the rear of the house for the night. A narrow bed is uncovered, draped under a dusty canvas as if put away long ago. Ann hastily explains it will be Rufus' room when he is old enough, as she wields her broom, cleaning and rolling out a braided rug made from scraps and rags. Crates are stacked to the side and the window opened, airing out the room. When all is done, Ann complains of the dust and rubs her eyes, face turned to her husband's shoulder.

I am not accustomed to young women of her age, but I know by the smile Edward forces upon his face this was the room promised to a child who never grew old enough for it. As Ann stands in silence, she reminds me of Viola in *Twelfth Night*:

She pined in thought,
And with a green and yellow melancholy
She sat like patience on a monument,
Smiling at grief.

The Bard meant, joy and sadness endured in the same moment turns the face to stone.

Martine brings Wait in by the hand, brushing against Ann who brings her hand to her mouth and leaves the room. Martine sits Wait upon the bed, kneeling next to him. Topheny follows with quilts and a wool blanket, more than enough for the mild night.

"It has been quite a day of adventures, Wait, has it not?" Martine says, patting the bed. He needs little encouragement. He yawns and stretches out. Then he seems to take notice of me.

"Freegift, don't you want the bed?" Wait asks, up on his elbow.

"Hardly," I say. "Too soft for a riverman like me. I like hard wood beneath my back. Please, Wait, leave me to the floor."

"You'll stay here?" Wait says, needing little convincing.

"Right here," I say, spreading my blanket and quilt.

"And you Martine?" Wait asks. Martine sits at the end of the bed, arranging his covers. "Will you stay?"

"Of course not," she says. "It would not be seemly for a girl to sleep in the same room as two men, Wait Jenkins. How dare you!" She tickles him, and they laugh like two children. I laugh too, and consider that we are all children, or would be if we had parents with wealth and time enough for us to grow into men and women. But for the likes of a stolen boy, an Indian, and an African, we must find our own path. I cannot say I have had childish thoughts in many years and am glad that some may return to young Wait.

"Have you seen Freegift's tomahawk?" Wait asks Martine, after the tickling is finished. I had let him examine it, under instructions not to test the sharp blade. He had, of course, and now had a good nick as a lesson learned. "It has eagle feathers."

"Yes, I know," Martine says. "My mother made it for him."

"Will she make one for me?" he asks. "I mean someday, not right now."

"If she has a vision to do so, then yes, she will."

"Where will you sleep?" Wait asks Martine, disappointed in the answer, vague as it is.

"In the wigwam with Topheny," she says. "Maybe you'd like to spend the night with us one day. It's by the river, and you can hear the water splashing over rocks in the night. It is pleasant. Peaceful."

"A real Indian wigwam?" Wait asks. Martine nods, but his face screws up in thought. "But when? Will we come back here?"

"We shall," Martine says, and kisses Wait on the forehead. I am sitting on the floor, and as she bends over, her dark hair falls against my face. It is so unexpected I gasp, as if the air is blown from my lungs. This caress is even better than a kiss, I think, although I have no way of comparing. I feel the blood rush to my face as my gaze lingers on her lips, and I wonder if I ever shall. She pulls away and stands over me, the shimmering light of a single candle at her back.

"Good night, Freegift," she says.

I cannot recall what I managed to say, if anything at all, although I lie awake remembering the silken feel of her hair against my cheek.

"Freegift?" Wait says after several minutes. I look to him. "What did Martine mean? I don't know if I can come back and sleep in the wigwam."

"In truth, Wait, I am greatly confused by her." I say nothing else, since it would not be my place, but I think it likely Wait will never have to leave.

Morning comes, and I must work myself into an enthusiasm about joining the militia. Last night, hearing Edward's tale of Bunker Hill and fighting to the last bullet, my blood raced. Now it runs cold at the thought of fighting British Regulars and their long bayonets. Not that my father is now with them. No, it is simply that in the still light of dawn, I have no wish to die.

But there is sense in it. No one will question my place in New London once I put myself in the service of Connecticut. It is the surest way to show myself to be a freedman. And it will further mask my intent to cross the Devil's Belt as soon as I find a way.

So, resolved, I find myself in an open field with Edward. And of course Wait, who at the mention of a musket is instantly at our side. Edward bids him to stay behind us, and I spy Martine advancing across the field. She takes Wait by the hand, and now I have an audience.

"What musket do you prefer?" Edward asks, and I barely understand his question. He has only one with him.

"The type Mr. Stoddard had," I say. "It did not look like this one." True enough.

"This is a French Chareville," Edward says. I see the stock is made of a fine walnut, but other than that, the name means nothing. I nod, as if evident.

"It's a tad lighter than the Brown Bess, so it should suit you easily," he says. Perhaps he sees confusion race across my brow and takes pity upon me with Martine and Wait watching. "Here, I'll step you through it, the way we do it in the militia."

Again, I nod, as if that makes perfect sense. I watch and study his movements.

Edward cocks the hammer back and takes a piece of wrapped paper from a pouch. He bites off the end and pours out black powder into the pan.

"Just this amount, right?" he says. I agree. "Then lock down the frizzen." I see he has clamped a piece of metal over the powder so it will not spill. I nod encouragingly.

He sets the butt of the musket on the ground, and stuffs the paper wad into the barrel, telling me to be sure the ball is at the top, laughing that he once placed it in upside down. As if the joke were on him. My appreciation of this man grows by the minute.

"Take the ramrod and tamp the powder and ball down," he says. "That's all there is to it. Put the ramrod back, raise the musket to your shoulder, and fire." He does so, squeezing the trigger. The powder in the pan ignites and is immediately followed by the roar of his shot, smoke and fire issuing from the barrel.

He hands me the musket. I pull the hammer back, surprised at the tension. Edward takes me through the commands in a low voice, giving encouragement. Finally I bring the musket to my shoulder and feel his hand at my back. With the other, he points to thick oak at the edge of the field.

"Aim there," he says, his hand firmly at my back.

I do so. I squeeze the trigger, and the musket bucks into my shoulder with more force than I'd foreseen. Edward's hand steadies me. I am grateful to not end on my backside.

"Excellent!" Edward says, clapping his hands. "Again, and pick up the pace."

Now he becomes a sterner taskmaster, adjusting my stance, having me bear the musket upon my shoulder as if on the parade ground. After six more shots, the musket feels lighter. What seemed difficult and confusing is now understandable, motions sure and swift.

"Thank you, Edward," I say, as we walk back to the house, Wait at our heels. Martine has left, and I wonder if she gave up after seeing my first clumsy attempts. I almost ask Wait, but cannot bear to hear that she ran off laughing at the would-be soldier.

"You are welcome, Freegift," he says. "I hope you never need face an enemy more ferocious than that oak. Now, to the rest of your supplies."

Edward's root cellar doubles as an armory of sorts. The local militia is amply supplied by the French out of Newport, he tells me. His farm secretly houses a cache of powder and ball, along with other necessities of war. Such as a leather belt with pouches full of munitions and tools for cleaning the Chareville.

"And don't forget this," he says, withdrawing a gleaming bayonet from a sheath. He snaps it onto the barrel and hands it to me. "It may save your life when there's no time to reload."

Saving my life seems to be a very practicable thing. Although I feel a reluctance to do so by piercing another human being with this steel shaft. I realize that could be how I meet my own end and find that I may be able to manage it. The terror of my own insides spilled onto the ground outweighs the momentary savagery of that shrieking thrust.

After a fine breakfast, Edward has one more gift for me. A linen hunting shirt, the kind he says has become the uniform of the militia, if not much of the army. It is a long garment, loose and easy to move within, fringed at the seams, and the color of an ash tree. He forbids me to wear it other than when with the militia. But, since I will be put on the rolls today as a member, he allows me to don it as we prepare to leave.

I am every inch the soldier.

I cinch my leather belt, adorned with the tomahawk and my knife in its sheath. The bayonet hangs in its scabbard, and I practice the small drill Edward has taught me, with Wait barking orders as if he were a general.

"Present arms! Shoulder firelock! Fix bayonet!"

"Come, Wait," Martine calls from the house. "Help me harness Cricket. You two can play militiamen later."

"I do not play at this, Martine," I say, indignant. Wait scurries off to Cricket, the horse more interesting than my musket work.

"No, of course not, Freegift. I only meant Wait was at play," she says. The words are correct, but I think she laughs at me all the same.

"Think what you will," I say. "After all, I am in your debt for bringing me here. I hope it has not been too great an inconvenience, nor will the return trip." I strive to sound haughty, as if I have little care for what she thinks.

"Oh, you think you are in my debt? Do not flatter yourself, Freegift. I would have made the journey without you, gladly. Edward has a load of foodstuffs to deliver to the tavern. Squash, beans, carrots, all freshly harvested. Make yourself ready and we will find room for you and your blunderbuss," she says, and turns away in a swirl of skirt.

"It is a Chareville," I shout after her. "A fine French piece!"

I am every inch the fool.

· Fourteen ·

⊢——⊣

The ride into New London is full of silence. Except for Cricket, who neighs and whinnies with abandon, glad to be on the road. No one else seems to share her passion for it. Edward drives, and Martine sits upon a barrel, leaving me to dangle my legs off the back of the wagon. It is hardly a martial procession.

When we arrive at the tavern, I shed my hunting shirt and belt. I am sure soldiers often carry bushels of squash in an encampment, but I prefer to work as plain Freegift here on Water Street. Martine excuses herself, running up steps at the back of the tavern to her attic room where she stays when not out at the farm with her mother. She returns donning her apron, ready for the work of the day. She directs us to stack the produce in the kitchen. Edward busies himself with the owner, counting the bushels and arranging payment. Martine talks with the cook and gives instruction to a kitchen boy with more grace than she showed to me.

I retreat outside, waiting in an alleyway for Edward. It smells of rotten apples and fits my mood.

"Freegift," I hear. It is Martine, standing in the doorway. "Would you leave without a farewell?"

"I did not think you wished it, Martine," I say. "Since we were only together through happenstance, as you said." Otherwise I would wish to kiss you, I think. Then I worry I have said that part out loud, but as she does not run away, I am safe. I can still speak less, it seems.

"It is true that I would have gone to see my mother anyway. But I did not mind taking you. And I am glad we could rescue Wait."

"You rescued both of us," I say, stepping closer. When I hear her say *we*, a sense of joy overcomes me at the thought of the two of us bound together in her imagination. I reach for her hand.

"Come, Freegift, to the magistrate!" Edward says as he steps out from the kitchen, intent upon making me a citizen of this town. My hand drops to my side. Not out of embarrassment or a sense of propriety. Rather, I have realized that Martine made me a citizen of New London in a way no officer or magistrate could. I wish to be with her. I wish for nothing else.

Except one thing, and that is my mother's dying wish. I have a promise to keep, and wooing Martine can only keep me from the journey I must make. To be a British subject and citizen of the city of New York.

"Yes," I say in answer to Edward and turn away. But not before I see a furrow across Martine's forehead. How much can she know of what I am thinking? More than I wish, perhaps, if she shares any of her mother's visions.

Thoughts race through my mind as I board the wagon with Edward. I cannot look back for fear Martine is still watching me. Farewell she wished to say?

Oh, now forever
Farewell the tranquil mind! Farewell content!

Shakespeare's *Othello*. It is a not a happy play.

"Put on your shirt, Freegift, and look lively now," Edward says as we draw up at the courthouse. I do so, and he fusses over me as if I am a child putting on my Sunday best. I know that whatever I do will be a reflection on him, so I make myself agreeable, stand up straight, and shoulder my musket. My tomahawk fits snug in the belt by my right hand.

"Ready," I say, smiling proudly. I am determined to put Martine out of my mind. Which only places her more firmly there.

"Good lad!" I wonder at that.

We take the steps up to the courthouse door and enter. Wide-plank maple boards creak underfoot as Edward leads the way to the magistrate. He knocks on a door and enters. A man sits at a desk by the window, the southerly light and view out over the harbor perhaps easing the burden of his work. The desk is strewn with papers and a large ledger book.

He looks up, and I doubt the pleasant scene before him has had much effect. He squints and his mouth is set in a scowl. He is balding and possesses bad teeth. I have never met a magistrate, or given one much thought. But if I had, this would be he.

"Elias Fox, our chief magistrate," Edward says to me, giving the fellow a slight bow. "This is Freegift Cooper, newly arrived at New London and eager to join the militia."

"You know we don't accept slaves into the militia, Hardwick," says Mr. Fox, not wasting more than a glance on me. I remain silent, struggle that it is.

"Freegift is emancipated and has his papers," Edward says, nudging my arm. I present the document, having removed it from my pouch prior. Mr. Fox does not deign to take in from my hand, but motions with his bony jaw for me to place in upon his desk.

"Appears to be in order," he finally grants. "You vouch for him, Hardwick?"

"Yes, I do. And we're short of men," Edward says. Hardly a stirring recommendation, but it does elicit a nod from the magistrate, who reaches for his ledger. He asks where I have accommodations, and I tell him Shaw's warehouse, where I labor.

"That is adequate. Be sure to keep your place in decent society and cause no trouble for your betters." He dips his quill and fills out a line in the book.

"I said I vouch for him," Edward says, his jaw set hard.

"Make your mark, there," Fox says, ignoring Edward and turning the ledger, tapping an ink-smudged finger below his careful script.

"Gladly, sir," I say, and dip the quill again, giving me enough ink to write out my name in large, bold, flowing letters.

Freegift Cooper, freedman.

For the first time, Mr. Fox actually looks at me. I take my paper back, betraying no expression.

"Well done," Edward says as we leave the courthouse. "Elias is not normally the most pleasant of men. It was good that you gave him no cause to dispute you."

"If I have learned one thing since becoming free, it is that less speech is better than more."

"You are a wise fellow for one so young," Edward says. "Come, I'll walk with you to Shaw's." He takes Cricket by the lead, and we walk up to Water Street.

"May I ask, Edward, what you intend to do with Wait?" He does not answer at once, and I regret the query. He sighs and then speaks, willingly enough.

"We must discover if his mother is still alive. From what Martine heard of his story, it seems his father is dead for certain. Is that what he told you?"

"Yes, we both heard that. The *Badger* took the ship he was on. Perhaps there are records of the prize vessels?"

"Yes, everything is detailed so that payment can be made to the crews. But the *Badger* has had much success, and there are rumors they have not reported all their victories."

"Because some of the ships are yours," I say. "Ours, I mean."

"Likely," Edward says, taking no note of my mistake. "Wait's parents could have been Tories on their way to Canada, or patriots fleeing Long Island. Impossible to know. We could search ship records for any mention of a Jenkins family, but it is a common name. And if Captain Cowburn of the *Badger* did not report his prize, we will never know."

"Why would be not? How could he dispose of the vessel?"

"Easy enough to land the cargo, then sell the ship anywhere up and down the coast. Cruelty and confusion reign in wartime, I'm afraid," Edward says. He talks of the progress of the war, moving the conversation away from my question, which he does not answer in the way we both know I mean it.

"That's a fine tomahawk Topheny gave you," he says. Is he reminding me that we each have our secrets?

"I was honored by it," I say.

"She's been with us for twelve, thirteen years now," he says. "I was near your age when she came to us. Martine was a mere babe."

"Topheny is your bond servant?" I ask. Warily, since it is not properly my business.

"No longer," Edward says. "She was indentured up in Norwich, where I guess she and your mother met. Her bond was signed over to my father in payment of a debt. After five years, she was free to go. But it is her home, and she earns her keep. She can trap, tan hides, knows much about medicinal plants and the like. Don't know what we'd do without her, frankly."

"Does Martine know all those things?" I ask, in the most casual of voices.

"Some, but Martine doesn't plan on living out her days in a wigwam. She's between two worlds, as you may be, if you don't mind my saying. Your complexion marks you. It is lighter than most of your brethren."

"True enough," I say, knowing that most Africans have skin the color of the night sky. Older ones, at least. Some born in this land have begun to take on a slight tinge of their masters, not that it lessens their burden. "What does Martine want then?"

"A good life, as we all do. A decent man and a place to call home. How about you, Freegift? What do you want?"

I mumble something inconsequential. For I am too discomfited to admit what I want. Two things: Martine, and for Topheny's vision to come true. That my father will seek me out.

We part at the warehouse, but not before he tells me the militia will drill on the morrow, at nine o'clock at Fort Trumbull. Then, I will see what real soldiering is about, he says. Marching to and fro and digging great holes in the ground.

I expect I will understand his meaning in the morning. But for now, I consider his mention of cruelty and confusion as I enter to see what work Tink has for me. I am counting on the confusion of war to provide me with a way to New York. And in that confusion, I wonder if Martine may come away with me?

I will watch for my opportunity on both counts.

And speak even less.

· Fifteen ·

I am at the threshold of the warehouse when a man on horseback approaches me. An African man, riding a fine steed and well-turned out in a buff jacket and waistcoat.

"Young man, are you with Edward Hardwick's Company?" He may call me young since a fair amount of gray decorates his temples.

"I am, sir, as of this morning. Freegift Cooper is my name," I say, studying this man who must be free, and doing well enough for himself to judge by clothes, horse, and confident attitude.

"Jordan Freeman," he says, introducing himself with a brief nod. "I have a message for Lieutenant Hardwick, from Colonel Ledyard. Is he about?"

"He has departed moments ago for his farm," I say. "But he will be back tomorrow morning for the drill at Fort Trumbull."

"I will ride to catch him, then," Freeman says as his horse snorts and shakes his head. "The colonel has orders regarding tomorrow. You are new in town, Freegift?"

"I am," I say, and find myself telling this stranger my story, in the briefest terms. Perhaps because he sits upon his horse like a proud lord, and this is not a thing I have seen any African do. And it is something I aspire to before my hair shows gray.

"I am glad to meet you, Freegift," he says, leaning down to offer his hand.

"And glad to see another freedman in our community."

"Did your freedom come as part of this Revolution as well?" I ask.

"No. William Ledyard gave up his ownership of me before the hostilities began. I now am employed as his servant, and glad of the chance to help with his militia duties. He commands all the militia in the area, you know. So, I must depart, I have other messages to deliver as well. Fare well, Freegift."

With that, Jordan Freeman tips his tricorn cap to me, spins his mount around, and rides off, as sharp as you please. Yes, I do hope to fare well, I think, as I set my hand upon the latch.

By God," Tink exclaims as I enter his office. "Here I was thinking Gill had taken you out to sea and fed you to the fishes. But now you stand before me a soldier! Freegift, you are a fellow full of fine surprises."

"I have joined the militia," I say. "At the suggestion of Edward Hardwick."

"Most sensible," he says. "Did old Elias give you any trouble?"

"The magistrate? No, not really. He did ask some questions which I judged foolish, but what can you expect from a man who sits in a room and squints at ledgers all day long?"

"Profits would be nice," Tink says, waving his hand across his own columns of numbers. But he laughs, knowing I do not mean him. He labors with his hands as well as his mind, judging by his calluses. "Elias Fox was reluctant to embrace the cause of liberty. When he finally did, I think it had more to do with not wishing to flee his home in New London than any scruples."

"So there are no loyalists here?" I ask, hoping I might find a kindred spirit.

"What Tories we had fled for Nova Scotia early on, or over to Long Island if they had kin there. Loyalist property was taken or sold to finance the war. If there are any remaining among us, they hide their beliefs well."

"A wise course in a town which loves liberty so. Mr. Fox at first thought me a slave and said they were not allowed to serve in the militia," I say.

"That is true," Tink says, then stops, nodding slowly. "Ah, Freegift, we must be friends for you to aim such a gentle barb at me. Yes, I take your point. The liberty we fight for is not liberty for all. But this revolution has pricked the conscience of Stoddard, and others."

"There's truth in that, Tink," I say, glad he has not taken offense and called me friend as well. I find it simpler than I thought to be at ease with this man, and Edward also. Perhaps they are my friends. Never having one, I am not certain.

"Now, to work. We can jaw some more later. Captain Saltonstall brought the *Minerva* in last night, heavy with a prize cargo. She's at the dock, ready to unload," Tink says, rising from his desk. "Unless General Washington requires you elsewhere."

"I daresay Admiral Tink out-ranks him," I say, and make for my room where I lean my musket in the corner, remove my belt, and hang my hunting shirt on a peg. The tomahawk I secret beneath my mattress, in case of unsavory visitors. I spend a moment taking stock of my possessions. I have never had so many, and with the money from my labors, I am richer than I ever thought to be.

If I had Martine, I would be Midas.

Taking the stairs from the wharf, I see the *Minerva* at the dock. A two-masted brig, she is sleek and narrow, possessing a swiftness evident even with her sails furled. Her lacquered wood is trimmed in green and yellow, and crewmen are busy washing the decks and running about, doing whatever sailors do with all that rope and canvas.

Of that, I know nothing. But I easily spy my work. The deck is thick with barrels, stacked one upon the other. Crewmen slide boards down to the dock, ready to roll the barrels along the gangplank.

Tink and a man who could only be the captain stand by the barrels and other goods, counting. The gentleman is dressed in a fine blue coat, a sword at his belt worn over a red sash. His tri-corner hat sits atop a mane of gray hair, tied back with red ribbon. He holds his head high, nodding in agreement with Tink's calculations.

"Ten hogsheads of ale, four of wine. Twelve tobacco hogsheads," Tink counts as I approach the gangplank. "Five barrels of salt pork, seventy wool blankets, and eighteen casks of gunpowder."

"Correct," Captain Saltonstall says. "The sooner you get the papers ready to sign and be witnessed, the sooner we can put back to sea."

"We will get everything stored away and attended to," Tink says. "Pity you couldn't salvage the ship."

"Smashed on the rocks off Block Island, worse luck," he says. "That fool of a Tory captain got himself drowned. Otherwise he'd have been good for a prisoner trade. Now, I must attend to the magistrate. My first mate will assist you. Good day, Tinkham."

"Good day, Captain," Tink says to his back and crooks a finger for me to come forward. The captain strides past, in a great hurry, paying me no mind. In fact, I must step aside otherwise I will be knocked into the water.

"This is all from a Loyalist ship?" I ask Tink as I survey the barrels. The heavy, numerous barrels.

"Aye," a booming voice says, as a sailor emerges from a hatch. "Courtesy of the sloop *Nancy*, and there would have been more if her captain hadn't run her aground. The waves smashed her against the rocks, but we managed to salvage a good part of the cargo."

"Freegift, this is Michael Gordon, First Mate of the *Minerva*. Michael, Freegift is working for me, since my laborers all went privateering."

"The last I heard of those two scurvy lads, they went on a whaleboat raid to Long Island and never returned," Gordon says. He is a large man, broad at the shoulders and bearing a thatch of wavy black hair. "Dead, drowned, captured, who knows? So take heed, Freegift, should you wish for adventure."

"But this plunder, sir, surely this shows your adventure has been rewarding," I say.

"That it has, but we have a stout ship, an experienced crew, and a good captain," Gordon says. "There's no shortage of fools voyaging out into the Devil's Belt with much less, expecting much more, and lucky to make it back to port alive. And no, we have no need of any more crew." He laughs and orders his men to roll the barrels onto the dock. From there, my labors begin.

I roll the heavy barrels up the ramp and into the warehouse. They are too heavy to carry up the steps, so it is a long round-about trip. The sun is bright and warm, and this is hot work. As I descend the stairs, I survey the crew readying the ship, bringing supplies on board, and scampering up the rigging to do things with the sails I do not understand. But what I do understand, as I grasp another weighty barrel, is that these people travel where I wish to go.

The brig *Minerva* is well armed, sixteen cannon in all. She looks fast, but any ship with sails appears swift once you've floated downriver on a raft. I begin to hope some of these fellows will quit the sea and leave an opening for me. I can swim, after all, and it would be easy enough to slip over the side at night, if Captain Saltonstall brings his brig close in to the Long Island shore.

Once the hogsheads are put away in the warehouse, I rest myself for a moment before proceeding with the piles of blankets and casks of gunpowder. I have grown weary and avoid sitting on the blankets for fear I will lie down and disgrace my employer with my laziness. So I sit on a gunpowder cask, which in no way tempts me to close my eyes.

"Freegift," Gordon shouts from the deck, beckoning me. "Water." I dart up the gangplank and see an oaken bucket, with a tin cup tied to it, hanging from the gunwale. I drain the cup, then drink again.

"Thank you, Mr. Gordon," I say, not from an excess of politeness, but since I have heard first mates are always called mister. In truth, he is perhaps ten years older than I, no more.

"You look equal to the work Tink's last two laborers managed, if not more," he says.

"I am used to hard work," I say. "My last employer was a cooper, and I felled trees for him." I do not wish to lie, but neither do I wish to utter the word owner.

"There's nary a cooper in New London," Gordon says. "Are you here to start your own cooperage?"

"I had thought of it," I say, although I have none of Mr. Stoddard's skills and do not plan to stay long here. But that is not how I want people to think of me. "But a cooper needs to be close to a good wood supply, and the forests here appear to have been cleared for the town and farmland. Further afield, perhaps."

"True enough," Gordon says and helps himself to the water. "Mind you, I was serious about those two boys not coming back. Don't be tempted by dreams of easy riches."

"There are many who are?" I ask.

"Too many," says he. "Some are inept sailors and are out-raced by their quarry. Or taken themselves, by Tory privateers. Then there are those who have experience and a good ship, which only means less for us, eh?" He claps my arm and laughs. He is in good humor, perhaps due to his nature, or the first mate's share of the cargo taken.

"Do you know of Captain Cowburn and the *Badger*?" I ask. "They seem to be experienced seamen."

"Aye, experienced in thievery," Gordon says. "Friends of yours?"

"I am acquainted with a man named Gill and a skinny fool name of Tom," I say. "They attempted to rob me of a shipment of staves."

"Well then, you are a rare lad. Not many live through their depredations, much less get to call it attempted theft. Thin Tom, they call Gill's shadow. How'd you manage against them?"

I tell Gordon the story of my raft, and the subsequent chase on Water Street, even mentioning Martine and her whip, along with Wait's excellent aim with a stone.

"Damn, I wish I had seen that," Gordon says, appraising me with a newfound interest. "Best be careful, Freegift. Gill is a mean devil and his captain no better. Neither will like that story getting around. It makes them look weak."

"I will stay alert, and I have joined the militia," I proclaim. "I am well armed."

"You don't have to worry today, we passed the *Badger* at sea. But know you this, they won't come when you're marching among the militia with your musket at your shoulder. They'll come at night, to slit your throat while you sleep."

· Sixteen ·

⊢——⊣

Tink invites me to sup with him at the tavern, where he is to meet Michael Gordon to deliver an accounting of the inventory. While the haul of Tory cargo means shares for the captain and crew, Tink benefits also. He charges for storage, which will come from the sale of goods as soon as the governor authorizes it. This privateering business is good for all.

Even myself, since Tink will pay for my supper as reward for the heavy work. I think of it as my share of the piratical booty and am quite pleased with myself. But not pleased at the thought of seeing Martine, oddly enough because she pleases me so much. I am determined to resist her beauty, not that she has offered it up to me.

And we must talk about Gill. I had thought Wait safe at the farm, but now I wonder. I am at a loss of what to do, other than hope the *Badger* is taken or sunk, with all hands lost. I know not if they are all evil men, but as I have heard said, a rotting fish stinks from the head.

Tink waits while I wash away sweat and grime at the pump by the side of the warehouse. I don a new shirt and button my waistcoat, making myself as presentable as possible. If I was a privateer, I would purchase shirts and breeches for every day of the week. A lucky privateer, that is.

"Do you think those boys who worked for you are dead?" I ask of Tink, as we walk to the tavern. I spy two Africans in the street, each walking in a different direction. One hurries, his shoulders hunched, and his head bowed. The other fellow strides with his shoulders back and head held high. He enters the tavern ahead of us. Slave and Freedman, it is writ in their movements, wary and easy, each according to their station.

"If they are, they didn't succumb from hard work," he says, taking no notice of the dark-skinned men and how they show themselves. "They weren't lazy all the time, but they were thick-headed all day long. If they didn't keep the few wits they possessed about them, they may have been killed or taken prisoner. Or left behind, as may be."

"By their own shipmates?" I ask.

"If a Tory mob is bearing down on you, and the only chance for your crew to get away is to shove your whaleboat off the beach and row out into the Sound, you don't wait for any laggards. Remember that, Freegift," Tink says, stopping and placing a hand on my arm. "I saw the look on your face today. Instant riches, you were thinking."

"It was hard not to, you must admit."

"Yes, yes, but think, Freegift. There have been voyages when Captain Saltonstall came back with little or nothing. And half the shares go to the owners. After that, the captain takes sixteen shares, the first mate and other officers ten or so. Able-bodied seamen get two shares and the rest of the crew, one share each."

"And one share is not much, then?" I ask, resuming our walk, for I am very hungry and thinking of Martine, even if I must act cold in her presence.

"Not much, no," Tink says.

"But how much?" I ask. "You have tallied the inventory and know the value of such things. What would the lowest among them have for their share?"

He did not answer right away.

"Tink?"

"One hundred dollars, Freegift, if you must know. Perhaps a touch more."

"That is a fortune, Tink! Or are those the worthless Continental dollars I have heard of?"

"No. The shares are paid out once the goods are sold off. In gold coin."

Gold. I would have to work months to save that much, and only if I subsisted on water and air. One hundred dollars in gold. Would such treasure tempt Martine to travel away with me?

"Did you hear me, Freegift?" Tink demands.

"Yes. Gold coin, you said."

He shakes his head as I open the tavern door. I take it he spoke of something else, which I missed as visions of shining gold and silken black hair shone in my imagination.

Gordon sits at a table, his hand on a tankard, his eyes fixed upon Martine. For her part, she smiles as they converse, one hand resting upon the table, as if she takes her ease with this man. I follow Tink, my head bowed, wishing I did not come.

She swirls away from the table, greeting Tink as she passes us on her way to the kitchen. She says nothing to me. Nor I to her. I am determined not to engage in conversation with her but find myself unaccountably angry she does not speak to me. Especially when she spoke so casually to Gordon mere seconds ago.

"What say you, Tink?" Gordon says, his tankard raised in salute. Then a nod to me. "Freegift, sit."

As if I had intended otherwise.

Tink and I sit opposite Gordon, whose eyes travel past us. I make myself ignore the direction of his gaze.

"I think you'll find everything in order," Tink says, passing papers to Gordon, who quickly attends to business. He runs his finger down the page, speaking softly to himself. He is not a fast reader and must sound out the words. Still, he perseveres. I cannot fault him there.

"All in order," Gordon pronounces, slapping his palm upon the table.

"Your tally agrees with mine. Well done."

"Does the captain not do his own tally?" I ask and see Tink smile. "I am only curious, being new to the way of privateers."

"Freegift, the cargo is the responsibility of the first mate. On the sea, the captain is lord and master, and we all step lively at his bidding. But when a ship comes into harbor, he has little to do. I and the second mate keep the crew busy, and the captain is free to do whatever he wishes. Captain Saltonstall is likely arranging supplies for our next voyage."

"When will you go?" I ask, having some interest in when Gordon will take his leave of us.

"Within days, I think," he answers. "There's many a ship trying their hand at privateering. Not to mention the whaleboats lying in wait at night. The captain thinks the British may soon send warships against us, so best to scour the seas while we can."

"Cider?" Martine says from behind me. She surprises me, and I am startled. I nod, hoping she has not noticed. Tink agrees. In his brief grin, I see he has taken in my discomfort. My face flushes, and I wipe my brow to disguise it as Martine sets down the sloshing tankards.

"Freegift has joined the militia," Tink says. "If Saltonstall is right, you may have done so just in time to see a fight." He claps me on the shoulder, as if this be every young man's dream. Not mine. I feel myself a fool here in New London, going soft in the company of people, however well-meaning, who are keeping me from what I need to do. If I mean to join my father in New York, the worst thing to do would be to stay here and train to kill Redcoats. I must get to a boat. But I cannot give myself away, either.

The meal tonight is smoked ham and squash. Likely the squash from Edward's farm, which I helped bring into the kitchen. Martine sets the plates before us and pauses, long enough to grace Gordon with a smile. Without a word to me, she flounces away. She returns to the table next to us, delivering cider.

"Tink, I may sign myself onto a privateer," I find myself saying, in a voice that cares not if it is heard beyond our table. "If I could find one to take me."

"I understand, Freegift," Tink says after a moment, nodding his head sagely. "It is hard to argue with what you've seen of the *Minerva's* success, I know that. But the only captain to take on a landlubber such as yourself might prove to be a fool, or a knave."

"Cowburn of the *Badger* is rumored to have slit the throat of a new crewman for nothing more than to take a few silver coins he had hidden in his belt," Gordon said. "But you already know to steer clear of that lot."

"What about the whaleboats I hear of?" I ask, conscious of Martine walking behind me. Slowly, with an ear to our conversation?

"Sometimes it's no more than a few lads who decide to row across the Sound and loot what they can from a Tory household," Gordon says.

"There are others more organized," Tink says. "Jeremiah Moore's crew has taken to the whaleboats since his ship was burned."

"Moore? Mr. Stoddard's daughter Rebecca is married to him," I say.

"Stoddard?" Gordon asks.

"Freegift's previous employer," Tink puts in.

"Owner," I say, unwilling to have Tink lie for me. "I am newly emancipated."

"Well then," Gordon says. "No wonder you joined the militia. You understand more than most the desire for liberty."

"Yes, liberty is a desirable thing. So would be the feel of gold coin. Tink pays me fairly, more fairly than I might find elsewhere. But a share of Tory cargo would allow me to enjoy my new-found liberty wearing fine shoes and a warm coat."

"Well said," Gordon replies. "But Moore's crew will not take on anyone new. They have men working on the repairs, while others take turns going out in their whaleboats. Newcomers would not be welcome."

"If you hear of a decent crew looking for a strong young man, do tell Freegift," Tink says. "With my blessing. Until then, I will continue to pay him fairly. After all, he works hard and quickly, as you saw."

"What was your work with Stoddard?" Gordon asks.

"Mr. Stoddard is a fine cooper," I say. "It was a shipment of his staves that I brought downriver to Tink's warehouse."

"Did he teach you that skill?" Gordon says.

"I was employed to bring wood to him," I say, reluctant to speak about Mr. Stoddard's reasons for not instructing me in his trade, but not wishing to appear the simple-minded manual laborer. "He entrusted me with the selection of the right wood for his work. I know trees and their grain well."

"You must," Gordon says, nodding in agreement. "And I'd guess you'd be handy with an axe, then."

"Of course," I say. "The felling axe and broad axe are tools of my trade. Or were."

We speak of axes and the art of dropping trees so they fall freely to the forest floor. Based on his words, Gordon is intent on discussing the art of wielding an axe. His eyes, however, wander to wherever Martine is in the room. I find that as he shows interest in her, my own resolve not to do so lessens by the minute.

We have another round of cider, brought by Martine. She inquires as to Tink's health, asks Gordon how he liked his supper, and looks to me. Her eyebrows rise in expectation. Of what, I am uncertain, so I fall back on what has been sound advice.

"Hello, Martine," I say, speaking as little as possible. Then I gulp my cider. I chance a glance at her. Her jaw is firmly set, her dark eyes narrowed. For a moment it looks as if she may speak, and that her words could well be unfriendly. Instead, she takes our empty tankards and walks away, shaking her head.

"Freegift, I thought you and Martine were on friendly terms," Tink says, leaning in to study my expression.

"Friendly enough," I say and drink more cider. I have no wish to explain what I hardly understand myself.

"She's a comely lass," Gordon says. "Part Indian?"

"Pequot," I say, perhaps more quickly than I intended. "I believe."

"Too bad you pay her no mind, Freegift," Gordon says. "Being as you both are half of one and not fully the other. It would be a good match."

"I'll make my own match, Mr. Gordon, when I wish," I say. And gulp more cider.

"No offense meant," Gordon says, waving his hands. "I understand. You have no interest in her at all."

That is not exactly what I said, but I leave it at that.

We part ways, friendly enough. Gordon goes back to the *Minerva*, Tink to his home, and I to my room at the warehouse.

But I must walk. I am not tired, and truth be told, two tankards of cider is more than I am used to in the way of spirits. I walk along the wharf, glancing at the *Minerva*, where a few crewmen are assembled on deck, standing watch. If they call it that while safely tied up on the moorings.

I walk on, past a sloop where sailors dance on deck to a fiddle played sharply by a one-eyed man. A frigate flying the flag of Spain is the largest craft in the harbor, anchored a stone's throw out in the river. Lights twinkle at the portholes as the sky begins to darken.

Farther on, I stop to watch the glow of lights along the water. A campfire shoots sparks skyward from the parapets of Fort Griswold, on the heights across the river. Downriver on my side, the glow of a fire sends yellow shadows dancing against the earthen walls of Fort Trumbull.

I follow the path along the embankment, the rising moon lighting the waters. I spy two fellows, about my age, pulling a row boat onto the rocky shore. It is large and oddly shaped, seeming to have a bow at both ends. Tink has told me how whaleboats are so constructed, allowing rowers to switch direction with ease. Useful for hunting whales. Or ships, I venture.

I stop to watch as they drag the long row boat and secure ropes around the largest rock.

"Good evening," I say. "Is that craft a whaleboat?"

They stop, eyeing me and then each other.

"Of course," one says. He is thin and sandy-haired, ill-clothed in a sailor's duck trousers and short-waisted jacket, frayed at the seams. "Don't you know what a whaleboat is?"

"Certainly. But I have never seen one up close is all," I say, jumping down onto the beach. "Are you whalers then?"

"You're that African what works for Tink, aren't you?" he says, ignoring my question.

"I do work for him, yes," I say. "Freegift Cooper is my name."

"Henry Geer," the lad says, extending his hand. I take it as the other tells me his name is John Gallop. He is stocky, with dark hair trimmed short and breeches that show a good deal of dirt ground into them. A farmer, I guess.

"We've heard of you," Gallop says, leaning against the whaleboat. "They say you bested Gill and his fellows."

"Twice," Geer says, and they laugh. "Is it true?"

"Be they friends of yours?" I ask, taking a small step back, ready to flee or fight, depending on circumstances.

"Hardly that," Gallop says, and they laugh again. I sense they are nervous. At my presence?

"Gill threw me in the harbor once," Geer says. "For the sport of it. If you had the advantage of them twice, watch out for the third time. He'll kill you."

"So I have been told," I say. "And I thank you for your warning as well. Now, what are you about here?"

"We are about getting rich, Freegift," Geer tells me. "We have the use of this whaleboat for three days, and we mean to go privateering."

"The two of you?" I ask.

"We have three others who will be here tomorrow," Gallop says. "We will stay with the boat tonight and shove off tomorrow before dark. Join us, Freegift. You've shown yourself to be a stout one in a fight. We could use another at the oars."

"Aye," Geer says. "The other boys will be glad to hear you've joined us. Everyone's talking about your fight with Gill."

"Where are you bound?" I ask, flattered by their comments, but keeping my face a mask.

"About eleven miles out into the Sound," Gallop says. "We'll stay in the lee of Gull Island and wait for a ship to come by."

"Will you land on Long Island?" I ask. "I hear there's Tory property for the taking over there." Could this be my conveyance to New York and my father? It seems so easy.

"No," Gallop says firmly, shaking his head. "There's too few of us. If we're found over there, we're dead men. Better to take a small ship, a sloop or whatever, and bring her back. Then we'll be rich."

"Have you done so before?" I ask, with a fair idea of the answer.

"No. But we've not had a whaleboat before," Geer says, as if that excuses all their inexperience. "Will you join us?"

"I thank you both and am glad to have made your acquaintance. But I recently joined the militia and also have my responsibilities to Mr. Tinkham, so I must decline. I wish you luck," I say. I believe they will need it.

They accept my statement, and we chat amiably for a few more minutes. By their glances and the secluded spot they have chosen, I think the whale boat must be stolen. Or perhaps borrowed, without the owner's knowledge, since they are firm about returning it after three days. When I expect the owner is due to return from his travels.

I stroll back the way I came, happy to know that I am thought of as someone not to trifle with. The joy is leavened somewhat with worry about what Gill will do when he next encounters me. I have my knife at my belt and consider carrying my tomahawk as well, especially at night.

Then I worry about Martine. The thoughts come unbidden. She was part and parcel of my last confrontation with Gill, and she is well-known about town. Soon I move beyond worry and think about her. She bewitches me, and contrary to the impression I gave Gordon, she does interest me. We would be a good match. The English may never accept our white-skinned halves, and our darker hues may not be a perfect match, but therein lies much of what we have in common.

From what I have heard of the Pequots, they are a proud, though vanquished, people. She may wish no man other than a full-blooded Pequot, but they are mostly gone. Killed, run off, or enslaved and sent to the hot islands of the south.

Why not me? I say it to myself again, as if doing so will make it true. Indeed, why not me?

I start to walk to the tavern, determined to tell her all. My plans, my fears, my joy and confusion when I am in her presence. My consternation at wishing to fulfill my mother's dying wish—indeed, my need to do so—and my desire to remain in New London, to woo and win the heart of Martine.

No, I tell myself, turning back as the lights of the tavern windows come into sight. No, do not be a fool. Speak less. It is the only way to be certain she will not laugh at my confessions. I walk with determined steps to the warehouse, ready to throw my head upon the pillow. I take my key in hand and stop.

I put the key in my pocket.

I turn around.

Damn this foolishness. I will speak to her.

I come to the tavern door, taking deep breaths to calm myself. I go in, scanning the room for Martine.

It is quiet, only a few solitary drinkers and three men playing at cards. Their pipe smoke fills the room, and the kitchen boy brings one of them a tankard. Martine is not at work.

I go outside, around to the alley, and make my way to the small courtyard out back, where wooden stairs lead up to her attic room. Candlelight glows from a small dormer window, and I take a moment to ready myself, wishing to appear unflustered. I take a breath, let it out, and step forward.

Then back, as the door at the top of the steps opens, and light spills out onto the landing.

Back into the shadows, where I watch Gordon shut the door behind him and descend the stairs. He strides by me, close enough to touch, but the darkness hides me.

His footsteps fade away, and I feel my heart pounding against my chest. I am too late. While I plotted words, Gordon took action with deeds. I look to the window and see a blurry form pass before the light. Then it is extinguished. As are my hopes, foolish as they were.

I wait, moving not a muscle, until I am certain Gordon is gone. I cannot look at the darkened window any longer. I turn away, as silently as can be. As if I was never present. As if it never happened.

I walk slowly, so it takes time to return to that spot along the shore.

"Geer! Gallop! Are you there?"

"Aye, Freegift," comes the answer, and I make out a blanket thrown back from within the gloom of the whaleboat.

"What time do we depart on the morrow?"

· Seventeen ·

I have never seen soldiers march in formation, but I cannot believe it looks anything like this company of militia. We drill at the rear of Fort Trumbull, a great pile of earthworks facing the river. Edward Hardwick rode in from the farm early this morning, but he does not act as the friend that he was. He acts like an officer, barking orders and causing us to line up in various sorts of rows and columns. Some are familiar with the routines. Others seem newly acquainted.

I am in my own category. The commands signify little to me, even as I try to follow what my companions on either side do. The clumsier I appear, the louder Edward shouts. Or so shouts Lieutenant Hardwick, I correct myself. It would not do to call him by his given name while in ranks. On the way here, he confided in me that Colonel Ledyard worries about the quantity and quality of militia defending this fort. Such was the message Jordan Freeman bore, calling on Edward to recruit more men and train those he had the harder.

Attention! To the Left—Dress!

We are instructed that at this command, the proper soldier turns his head briskly to the left and brings his right eye in the direction of his waistcoat buttons. Well, I wear my hunting shirt, but I do recall where my waistcoat buttons last were located. However, by the time I consider that, we are off to another command. And another.

To the Right—Face!

I must turn smartly on both heels to the right, lifting my toes but only a little, making a quarter circle with them. Then bring the right foot back flat on the ground, but without stomping. Edward prefers no stomping. The stomps of thirty men would sound quite martial, but I think it best not to offer my opinion. Speaking less is expected of the common soldier.

Then marching by files, marching at the quick step, and the oblique step. The entire purpose of which is to bring our muskets to bear as quickly as possible, warding off an enemy who may approach from any side.

Sensible, if confusing.

We go through the fifteen motions of priming and loading our muskets, but we do not actually load or fire, much to my disappointment. These steps I manage to master, since Edward has already instructed me in the basics, and since you may stand in one place to accomplish them all. Of course, being under fire from disciplined British Regulars might make standing in one place a less than pleasant experience.

I put that thought out of my mind as I go through the motions. There are other thoughts I also work to displace, thoughts of Martine and Michael Gordon. They are harder to dislodge.

"Lieutenant Hardwick," a voice booms from behind us. Edward commands us to *Rest*, which is a relative term, meaning we may stand in place and move our feet and hands only slightly. A strange resting.

"Colonel Harris, sir," Edward replies, standing smartly and saluting. I can see him, but not this colonel, since Rest does not allow for the turning of the head.

"It is time to replace the musket with the spade," Colonel Harris says. "I think these men will do better with a simpler implement." I hear the *clip clop* of horse hooves and slowly the officer comes into my line of vision. He wears a sneer upon his face, a resplendent blue jacket with red facings, white breeches, and a matching waistcoat, the buttons of which do battle with his girth. "There's much work to be done."

"Yes, sir," Edward says, and calls us to attention as Colonel Harris rides away, his horse's tail twitching in our direction.

Edward instructs us to *Fall Out*, which is an easy command. *Stack Arms* is more complicated, requiring us to balance muskets against each other, without having them clatter into the mud. We manage that, and Edward orders us to a shed at the base of Fort Trumbull, where picks and spades are handed out. There is no manual of arms for these.

I consider the manual labor we are about to embark upon, using our God-given arms, and laugh.

"What is funny about this, I ask you?" The question comes from a sparsely-haired fellow name of Bailey, who trudges along beside me. I fell in with him on the road from town, and we spoke of the chance war would come our way. He judged it unlikely and saw little need for drill. Less for spade work, it seems.

I explain my double play on words. He is not over-awed.

"A waste of time, if you ask me," Bailey says. I have noted that only people who have not been asked use that phrase. "Fort Trumbull has guns enough, I think."

"They have several good ones, Bailey," Edward says, moving quickly ahead of us, pickax in hand. "And they are well-placed, if the British oblige by sailing past the fort. Do you see the problem, Freegift?"

I look to my left, where the water widens before emptying into the Sound. The problem is clear, especially from this vantage point as we tramp up a steady incline.

"If they land to the south, they can take the fort from the rear," I say. The earthen walls appear stout, but the fortification is open at the rear.

"Yes," Edward says. "So we are to finish the earthworks at the top of this hill, to defend the landward route." He moves quickly ahead, ready to wield his pick.

"He's a good officer," Bailey proclaims. "Doesn't mind getting his hands dirty."

"And that colonel?" I ask.

"Ha!" Bailey glances in every direction, making sure he is not overheard. "Colonel Joseph Harris, a wealthy man who does little but order us about, to no effect."

"But is he a good soldier?" I ask.

"Ah, he's no soldier at all. When we went off to fight the French and Indians, over in New York, he stayed home. Did the same when we all went up to Boston with Lieutenant Hardwick. Harris never heard a shot fired in anger, but wears his tailor's handiwork well, don't he? Ha!" Bailey spits and that concludes our conversation. I am happy to hear no more, hoping he is wrong, or at least a born complainer. I prefer my colonels, if I am to have them, to be martial, fearless, and competent.

Edward directs us to our tasks once we reach the top of the hill. Trenches have been dug and the earth piled high, bound by logs and saplings wound between them. This breastwork is a haphazard affair, and I hope the safety of New London does not depend upon this small fortification. A single twelve-pound cannon stands to the rear, an oxcart holding its supply of shells and powder.

We hack away at the soil, taking away more rocks than dirt. Bailey and I carry logs from a pile and work to expand the breastworks even further. The slope down to the river has been cleared, giving us these lengths of maple and oak, while at the same time providing a clear view of whoever might advance upon us.

I think of Redcoats marching in columns with drums beating. I look around at my fellow militiamen, dirty and discouraged with their shovel work. I think we are wasting our time. If the British do come, they will surely bring enough men to overwhelm our small company, breastworks or no.

"Well done, men," Edward says as he surveys our handiwork. He has been prying boulders from the earth, a task well-borne by a New England farmer. Sweat streaks his brow. His hands are as dirty as mine, but all I can think is that a British officer would never lower himself so. It is a practical matter as well, since they have no shortage of common soldiers to do their digging.

Unlike us.

Edward instructs us to leave a cut-out in the new section of wall for the cannon, which will be aimed along the river road.

"Just one, Lieutenant?" I ask. I cannot imagine a single cannon will make much difference in a fight.

"Just the one," he answers. "They need the rest for Fort Trumbull itself, to defend against broadsides from British men o' war. This piece is all that could be spared."

"What nonsense, eh?" Bailey says once Edward is out of earshot.

"I am not sure I agree," I say. "Lieutenant Hardwick is experienced, is he not? If he thinks one cannon will do, who am I to say different?" I have no wish to sound like an officer's lackey, but neither do I want Edward to be the subject of derision.

"No, you mistake me, boy," Bailey says. "I was making a small joke, and not at the lieutenant's expense. This poor excuse for a fortification has been dubbed Fort Nonsense. Since no man who has labored here can see the sense in it. Understand?"

"Of course," I say, glad to avoid an argument. "Do you mean because it is unlikely the British will attack here? Or this is a poor location for a fort?"

"Well, I suppose they could attack us," Bailey allows, as we place a log across the breastworks and tamp it into place. "But why, when all the fighting is down south these days? And if I have to dig in the dirt, I'd rather be doing it on my own land. I signed up to march about and fight if I had to, not wield a shovel while his highness Colonel Harris swans about on his horse. So Fort Nonsense it is."

Bailey's case offers a certain logic, but as I view the open river road, I think Edward's does as well. I dig, not as excited as Bailey with the notion of marching about all the afternoon. Within the hour, men have rolled the cannon into place, the earth covered in split logs to keep the field piece from sinking in mud. The muzzle of the cannon looks out over the open ground, and I suspect it may get a few deadly volleys in before the glinting bayonets of the lobsters—as the militiamen call the British, for their red coats—settle the issue.

I am glad at the thought of making my way to New York. However arduous the journey, it will be better than facing line upon line of the British or their Hessian mercenaries.

"Water!" Edward announces, as two oaken buckets are brought to us by young ladies, likely from a farmhouse on the ridge. We take our turns with the ladle, and the girls smile and laugh. I see their mother a few steps back, her eyes not straying from her charges. Brave militiamen we may be, but we are also men, soiled and dirty. Some have removed their waistcoats, which makes them nearly naked by the standards of these city folk.

A cannon shot echoes out over the water. Everyone turns to the river.

Then another, and I see gray smoke drifting up from beyond the trees.

A third shot sounds, and everyone cheers. Except myself, as I am ignorant of what my comrades seem to take as common knowledge.

"What is it?" I ask.

"Look there," Edward says, pointing to where the trees give way to a full view of the river. A ship comes into view.

"It's the *Badger*," Bailey shouts.

"What did the cannons signify?" I ask, as I watch Captain Cowburn's brig sail upriver. I had hoped they would be at sea much longer. Damn their luck.

"It's the privateer's signal," Edward answers. "A three-cannon salute means they bring in a prize. There she is!"

A sloop appears, her sail full with the wind, a pretty sight, even if Gill may be aboard.

"What happens to the crew?" I ask.

"Captain and First Mate are worth something," Bailey says. "The others, I doubt Cowburn or Gill would bother with. Over the side, and they'll claim they fought to the death."

"It can be a brutal war, especially when people who once had been neighbors find themselves on opposite sides," Edward says. "It gives men like Cowburn and Gill an excuse to legalize thievery. But for now, let us finish here and make our way into town. Everyone will be at the docks."

We work another hour, and finally it is time to lay down our spades and march back, muskets on our shoulders. There is much talk of the prize sloop, and what cargo she may carry. The riches she brings benefit not only the crew of the *Badger*, but the town itself. The tavern and shops where crewmen will spend their money, and the farms and laborers who supply them, all reap the reward of the privateer's endeavor.

We march to the town green by the Congregational Church, and Edward orders us to fall out. It is the easiest command of the day.

"Freegift," he says, as the men disperse. "Tomorrow being the Sabbath, why don't you come with us for dinner after services? Martine will ride back with us as well."

"Thank you," I say. "But Martine's presence is not something that would persuade me. And I do have plans for the day already. Please give my best to your wife and Topheny."

"That I will," Edward says, his brow furrowed in puzzlement. "I am sorry, but I thought the two of you enjoyed each other's company."

"It is not only mine she enjoys," I say, and instantly wish I had not spoken. A lesson I still have not fully learned.

"Freegift, don't be foolish," Edward says.

"Nor will I be played for a fool, Edward," I say. "I am sorry I cannot accept your invitation."

"As you wish. Remember to attend services, though. It is expected, and they may levy a fine if you are thought to be a non-believer, or simply too lazy to sit through the sermon."

"I am a believer," I say, failing to mention what beliefs I hold to be true.
I know Edward does not favor the long Sunday services himself and
offers good advice. He cannot know what a brief visitor I plan to be.

"Fare you well, Freegift," says he. "The offer still stands, should you
change your mind. Or come to your senses." He smiles and gives me a
playful hit upon my shoulder.

We part, Edward to his horse and me to walk downhill to the
warehouse. He is a good man, as is Tink. Perhaps Gordon is even a good
man. I cannot blame him for seeking the affections of the woman I care
for. Would I not do the same?

Still, my anger rises as I near the warehouse, glad only that Martine has
revealed her intentions in time for me to see what a mistake it would
be to stay. I cannot wait to launch out into the river and see if Geer and
Gallop will draw near enough to Long Island for me to make my escape.

I am filled with determination. I gladly will leave this behind and seek
out my father. I must, in any case. What son can deny his mother?
What son could ignore the command given with her last breath of life?

Not I is the vow I make to myself.

Steps from the warehouse, I see Martine. She is running arm-in-arm
with a younger girl I recognize from the tavern's kitchen. They are
smiling and laughing, off on a merry jaunt to see the privateer's prize.
Her black hair floats behind her, her laughter a halo of joy borne into
the midst of the gathering crowd.

She and the girl disappear into the throng. I wish to never see her again.
I pray I will not, since my heart is broken all over again at the sight of
her and the thought of what might have been. For what some have said
is true. We are both halves of something, and from the moment I saw
Martine, I knew together we could be as one.

But she must feel herself whole already, with no need of a half-African
lad at her side.

· Eighteen ·

├────┤

I wait for darkness. I dress in my hunting shirt and a clean pair of breeches and worry about what to do with my papers. If I am lucky, I will make my way to Long Island tonight. From there, I will need to prove I am a free man. My emancipation document is wrapped in oilskin, secure in the pouch about my neck.

But if I end up in the water, will it be safe? A journey by rowboat with these boys may not be entirely dry. And if we do take a ship, might we not take a dunking as well? I cannot leave without it. I could be sold into slavery again, and that would be the last journey for me. So I re-tie the pouch, my emancipation paper inside, snug next to the old newsprint. It is my hope Benedict Arnold—my father, it is still not easy to say—will recall the wording. Sold for no fault but being saucy.

I leave the musket, since it is not my property. I think about writing a note to Tink, but there is a good chance I will return tomorrow after a fruitless voyage, and things will proceed as normal. Until I find another way, that is. If I do not return, it will mean I was successful, or drowned. I can see him shaking his head at my foolishness, regretting the loss of a good laborer.

Perhaps I do him a disservice. He might regret the loss of a young friend.

And Edward as well. I am sorry I could not reveal my plans and give him my thanks for his friendship, but all preparations must be made in secrecy. This small boat has no privateering Letter of Marque, nothing official to keep us from being branded pirates. If we take a British ship, no one will care. If we fail quietly and row back empty-handed, no one will care. But if something goes wrong, there will be blame enough.

What could go wrong, I wonder, as I walk down the darkened road along the river. We could lose the rowboat, which I am certain is borrowed without the owner's knowledge. Which is to say, stolen. Or Geer and Gallop might pounce upon a patriot ship, not caring for whom the cargo is intended. That is the very definition of piracy.

I hear the celebrations by the wharf, where the *Badger* and her captive prize are moored. Other crewmen are likely at the tavern, downing rum, ale, and cider by the gallons. If Gordon is to press his suit upon Martine, I hope he has the decency to linger at the tavern and protest any drunken sailor's untoward advances. I know I would.

If I were the one pressing my suit.

I jump down from the rocks and walk along the stony shore, squinting in the dark to make out the place where the rowboat is hidden. There is no sound but the lapping of waves and the pull of pebbles tumbling against one another. The wind is slight, but I feel it against my face. The Devil's Belt will not be a calm pond tonight.

I see no one. I am half surprised at myself when I am relieved. Perhaps they returned the boat. Or left without me. Perhaps this is not my night to cross the Sound.

"Freegift, here!" It is Gallop, who walks out of the shadows. "Come, everyone is ready."

"Did you see what the *Badger* brought in?" Geer asks, too excited to wait for an answer. He gives me a hurried introduction to three other boys. Jedidiah and Moses are brothers, both rail thin and wearing the worn wool clothing of a working field hand. They carry axes and knives stuck in their belts. Kitchen knives by the look of them, perhaps stolen from their mother's kitchen. The two of them are jittery, glancing at each other as if to confirm this is really a good idea. Trouble will be waiting if they don't return with the riches they expect. Matthew is the third, more well-dressed and armed with a gaff, the sort used by fisherman. It will spear a sailor as well as codfish. Matthew is a few years older than me, his attire more appropriate to a shop than farm work. He nods to me, his sharp blue eyes flitting from one lad to the other. He is nervous, but eager.

We drag the boat into the water and board, pushing off from the rocks and plying our oars. It takes us a few minutes to get used to the boat and begin to work together. The benches are wide, each of us situated with our own oar, three to a side sitting alternately. I have never rowed in such a boat, but it is surprisingly swift once our strokes are in unison.

I am in the middle on the larboard side, with Geer behind me and Matthew in front. Beneath our feet are more gaffs and a heavy pike. Geer explains we will use these to snare the rigging of the vessel we are to board, as we draw close. He also has a grappling hook at the end of a coil of rope, to be used as well. These are implements of deadly intent, and I shudder at the thought of what will follow the boarding. Too late for such worries now, for I am committed to this venture. I have given my word.

We are soon in open water where the river widens as it empties into the Sound. The waves are moderate, and they slap against our craft, making the going hard. Matthew groans as he pulls on his oar.

"Hush," Gallop says. "Sound carries out on the water. More than you'd think."

Matthew nods and we press on. Where we went in a straight line on the river, our progress now is a good deal of up and down on the waves. Sometimes I work my oar and find only air as the crest of a swell lifts us up, then slams us down to bounce on the bench, with some force. I myself groan, the sound lost in the wind and sloshing of water.

Salt spray coats my face, and I squint to keep it out of my eyes. Shimmering lights appear off to the side, and I widen them to focus. Is it a ship?

"There!" I say, nodding my head in the direction of the glow, low to the horizon.

"Fisher's Island," Geer says. Of them all, he appears the most nautical. "Just a few farms. The Tories have raided it twice. Watch for rowboats or small craft, we may be able to ambush them."

How I might see anything in the rolling swells is beyond me, but I do try. All I see is an endless array of whitecaps each time the clouds part and the half-moon shines upon the waters.

Time passes. I have no idea how much. Geer gives directions now and then, telling one side or the other to ship oars, which I learn means to take them out of the water. How he knows where to go I know not, but he seems confident. So I take comfort in that.

Matthew retches over the side. I take comfort it was not in the boat.

The clouds are thick, and little moonlight filters through. The darkness is total, as if we are adrift in the middle of the great Atlantic, with not a light visible anywhere. The wind picks up, pelting us with spray, and even with the exertion of rowing, I shiver.

I begin to see this was not a good idea.

"There it is," Geer says. I know not what it is, but I am glad he has sighted anything within this soaking darkness.

"Little Gull Island," Gallop says, answering the question we were all too cold and miserable to ask. I glance over my shoulder as I row and spy breaking waves. It is land. But how close to Long Island?

We row away from the breakers, Geer warning us we should not get caught up and smash the boat. This makes eminent sense, and we pull even harder, going around what I guess to be the eastern side of the island. Once we get around the crashing waves, the water is calmer. This must be what they call the leeward side of things, away from the wind and waves, the island itself protecting us from the weather coming in from the ocean.

For this, I am thankful. As are we all, slumping over oars and letting the boat drift idly in a small bay cut into the rocky shore. Yards away, I can see a white beach curving into the night. It is almost peaceful.

"A few more strokes, boys, and we're on dry land," Geer says. We obey, and in moments he and Gallop are over the side, pulling the bow onto the sand.

"What are we doing here?" I ask as I vault over, soaking my shoes. It does me good to have the feel of solid shore under my feet, but I see no booty here. Nor is this Long Island, from what Geer says.

"Come with me and see," he says. Gallop moors the boat to a rock as Matthew hangs over the side, spitting up what is left in his stomach. Not a man of the sea, that one. Jedidiah and Moses show no interest in exploring and lay themselves prostrate in the sand.

I follow Geer as he scampers across sand and stone. The island is entirely flat except for a small rise on the other side, which we reach in less than a minute. There is no habitation here, other than evidence of sea birds and gulls. Oyster shells and droppings give the ground a whitish-gray glow in the scattered moonlight.

"Let your eyes find the light," Geer says, pointing out into the Sound. I listen to the waves crashing against the shore and the wind whistling by my ears. I look to the west and see the thin line of light appear at the horizon.

"Dawn already?" I ask. It seems too soon.

"You've not been to sea, Freegift," he says, grinning with the joy of knowledge imparted. "That's dawn somewhere out in the Atlantic. The sun's still far below the horizon, but she lights up that thin line between water and sky. You can't see anything like it on land, what with trees, building, and such."

"So this is where you can spot a ship coming in from the east," I say.

"Exactly so, Freegift. We are still in darkness to them, but there's enough light at their backs for us to spy their sail."

"How can we hope to intercept them? They may go on either side of us." I gaze out over the water, the thin line of the horizon clear with the faint dawning glow, while above all is inky black strewn with stars. I never before, in the deep woods of Connecticut, grasped how huge and magnificent this world is. Maps are wonderful things, but this stark beauty is new to me.

"Look you," Geer says, gathering bleached shells and laying them out on the sand. "We are here, on Little Gull. Great Gull is southwest of us, about half a mile away. Four miles or so farther on, is Plum Island. Then we finally come to the North Fork of Long Island. Most British ships will thread their way through these islands on the way to New York. So, we know the route will be starboard. That's to our right."

"I know larboard from starboard," I say, although my seafaring knowledge goes no further. "But why should they go around these small islands? Isn't it harder to navigate in the dark?"

"Aye. But to stay in the middle of the Sound means they're closer to Connecticut and all the privateers ready to sail out after them. And in North Fork, they have British warships close by."

"There's Redcoats not ten miles away?" I ask, pretending to be frightened that they should be so close. Although I have little difficulty achieving this pretense. Still, it means I may not have to trek across the length of Long Island before finding my father's army.

"Sure," Geer says. "There's a fine bay in the lee of North Fork. They say a few frigates are anchored there. Not to mention the traitor Arnold headquartered in Oysterponds."

"Benedict Arnold you mean?" I can barely gasp out the words.

"One traitor name of Arnold is enough, don't you think?" Geer laughs. "Aye, that's him. Rumor is General Clinton sent him there last month, with a regiment of Redcoats, a Tory legion and more Hessians. He needs all them bastards to protect him, don't he?"

"It is hard to believe the most scorned man in America is but ten miles away," I say. I feel the heat of Geer's hatred for the man who sired me, and I cannot help the shame that burns on my face. I am glad for the darkness. At the same time, it is as close as I have come to him. Since my father sold my mother with me in her belly, that is.

It may be this insane, drenching venture, but I feel a stirring of sympathy for these patriots. For the pull of liberty that Mr. Stoddard felt and acted upon. Perhaps it will suit these English of America well. Or perhaps they will be satisfied with liberty only for themselves and leave slaves and Indians to suffer as they have before. I like the people I have met and befriended. Their society and their god, I find less likeable.

But I can understand how Geer hates my father. He betrayed his own people, and that is a fierce betrayal indeed. I will have to query him, once I determine the best way to ask a father to accept me and explain his traitorous conduct at the same time.

Ah. Speak little. It may serve me well with Father Arnold.

We watch the horizon as my thoughts drift to Martine. I spoke little to her, and now I flee her company. Perhaps if the answer is to speak little, one must say that little sooner than later.

Geer cups his hands about his eyes. He sees something, but I do not.

"Where?" I whisper, as if the sailors may hear. He points, and I stare across the waves.

I see it.

"A sail," I say. It seems distant.

"Aye. Far away, or a small vessel, perhaps. Look how it turns to the so'west."

"To larboard," I say.

"Aye," Geer says. "And that's a single sail. A sloop, maybe. Easier for us to board, harder to come alongside, since she'll be fast."

"Is she heading for Great Gull?" I ask, falling into calling the ship as a woman quite easily. I feel myself piratical.

"I'm not sure," Geer says. "Wait! Look at her move. Damn and hell, it's a cutter, making for North Fork and Oysterponds, I'll wager. Come, there's not much time."

"We have a single-masted cutter, making for the North Fork," Geer

exclaims as we return to the boat. Gallop springs into action, being
the only one who understands the implications and pulls the line from
around the mooring rock. Geer boards and takes the gaffs and pike
from under the seats, keeping them close at hand. Gallop and I push off,
as Geer explains.

"If she's going to the bay at North Fork, we can intercept her," he says.
"The cutter's a small vessel, built for speed. They use them to carry
military messages up and down the coast, sometimes all the way from
Nova Scotia."

"No cargo?" Matthew asks as he strains at the oars. We are soon out of
leeward and back in the Sound.

"Not much," Geer says. "But not a big crew, either, lads. And her
gunwales are low. We'll be over the side and on deck before you know
it."

"It's a ship we can take as a prize," Gallop says. "Worth more than cargo,
not to mention what letters from generals up in Canada will fetch."

"The hard part is closing with her, since she's moving fast. We toss the
grappling hook into the rigging and grab on with the gaffs," Geer says.
"Up and over. There's likely only the watch and helmsman on deck.
We'll have the captain and crew trapped below decks, and the ship will
be ours, boys!"

In spite of the previous injunction to quiet, we all whoop and holler,
giving little thought to any outcome but the one Geer lays out for us.
Soaked clothing, salt caked upon faces, aching muscles, and blisters on
palms are forgotten as we row, oars cutting through water in unison,
the thrill of the hunt bringing us together in a rhythm so natural we
seem as one, propelling our craft through the waves like a missile.

"Larboard side, hold," Geer orders, and three of us lift our oars from the
water. The starboard rowers continue, altering our course, until Geer
tells us to press on. I glance back and see him casting a quick eye toward
the horizon, tracking the sail. He knows these waters well and seems
to be a good judge of speed and distance, since we are soon within easy
sight of the cutter.

"The wind's lessened," Gallop says.

"Aye," Geer says, and tells us all to hold. "Coming more from the west as well. She'll be working to windward, keeping the helmsman on his toes."

"Good news for us, boys. She's slowing now, beating against the wind. We'll come up on her nice and easy," Geer announces.

"They won't see us?" Jedidiah asks.

"Not likely," he answers. "We can see that big sail against the horizon, but they're still staring westward into the dark. Don't you worry."

I pull at the oars, knowing that when a man tells you not to worry, it is a sign you should commence to do so. When a boy who has never felt a razor on his cheek tells you, it is likely too late for worrying to do much good. So I row, and try to ignore the fear rising in my gut.

"Quiet as you can, boys," Geer whispers, and we dip the oars as silently as possible, avoiding the loud splash and spray of saltwater. My eyes are accustomed to the dark, but I sense now that light is filtering across the horizon. The sun has advanced across the Atlantic, and now must be touching New England.

I ask my ancestors to hold the darkness in place for a few more minutes. Then I look over my shoulder.

We do not need another minute. The cutter is nearly upon us. Its sail billows out and the ship leans to the side as it slices through the cresting waves.

"Oars in," Geer says, his voice low and urgent. He gives a last stroke with his, and we are positioned perfectly, lined up with the larboard side of the cutter. This is the lower side, the wind pushing the vessel as it is steered against the wind.

It grows huge, coming toward us from a blood-red dawn. It is light enough now to see everything, but my eyes are fixed on the bow of the cutter, seeming to come straight at me.

Geer stands and twirls the grappling hook. He sets his feet wide and waits until the bow is abreast of him. The spray sends a torrent of water into our boat, but he does not falter. The grappling hook flies and snags in the rigging. From the deck to the top of the sail is a profusion of knotted rope, and the hook has a good purchase. Geer ties the line to our craft as Gallop snares a gaff into the lower rigging. We are now being pulled by the cutter, and I am glad the whaleboat has a bow at both ends.

"Now," Geer says, grasping the line and pulling himself up. Gallop has a firm grip on the gaff, and the rigging is within reach. First Jedidiah grasps it and launches himself into the rigging, taking hold with both hands. He gets one leg over the gunwale and Matthew hands him the pike as Gallop secures another rope from the rowboat to the rigging. I climb up that rope, pulling myself into the rigging.

Geer is on the deck. All is quiet, and it seems we have achieved surprise.

"Williams?" The voice comes from the stern, and footsteps sound against the wooden deck. A figure in a red coat advances toward us, mistaking Geer in the dim light for a comrade.

"Aye," Geer says, making his voice hoarse. It does not fool the Redcoat.

"Boarders!" Comes his shout, and he lifts a musket. Sailors on watch we had expected. Armed sentries, no.

"Prepare to repel boarders!" More shouts issue from below decks, and a hatch springs open. More Redcoats, more muskets. Our axes and gaffs are no match for these.

"Back," Geer yells and jumps to the grappling line. Jedidiah does the same, sliding down the rope and falling into the rowboat.

I stand in the rigging, transfixed. I think I may announce myself to these men, ask for sanctuary. These thoughts fly through my mind as I see the soldier adjust the aim of his musket, away from where Geer stood. Confusion fills the air. More Redcoats spill out and orders are issued, questions asked.

Where are the devils? What ship? Where's the watch? Helmsman, steady on.

The barrel of the musket settles upon me. We are yards apart and the scene is ill-lit, but I do make out the whites of his eyes as he widens them. I see his finger tighten. Shouts come from the rowboat and commands from officers on deck. I feel as if I could remain hanging from the rigging forever, staring at this Englishman who seems not to wish to kill me.

He pulls the trigger. The flash rises from the pan, and I clamber down the rigging as flame and noise pursue me, the bullet passing above my head with the sound of an angry hornet. I hang from the rigging and drop, holding onto the gaff still fixed to the cutter's ropework.

"Push off!" Matthew screams, as Geer works to loosen the knot securing the grappling line. Gallop does the same with the rope he has tied to the rigging. Until these are both dealt with, we are bound to this vessel and no good will come of that.

Two men lean over the gunwale, muskets aimed at us. I take the pike and launch it at them, and it proves a distraction. Moses and Jedidiah do the same with their gaffs, which gives us a few precious seconds. Gallop unhitches his knotted line and we are free of it. The rowboat swings about, secured now only at one end. Geer stumbles, and I cannot tell if he has the line undone.

"Watch out!" Gallop yells to him as more muskets are aimed over the side, this time from the stern, too far for us to throw anything. Two muskets fire, to no effect. We are swinging back and forth, the wake of the vessel tossing us about with no mercy.

More shots.

Geer is struck. Square in the chest, his life's blood sprayed like seafoam across the rowboat.

The line is under him, tangled around his arm. It is still knotted to the bench, and I jump toward it, hoping the motion will not toss me into the sea. I take my tomahawk, hold the line against the bench, and cut it through.

More muskets fire at us, but the cutter is moving away as we drift back.

Shots drop in the water around us.

"Row," Gallop shouts, and no one needs encouragement, not with poor Geer dead of a musket ball. Another volley sounds, and I duck, as do the others.

I hear a sound like a rock hitting a ripe melon. I look up, and Matthew stares at his shoulder, a blossom of blood issuing from him, his arm limp and useless. Moses cries out to his god, who is nowhere to be seen.

"Row, damn you," Gallop says. "Unless you want one too."

I row.

· Nineteen ·

———

Four of us row. Matthew groans and grimaces. Geer lies dead. The sun is full up, and it has dawned over a calm and placid sea, marred only by the wisps of fog floating over the water. It is a fine day, except for the dead, wounded, and miserable. And the lost, I must add. Geer was our master mariner and navigator, and he is now on a different journey altogether. To where, I do not know, no more than I know where we be bound.

"The sun rose there," Moses says, not for the first time. "In the east. So north must be that way. New London should be due north of us."

"What are we going to do with Geer?" I ask. We ignore Moses and his pointing, since it is impossible to know where on the flat and hazy horizon the sun actually came up. His version of north is as likely to take us past New Haven or Newport.

"His family will want to bury him," Jedidiah says. "We must take him back."

"He has no one," Gallop says. He gently arranges an errant lock of hair that has fallen across his dead friend's face. "No one who cares, at any rate. Except for me and a few souls he worked the clam beds with."

"But he does have family, even if they do not care about him?" I ask.

"His mother died bearing him," Gallop says, looking out over the water. "She was a serving maid in his father's house, out in Rhode Island somewhere. He's a cod fisherman, has a few boats. The old man didn't like a bastard son underfoot, so he sent Geer off to work as a servant when he was still a small boy. If he didn't want him when he breathed, I doubt he'd want him now, all cold and gone white."

We bob on the water for a while, Matthew rocking the boat as he tumbles about, grasping his shoulder. His wound is not as terrible as it first looked. The cutter was some distance away at the last volley, and the ball was nearly spent. It broke the skin and embedded itself in Matthew's flesh, but fell free when he clawed at it in his panic. Still, the wound is bloody, his chest bruised purple, and bones are sure to be broken.

"Matthew, we must cleanse the wound," I say, reaching for his good shoulder. "Otherwise it may worsen."

"With what? We have nothing," he says. We drained the last from a jug of water an hour before.

"Salt water," I tell him. "I will run the seawater over it, cleaning out any bits of your shirt and waistcoat stuck in the flesh. It will sting a trifle, but it is good for you."

"He's right," Gallop says from behind Matthew. "We can bind the wound with your shirt. Don't worry." He moves to help him remove his clothing and is rewarded with a hard shove delivered by Matthew's good arm.

"No! Leave me be," Matthew shouts, and Gallop is sent sprawling between his dead friend's legs, which does not improve his humor. He tells Matthew he is a damned fool, and we have enough death clinging to the boat already. He gains his footing and restrains Matthew as I unbutton his waistcoat. Matthew turns his face away from us and whimpers. I know he is in pain and fears the sting of the salt water. But if he braved the Devil's Belt for plunder, then he should put on a brave face now, I think. His cries are unseemly, even for a wounded privateer.

I rip the linen shirt away, knowing it will be in shreds anyway as a bandage.

Then I see why he has not wanted the shirt removed.

His back is strewn with scars, thick welts of knotted flesh one upon the other. Someone has laid into him, and changed hands when he grew tired. Many lines are left to right, others right to left. Matthew weeps, and I lay a hand on his shoulder. I feel the hard lines of poorly healed scars at the base of my hand.

"My God," Gallop says, falling back onto his bench. I hear Jedidiah and Moses gasp as I lean in to try and meet his eyes.

"Who did this, Matthew?"

"Father," he says, tears and snot gushing from his face. I tear a length of linen for him to use. "Father," he repeats. A name, peculiar to one man. A word, common to all who are born. But so widely differing in how they teach their boys.

I wish to know why, but how could there be a reason for such brutality carved into the flesh of one's own flesh? The answer would be poor and paltry, for how could a son answer?

"He hasn't beat you in some time," I say, surveying the map of paternal rage Matthew carries with him. There are old scars and newer scars but none fresh and unhealed.

"I ran away," he says, rubbing his face clean.

"And came some distance, I hope," Gallop says.

"A goodly distance, yes. I won't say from where, if you don't mind. I trust you boys, but there's no reason to say something that could be repeated by a slip of the tongue. He's likely out to find me. I took some money."

"Surprised you didn't take his life," Gallop says. "I'd be tempted."

"All I wanted was to get away," Matthew says. "It was enough to get to New London. I have a job at the printer's, and it suits me. Better than what Father had planned."

"What?" I ask.

"To follow him in service to the Lord," Matthew says, a crooked smile on his face. "He was beating the devil out of me, or so he said."

"I think the devil was in him," Jedidiah says. "If you don't mind me saying so."

"The thought occurred to me as well, on a regular basis," Matthew says.

"Being as you are used to pain, you won't mind the salt water so much," I say and pat him on his shoulder.

"Be just like home," Matthew says, wincing as he sits up straight. He nods his readiness, and I dip the jug into the seawater. I push him back into Gallop's arms and stand over him, letting the water run in a torrent from the jug onto his shoulder. He clenches his teeth but utters not a word.

The wound looks good, no stray fibers of wool or linen left inside. I dunk the jug and repeat again, the water washing away Matthew's blood. When the preacher does this to a newborn in church, splashing the baptismal water on the wailing child, he recites, in that sing-song cadence, *In the name of the father and of the son.*

What foolishness. Did Matthew's father pray while he seared the flesh of his son? Was it done in his name and Matthew's? What these English do in their churches they take seriously. Except when they leave and spend the next six days wreaking havoc.

I tie off a bandage around Matthew's shoulder and ease the waistcoat back on him. It covers most of his agonies, but the edges of scars appear when he moves, as if writhing creatures decorate his back. He rests his head and sleeps, exhausted.

"Where are we?" Moses asks, after minutes of quiet. He has finally given up pointing.

"I'm not sure," Gallop says. "We're drifting, but I can't tell where the current is taking us."

"We should row in the general direction of north," I say. "Otherwise, we could make landfall on Long Island." Which might suit me another day, but if the Tories spot us, they'll promptly kill us, my paternal protestations notwithstanding.

"Look," Jedidiah says, pointing starboard, where we think east still is. "Land, is it not?"

"It is," Gallop says, shading his eyes. "No way of knowing if it's one of the Gulls, Plum Island, Fisher's Island, the North Fork of Long Island, or any of the little islands along the Connecticut shore."

"Let's row," I say, if only to take some action.

We row, keeping the sun on what we take to be the eastern side. The land Jedidiah spotted fades from view, and we settle into a steady stroke. But it does not last long. We are exhausted, thirsty, hungry, and frightened. Fog rises like steam from the water. Glimpses of land play out on the horizon, appearing and disappearing as we move.

We halt the rowing and scan the horizon in each direction. Nothing but haze and glare.

"We should do something with Geer," Gallop says, returning to the unresolved topic. "He loved the sea."

"Sailors have a burial at sea, I hear," Moses says. We all nod. Matthew is awake and adds his assent.

"It will make the boat lighter," he says, combining the spiritual with the practical.

"He'd want it this way," Gallop says. "He'd want a burial at sea, and he'd want to help us. This raid was his plan, after all. He'd feel responsible."

Silence reigns for several minutes. The logic is undeniable, but no one moves to take the first step. The sun, high in the sky, beats down on us through the haze with shimmering, thick heat, making every movement and decision arduous.

"We don't have a shroud," Gallop says. "There should be a shroud."

"Man comes into the world naked," Matthew says. "No reason he can't leave this world naked."

"It seems right," Moses says. "Maybe the next best thing to a shroud is nothing at all. When he gets to heaven, he'll have robes and all that, right?"

"Right," his older brother answers, in a manner which tells us all to hold comment on Moses' grasp of theology.

"So, naked it is," I say, watching Gallop for the final approval, as is his right being Geer's friend and partner in this endeavor. He nods, and we begin to disrobe the body. It is a simple matter, the duck sailor's trousers pulled off easily along with the blue jacket. The shirt is torn and bloody. We tear at it and toss it over.

"Wash him," Matthew says. I obey, sensing something biblical in the injunction. He is our expert in such matters, however hard-won the knowledge. So I dunk the jug again, and douse Geer with the ocean water, sluicing it across his bloody chest, anointing his forehead.

Finally, we are ready.

"Anyone know a prayer?" Gallop asks. I do not. Matthew shakes his head, which must be full of them. But we are seeking tenderness, not the wrath of the god he learned.

"I do," Moses says. "It's our bedtime prayer."

He looks to his older brother, who tells him to proceed.

Gallop and I ease the thin body overboard. We let him into the water as gently as we can, and I give him a small shove away from the boat.

Moses prays.

Now I lay me down to sleep,
I pray the Lord my soul to keep,
If I should die before I wake,
I pray the Lord my soul to take.

No one says a word. Moses wipes his eyes, as do I. We watch Geer drift away, his pale body a tiny island in this watery terrain.

I feel even more alone. Strange that a corpse gave me comfort. He had been so confident, knew so much about the sea, and now he is gone forever.

"We should row," Gallop says.

"Aye," I say, adopting the nautical term Geer used so often.

"Which way?" Gallop asks. With the sun straight above us working to burn through the foggy haze, it is hard to tell. Everything is a confusion of blinding light, constant horizon, gray sky and dark water.

"It is hopeless," I say. "Choose a direction, and we'll trust to luck."

"No," Moses says. "We should follow Geer."

"What?" Gallop says, irritation in his tone as his friend being made light of.

"Look," Moses says, pointing to where Geer is now drifting. He is moving faster than our boat.

"The tide?" I ask. No one knows. There is no better choice, so we row with what strength we have, following the steady progress of the only one of us who knew the way home.

· Twenty ·

———

Wе follow Geer on his steady course. Whether it is the tide, or the current, or perhaps their god deciding to intervene, he leads us in the right direction. We row as the fog and haze blows away and his body sinks deeper in the water. The pale, drifting ghost finally disappearing beneath the surface. Geer is gone, but ahead the shoreline of Connecticut and the mouth of the Thames River appear as the sky gradually clears. He has brought us home.

"Jedidiah, Moses," I say, as I strain to row the last mile or so. "Have you boys a mother and a father?"

"Both," Jedidiah says. "They'll be right angry when we get home."

"I thought I'd bring Mama a gold bracelet," Moses says. "Then maybe she wouldn't be so mad."

"And your father?" I ask.

"I suspect he'll be glad to see us return," Jedidiah says. "There's lots to do in the fields and with the animals. Doesn't mean he won't take the switch to us. But not like. . . you know."

"Not like me," Matthew says, opening one eye. "Don't worry fellows, it takes a rare father to make these scars. A few strokes on your backsides will leave everyone feeling better about things."

"Papa don't stay mad long," Moses says, nodding his head in agreement.

"Of course, we never done anything like this."

"How about you, Gallop?" I ask.

"Pa left on a whaler when I was five. Never came home. Ma says the ship sank, but I'm not sure about that. Maybe he's still out there somewhere, thinking of us now and then."

How strange it is. In this small boat, there was one son not wanted by his father and cast out. Another son's father left him or was drowned before he could come back. Another beat his son without mercy, in the name of their god. One father seems to be made to order, stern but quick to forgive.

And then there is mine, who does not even know I exist. Which father shall he be? Worse yet, will he deny me, deny he knew Maame, who he called Sally? I do not know which would be harder to bear.

I may never know. I came close to his people last night and barely escaped a musket ball. Next time, I will need a better plan. And a boat I do not need to row so far.

We row to Tink's warehouse; Gallop will then take Moses and Jedidiah across the river to Groton, where they will make their way home. The boat will be returned in fine shape, except for a musket ball embedded near an oarlock.

"I will help you to the doctor," I tell Matthew, who looks anxiously about as we pass by ships moored at the wharf.

"No, I can't go," Matthew says, shaking his head with determination. "Get me to my room, please, and I will be fine."

"You will not," Gallop says. He points to my raft, secured to Tink's dock, and we head in. When I put her together—all ships will now forever be female to me—I thought the river journey to be the height of my waterborne exploits. Now it seems quaint. "You will die if the wound goes bad. You must go."

"No, I will not," Matthew says. "I thank you, but if I do, people will talk. Our expedition will become common knowledge. If someone speaks of the printer's apprentice, word may get to my father."

"He knows you work with a printer?" I ask.

"He knows I wished to. He forbade it, of course. I cannot take a chance."

"Matthew, are you not of legal age? Why do you fear your father now?" Gallop asks.

"I fear him no longer," Matthew says. "But I do know I will kill him if he tries to lay hands on me. And I have no wish to murder my father, no matter the pain he has caused me. So please, Freegift, make no attempt with the doctor, I beg you."

"You have my word," I say. "I know of another way." Knowing Matthew's desire for secrecy, I do not explain myself. I speak little, and again find Tink's advice useful.

We pull up to the raft, and I help Matthew, who climbs stiffly out of the whaleboat. Gallop and the two boys wish him well and push off. What is left unsaid is what we all know. Never again will any of us venture into the Devil's Belt with such a small boat.

I take Matthew's good arm and drape it over my shoulder, helping him up the steps to the warehouse. It is not busy, being the Sabbath. A few sailors stand on decks, most gazing out over the water. We draw no attention to ourselves as I help Matthew to the door and unlock it.

"Is this where you live?" asks Matthew, as I lay him down on my bed.

"Yes, and where I work. You will be safe here. The manager is a good man."

"They say that of him, the fellow everyone calls Tink. And most speak of you well also, Freegift."

"Only most?" I say with a grin, as I light a candle. The sun is still up, but the one window does not admit much of its light.

"Not the men of the *Badger*, or a few who are suspicious of Africans. They say you may be a runaway."

"What do you think?" I ask.

"That it is quite funny people should confide such thoughts to me, a son who has run away from his father. I believe you have been freed. I've heard of it being done enough since Bunker Hill, so I have no reason to doubt you."

"Why did you come on this voyage?" I ask. I sense Matthew is a decent lad, intelligent, and possessed with wit enough to see the world as it is—a cruel and unsettling place.

"To see where it would take me," he answers. "To see if I could survive it."

"What about riches?" I ask.

"I would not turn them away," he says. "But what I wanted most was to cast myself out into dangerous waters and see if I might live through it."

"As you have cast yourself out into the world," I say.

"Yes. Now, I know. If Father did not kill me, and this expedition did not, I stand a fair chance of thriving in this world, on my own account. It is a refreshing thing to know, even at the cost of this," he says, waving his hand over his bandaged wound. "Will you tell me what you plan to do with me now?"

"I will bring you to a healer. But first, I must get some food and arrange our transportation," I say, making for the door.

"Thank you, Freegift," Matthew says. "You don't have to do this, which makes me even more grateful for your aid."

"Actually, I think I must do it," I say. "But I'll accept your gratitude nonetheless. Now rest, and I will be back with food and drink."

"Freegift?" Matthew calls out as I open the door. "Why did you go?"

"That is a long story," I say. One that I have not yet told to a soul. I close the door and step into the street.

As a brisk wind blows off the water, I am quite glad to have solid ground underfoot. Hunger gnaws at me, and I make for the tavern, the only location to obtain food on the Sabbath. The bake shop and other establishments are closed, enjoying their day of rest. As I enter the tavern, I see that many rest everything but their elbows. The serving girl who accompanied Martine to the wharf yesterday hurries by, struggling with a tray filled with tankards. As the girl—Jenny by name—returns to the kitchen, I inquire after Martine. Jenny tells me she is expected this evening after spending the day with her mother at the Hardwick farm. She says this with a warm smile, brushing a wisp of hair back under her bonnet. I give her a penny and beg her to ask Mr. Hardwick to call upon me at the warehouse before he returns.

"Not Martine?" Jenny asks, wrinkling her brow.

"No. I expect Mr. Hardwick to bring her in the wagon, and then return to the farm. I must speak with him, do you understand?" She shrugs her assent and makes for the kitchen, leaving me to feel I have somehow disappointed her.

I look about for Tink, but he is not present. As the tavern keeper passes, I ask for two meat pies and a jug of cider to take with me. He takes my coin and I wait by the fireplace for the food and drink. Even though it is summer, the low fire is welcome after the chill and dampness of the past hours. The warmth in the low-raftered room soothes me, and I look about, recognizing a few faces from my brief time in New London.

One of them is Michael Gordon. He does not spy me, with his eyes intent upon a young lady at his table. It is not Martine, and I am at first seized with anger that he should flaunt his regard for another woman so openly. Then, I tamp down my anger and see the advantage in this. His dining partner is young and pretty, yellow-haired, and dressed in a fine garment. I am suddenly eager for Martine to appear, where moments ago I was relieved she had not yet returned from her Sabbath visit.

Another gentleman joins them. Gordon rises to clasp his hand, showing respect. The girl's father, perhaps?

The meat pies and jug are brought to me, and I make my way out, head down, wishing Gordon not to see me. But truth be told, there are no other Africans with long twists of black hair about, and he may see me by chance. What I do not want him to gaze upon is the look I must wear on my face.

Joy and triumph.

But no, this is not a triumph. I have a journey I must make, and all this does is put a firmer grasp on my desire to remain in New London, to be with Martine, and settle in among these people.

I must not give in. Maame, who is with our ancestors, is depending upon me to find my father. I cannot go against her wishes and risk the anger of all those who have gone before me. I know not what will happen after I die, but I am sure they will greet me then, when I must answer for all I have done.

I am torn. Between my dead mother and a girl who may not wish my company at all. I have no wish to return to my life as a slave of Mr. Stoddard, but again I see how simple that life was. Unlike this one, which finds me betwixt and between Maame's wishes and my own desires, while carrying vittles to a wounded lad lying in my lodgings. I have taken responsibility for this fellow I knew not, less than a day ago, before we both saw a man die and nearly departed this world ourselves.

No, this life of freedom is not a simple one.

Rain begins to fall, softly at first, then with a pelting hardness that makes me glad to reach my door. I keep my thoughts to myself as Matthew and I devour the meat pies and gulp cider. I had not thought I could be so hungry.

"What now?" Matthew asks, as he finishes the last bite of his pie.

"Someone will come soon to take us out of the town," I say, inspecting the hurried bandage I made from his shirt. It is caked with blood, but there is no foul smell, which is a good sign. "It will be safe, I promise you." I know it will be safe at Edward's farm, but what I cannot be certain of is if he will bring Martine to town. Since it is the Christian's Sabbath, he will not deliver a load of produce to the tavern. Perhaps Martine will walk or take the wagon on her own. I say nothing of this to Matthew. He is in no state to walk, and if there is no wagon, I will have to find another way.

"To someone who knows medicine?" Matthew asks. "Someone you trust?"

"Yes. Someone who knows medicines, and who has been long trusted in my family."

"Tell me about your family, Freegift. It will pass the time while we wait."

I see no harm in this, so I tell Matthew the story of Maame and her brother and being sold for being saucy, without mention of the Arnold family. Of my growing up and working enslaved for Mr. Stoddard, and how he taught me to read and to think carefully about what I learned in the pages of his small library. Of Shakespeare and maps. Of the trees of the forest.

Of Maame's death, speaking not of her last command to me.

Of the freedom I was granted, which was only my due. Of the wages Mr. Stoddard paid me for past years, unexpected, but again, only my due. Of my voyage downriver and my encounter, twice-over, with Gill, which he has already heard tell of. But by the time the story had come to Matthew, it had grown considerably in the re-telling. I told of bringing the boy Wait Jenkins to the Hardwick farm, hinting that Wait had a connection with them, not I.

Of Martine, I say nothing.

Of Topheny, I say nothing, since I do not wish him to rebel at the thought of being treated by a Pequot woman. He is wise to avoid the notoriety of the doctor on Bank Street, but at the same time, he needs medical care. That it will involve herbs and a moss poultice is best left unspoken until there is no chance of refusal.

"You've said nothing of your father," Matthew says, as I conclude with a long swallow of cider. I have not spoken so much since—ever, now that I think upon it.

"My father is an unknown," I say, which has some truth to it. I am glad not to have lie direct to Matthew.

"I understand," he says. "So are many, even when they are known for a lifetime. My own father, I cannot say I know what drove him. Madness? The devil? God himself?"

"What do you think?" I ask. Who else could know? Matthew is silent, staring at his hands. The only sound is the rain on the window. Finally, he looks me in the eyes.

"I believe it was his own father, God help him. And God help me should I ever carry on with my own son so. When I was very young, too much a babe for even him to whip, he warned me, saying his father had struck him hard, to beat sense and the Lord into him. It frightened me, but I took it as the sort of thing all fathers say to their boys. When he started to whip me, I still thought it was something every father did. Something necessary. One hot summer day, I saw three older boys at a pond near our house. They stripped bare and dove in the water. There was not a mark on their backs. I went home and asked Father how could there be boys so perfect they were not struck and scarred as I was?"

"What was his answer?"

"He said there were no such boys. It was the devil playing tricks with my eyes."

"Matthew, I sometimes wonder about this whole business of fathers, I must admit. Poor Geer and his father throwing him out. I was terribly glad to hear Jedidiah and Moses speak well of their own, otherwise I might give up hope."

"Give up on what hope?" Matthew asks, and my stomach feels to drop out of me. I have spoken too much, and too long. Like a man unused to strong drink, I have become drunk with words and memories.

"On... being a father myself," I say, recovering with a deep breath. A knock sounds at the door, rescuing me from any further explanation. I open the door.

Martine stands there. She is soaked through, her hair plastered against her face. She pushes it aside.

"Freegift," she says, out of breath, doubtless from the exertion of running through the downpour. "Jenny said you needed me."

Oh, Jenny.

· Twenty One ·

I bid Martine enter, reaching out with my arm to guide her through the doorway and in out of the rain. She brings herself full into my arms instead, the wind and water gusting at her back. Her thin cloak is soaked, and she shivers in the chill air.

No, not shivers. She is crying, warm tears mixing with cold raindrops.

"Jenny told me you asked after me and wished to see me," Martine says, raising her head from where it nestles on my chest. I never felt such warmth from a cold and drenched soul. Nor from any soul, I must admit, since I grew too old for a mother's lingering embrace. "I wished to say much to you, but you left so quickly when we came back from the farm."

"Martine," I say, closing the door and nodding toward Matthew on the bed.

"Oh," she says, her hand to her mouth, as if to keep more words from tumbling out.

"This is Matthew, who is in need of care. I thought Topheny could help him, if we had means to carry him to her," I say. Martine looks to me, perplexed.

"Matthew Rogers, at your service," he says, trying to stand and falling back into the bed. "Although what service I could provide presently would be a small one indeed."

"Why do you not go to Doctor Hayes? He is close by," Martine says.

"We have need of discretion," I say, as Martine steps closer to inspect the bloody bandage and the wound beneath. "It is important no one speaks of this or bandies about Matthew's name."

"You work in the printer's shop, do you not?" Martine says, lifting the bandage clear. Her face betrays nothing.

"Yes," Matthew says, tensing as she touches the skin around the wound.

"Are you a criminal? Does the magistrate seek you?" Martine asks these questions as she presses her face close to the wound and sniffs.

"No, he does not," Matthew says. "Someone does, but it is not a matter of law. Not exactly."

"Hmm," Martine says. "Not exactly is not exactly a convincing answer. But no matter, we must get this treated. It is not yet foul."

"I washed it with salt water," I say, and immediately regret it. There is no reason to speak of our absurd and deadly journey.

"Good," Martine says, seeming not to care where or how Matthew received his wound. "Is there a clean piece of cloth for a new bandage?"

I give her my spare shirt, and she rips it into pieces. In a violent manner, actually, and I see the anger in her eyes. Jenny has played the matchmaker poorly, and now Martine feels the fool, rushing over here only to find a patient in need of care, not a suitor. The shirt is a small price to pay.

She eases Matthew forward to wrap the bandage around him, then stops for a moment as her fingers touch the edge of the scars upon his back. A brief *oh* escapes her mouth, before she returns to her work, as if a back full of scars is a fully normal thing.

"I will take you to my mother," Martine tells Matthew. "She is a healer. We are a few miles north, and no one will know where you are."

"A healer?" Matthew asks, as she binds the remnants of my linen around his shoulder.

"Her name is Topheny," Martine says. "One of the few Pequot people left. And the last healer."

"You seem adept at medicine," Matthew says, attempting a smile as she knots the bandage. Her long silken hair falls close to Matthew's face, and he grins, even in his pain, as she smooths it back behind her ear and graces him with a smile. It seems men are drawn to Martine, as the river is to the sea. She does possess an arresting quality, a soothing nature that calms my breast with her very presence. And the breasts of others, I see. I find myself unaccountably angry with Matthew. How dare he compliment Martine so forcefully? Which only makes me think again of Michael Gordon, tromping down the wooden stairs at the back of the tavern.

Why will they not leave her alone? Why will they not leave her to me?

"I have sewn up fools cut open in a tavern brawl once or twice," Martine says. "But my mother is the true healer. I have the wagon outside. Can you stand?"

"Of course," Matthew says, bringing himself upright while keeping his hand on Martine's shoulder far longer than he has need to. "I am in your debt."

"No need," Martine says, avoiding my eyes as she speaks to Matthew. "You have helped me see things clearly by your very presence."

"I will go with you," I say, rushing to the door to open it.

"Do not bother yourself, Freegift," Martine says. "I understand now all you wish is to help your friend, to your credit. Matthew will be well, do not worry. You've done a fair job with him, however this happened."

"I will go with you," I repeat. "If only to visit young Wait." Her words are full of praise for my actions, but now empty of care for me outside of what I did for Matthew. She was warm at the door. Why so cold now?

"Suit yourself," she says with a sigh.

Love is a smoke and is made with the fume of sighs, as the Bard said in *Romeo and Juliet*. If the best I can expect from Martine is a sigh, I shall be satisfied.

I do suit myself and help Matthew into the back of the wagon. I dash back inside to fetch my musket, wishing to be armed as we navigate the roads at night. I return to find Matthew tucked under an oilskin, with Martine at his side, a soft mist falling over them. It falls to me to sit alone, snapping the reins and urging Cricket forward. She whinnies, and I imagine it a laugh at my own expense.

I have little to do but bounce on the wooden seat as Cricket navigates the rutted lane to the Hardwick farm, a route she knows well. I listen to Matthew, who previously endured the pain of his wound with a stoic silence, now uttering low moans and gasps, all the while assuring Martine he is fine. Certainly he is fine, dry beneath the oilskin with a beautiful girl nestled at his side. I would be fine as well. I would take a musket ball at the languid end of its trajectory if it would place Martine next to me. I hear the two of them talking in hushed tones, and wonder what they feel must be kept from me. Is her warmth now transferred to Matthew? Anger rumbles within my brain.

Although, I must admit, I am up here, closer to Cricket's rump than Martine's tender mercies, of my own accord. Have I not determined to leave everything New London has to offer behind? Was it not my choice to turn away from her, even before Michael Gordon made his advances and Matthew began his flirtatious behavior?

Yes, I tell myself. It was.

Then why do I feel this way?

Why do I wish to have been wounded, in order to be close to Martine? All I need do is woo her. But I know precious little of wooing. Nothing, in fact, other than what I observe. Michael wooed directly, spying Martine in the tavern and making his way boldly to her room. Matthew woos slyly, acting the hurt child to draw out Martine's motherly soothing.

What should I do? I am not forceful like Michael, nor shrewd like Matthew. The truth is, I am paralyzed in the presence of Martine. Her beauty chases the breath from my lungs, leaves my tongue still, and my mind perplexed.

I wish it would be as simple as telling her.

We arrive at the farm as the rain lets up. I am soaked. Matthew has overcome his pain well enough to have fallen asleep on Martine's shoulder, and she rouses him from his slumber with gentle words.

Candlelight sparks at the windows of the farmhouse, and Martine shouts out her presence while calling for Ann to come help. There is a confusion of questions from Edward clad in his nightshirt, musket in hand. Ann is instantly practical, taking Matthew by his good arm and guiding him inside. Wait stumbles out, rubbing his eyes, his blonde hair askew.

"Freegift?" Waits says, squinting his eyes. Then more awake, "Martine!" Every boy and man alive is more than glad to see her.

"Wait, run to Topheny and bid her come with her medicines," Ann says. He runs off barefoot, down the dark path to her wigwam. We are soon in front of the fire. Edward brings the embers to life with his bellows, adding kindling until bright, crackling, yellow flames cast their welcome warmth and light around us.

"What has happened, Freegift?" Edward demands. "Who is this fellow?"

"My friend, Matthew," I say, and even with Edward's eyes upon me, I must pause, since it is the first time I have ever called anyone my friend. Saying it aloud sounds strange. Yet comforting. "He has been shot."

I remove the jacket from his shoulders, my eyes upon Ann and Edward, sending a silent signal that they should prepare themselves. Martine bends down to Wait, whispering and drawing his attention away. I see eyes widen at the sight of the criss-crossed scars, then Ann scurries into the kitchen for a shawl which she places across Matthew's shoulders, guiding him to a chair.

I cannot predict Wait's reaction, but he is too young to rest eyes upon such a sight, nor to know what some fathers are capable of.

"Was it a ricochet?" Ann asks, her fingers testing the skin around

Matthew's wound as he sits close to the fire. "There is no bullet lodged inside, yet it looks like he was struck with a musket ball."

"Not a ricochet, Ma'am," Matthew says. "But a ball that was nearly spent. Still, I felt it, as I do now."

"Who did this?" Edward demands, and we are saved from explanation by Topheny's entrance. She brings a leather satchel and surveys Matthew's wound. Ann has cleaned the blood away, and mark of the ball is evident, the skin burst open, raw and ragged.

Wait returns with Topheny. She wastes not a word, but sniffs at the wound as Martine did, nodding her head in satisfaction. She pokes around his shoulder, then along the collarbone. This brings a sharp gasp of pain, nothing like the false cry engineered to elicit pity. She pays no attention to the scars. Perhaps her life has been so full of them she takes little heed.

"This bone is broken," Topheny declares. "The wound will heal quickly. The bone, slowly. You are lucky."

"I do not feel much the lucky man," Matthew says, eyeing the small pouches Topheny pulls from her satchel. "What are those?"

"Yarrow and Leopard's Bane," she says and sprinkles the dried herbs over his wound. "This will help the skin mend. Do not move." Matthew looks on with dread but remains still. Martine and Ann bring strips of cloth, already prepared as bandages.

"This must cover the open wound," Topheny says, taking a fistful of dried sphagnum moss from a burlap pouch. "Or the blood may poison itself, do you understand?"

"No, but I will do as you instruct," Matthew says. "I have seen people die at the hands of a trained English doctor, so I will give myself over to your healing."

"The forest and field hold medicine enough for all people," Topheny says, as Ann wraps cloth around Matthew's shoulders, holding the poultice in place. Soon Matthew's left arm is secured against his chest. "If they are smart enough to use it."

"Topheny is smart," Wait says, piping up from where he stands by the fire. "She showed me how to find all sorts of things in the woods."

"Will someone tell me what on God's green earth has happened?" Edward says, a cloak now draped over his nightshirt.

"These stupid boys went out as privateers," Topheny says, folding her arms across her chest. "I thought Sally's boy would show more sense."

"How do you know?" I ask and realize what I have admitted with my words. Why cannot I remember to speak little, or not at all?

"Look," she says, pointing to tell-tale white lines left by the salt water on our clothes. "How badly did it go? Is this the worst of it?"

"No," I say, unable to meet her eyes. Why did she have to bring up Maame? "A boy was killed. Henry Geer. We went out in a whaleboat."

"One whaleboat? What did you expect to accomplish?" Edward demands.

"We did board a cutter," Matthew says. "Almost took her, too."

"You climbed aboard a British cutter?" Martine asks. I see my chance to stand tall and answer proudly, in my most nautical manner.

"Aye, off Northfork. We rowed all night and laid in wait. Henry said we had a chance of capturing important dispatches."

"If not the cutter itself," Matthew adds.

"And now this boy is dead, and your friend barely escapes death," Martine says to me, hands planted firmly on her hips. "I did not think you such a fool, Freegift."

"It did not go well, I grant you," Edward says. "But if you managed to board a fast-moving cutter in the dark of night, then you almost had her. I'm sorry about your friend Henry, but it was a valiant effort, lads."

"Ohhh!" Martine exclaims. She stamps her foot and walks away, busying herself gathering blankets and quilts. I have never before been called valiant and wish it might have a different effect upon Martine. I do recall that Mr. Stoddard laughed the time I asked him a question about women. He said I had much to learn, and he envied me. Upon the first point, I judge him to have been fully correct. As to his second point, I so far see little to envy in my ongoing ignorance.

"You boys are soaked to the bone," Ann says, bearing blankets. "Salt water, rain, it matters not if you come down with the ague. We'll set you up by the fire and dry your clothes. They'll be fine by morning, though dawn is not so far off."

"It would not be proper, Ma'am," Matthew says.

"It was not proper to go off and get yourself shot, but you succeeded well enough at that," Ann says. I have not known her long, but from what I have seen, she is not a woman to be argued with. "Now strip."

Wait giggles. Martine tosses quilts on the floor at our feet.

"I will sleep in the wigwam," Martine says. "I have no wish to see such pale and puny bodies. It will ruin what sleep is left in this night."

"I am not pale," I say, somewhat louder than necessary.

Wait giggles again. Matthew laughs. I think I hear Martine choke back a laugh herself, and Topheny grins widely.

"You still do not understand why Sally sent you here, do you?" Topheny says this to me in a whisper and leaves with her leather satchel.

I am mystified.

"Can I sleep out by the fire too?" Wait asks. "I'll be quiet."

"No," I say quickly, knowing Wait would catch sight of Matthew's back. "We are exhausted, Wait, and must sleep. We shall talk in the morning." Ann takes a disappointed Wait by the hand and walks him to his room. Edward places another log on the fire and bids us good night. I think he is proud, no matter how foolish I have been. This makes me happy.

Alone, Matthew and I disrobe and hang our meagre clothing by the fire, shoes close to the hearth. Steam rises from the wool and linen like ghosts in the night. Matthew is upright against the wall, his movements constricted by the cloth binding his arm in place. I curl up under a quilt directly in front of the hearth. My limbs ache with exhaustion. My eyes feel full of grit, and it is impossible to hold them open.

But I cannot sleep.

"Matthew?"

"Yes, Freegift?"

"Is it our fault that Geer is dead?"

"I think it the fault of the Redcoat who shot him," Matthew says.

"But if we hadn't gone out with him, he might still be alive."

"If we had not gone, he and Gallop would have found two other fellows. Perhaps two even less adept than either of us, and then all might have died," he says. I tell him I see the sense in that but am not fully persuaded.

"Now a question for you, Freegift," Matthew says. "Why do you act so poorly toward Martine when anyone can see she is smitten with you?"

Smitten? With me? If I were not already on the floor, I would have fallen to it fast. I struggle to reply, but before I can summon the words, a gentle snoring comes from Matthew.

I stare at the flames, trying to understand this world I find myself in. I find myself unaccountably homesick for the old world of Mr. Stoddard's cooperage. The steady work, the sameness of the days, the routine as constant as the river's flow. I do not miss being owned, but the familiarity of my past beckons me with a rosy glow.

No. I cannot let freedom defeat me. I must find a way to speak my mind. Perhaps speaking little is not always the best course of action. After all, the Bard counsels us to say it thusly: *I know no ways to mince it in love, but directly to say 'I love you.'*

Henry V, a rousing play.

I am full of brave words as sleep overcomes me. I pray I will recall them in the morning.

· Twenty Two ·

⊢——⊣

I help Matthew dress in the morning. At first he waves me off, but then surrenders to my assistance, finding one-handed buttoning near to impossible. Our clothes are dry and smell satisfyingly of wood smoke. From Edward comes a shirt to replace Matthew's torn and bloody garment, and in short order we are close to presentable, although in need of a visit to the necessary house. When I have finished, I leave Matthew to work his own buttons undone and make for the kitchen. There I find everyone seated at the table. I send Wait out to help Matthew button up, and although he makes a face, he runs outside fast enough.

I tell them the story of Matthew's father, and how he fears his father will find him, leaving out the part about Matthew afraid he will slay the parson if he sees him again. I think it may not be true, or at least not a story that illustrates Matthew's character the best.

"I will take him back to New London, if I may have use of the cart," I say. "I am sorry to have burdened you with him, but I could not think of anything else. I knew Topheny would be able to treat him."

"He should remain quiet for three days," Topheny says. "To let the bone begin to mend. The road to town is poor and not the best for a broken bone to rattle over."

"Three days?" Edward says. "I think we can manage." His gaze drifts to Ann, seeking her opinion. She nods her agreement.

"You do bring such interesting visitors, Freegift," Ann says with a smile.

"Matthew seems a polite young man. But next time, come alone, will you? The house is getting full."

"How is Wait?" I ask, sensing that she is joking, while glad of the invitation to visit again.

"He cries out in his sleep," Edward says. "That's when the memories come, I fear. In the daylight, he professes to remember nothing of his parents being taken. He's a bright boy, eager to please. It's no trouble to have him about."

"What Edward means is that Wait is a joy," Ann says. "Thank you, Freegift, and you Martine, for bringing him to us."

Wait returns with Matthew in tow, and the table is full of talk and food. Matthew and I are pressed for our story, and we tell it as best we can, granting Geer the most heroic death possible within the bounds of the truth. We tell of the burial at sea, and how Geer's body floated away with the whaleboat in its wake, guiding us home. Wait's mouth gapes open, and he inches closer to Ann, who puts a protective arm around his shoulder.

"And here we are," I say. Silence falls across the table. Even Martine is quiet, no sharp quip coming from her about what idiots we boys be.

"Matthew, Topheny says you should stay with us for at least three days to heal properly," Edward says. "You are welcome to do so."

"I thank you all," Matthew says. "But I must return to work at the print shop. I am already overdue."

"No," Topheny says, chopping the air with her hand, which I know means she will brook no argument. "You have been stupid enough. Stop now. Rest, or your bone will not set well. Your arm will be crooked, and no woman will have you."

"Then I will stay," Matthew says. "I am in your debt, all of you. But especially to you, Topheny, when all the ladies swarm to my side." We laugh, and I wish I had Matthew's way with words. They flow like nectar, and we are bees hungry to lap it up. I glance to Martine, and she is smiling, but I am surprised that she is looking at me.

And that she does not look away, but rather shows me the warmth I have not seen since she stood in the rain at my door.

"I will go to your employer, Matthew," I say, covering my shock with a torrent of words. "I will tell him you met with an accident and will return to work as soon as possible. There's enough truth in that."

"Will he give your position to another?" Edward asks, ever practical.

"I think not. I do have some skill with a press and think he will be glad to wait," Matthew says.

"That's settled then," Edward says. "Freegift, I'd be obliged if you help Martine with her belongings in town and see her safely off."

"Pardon me?" I ask, not understanding.

"Martine is not safe in town," Topheny says. "That man Gill threatens her. She must come home. Did she not tell you?"

"No. Martine, I am sorry. This is all my fault," I say.

"Mine too!" Wait insists, and I credit him for Martine's trouble in equal parts.

"It was my choice, Wait Jenkins," Martine says, not addressing me at all. "I could not bear for you and Freegift to make fools of Gill and his men alone. Why do boys want all the fun for themselves?" She graces me with a smile, and I feel nothing could improve upon this moment.

"Has Gill hurt you?" I ask, overcome with a desire to protect Martine from all harm. Such is the magic her smile works.

"No, only sneers and threats from him and his men," she says. "The other night, Michael Gordon, a kindly fellow from the *Minerva*, came to warn me he overheard Gill plotting to kidnap me and take me aboard their ship. You must know him, Freegift, he is first mate, so he says."

"Gordon? Why, yes, I do," I manage to utter. I have been a fool. The night I vowed to tell Martine of my feelings, she was not in a dalliance with Gordon, and he apparently had no motive but that of a gentleman. Yes,

I am a fool, and have wasted precious time. "He is a good man, indeed. You were wise to heed his advice."

"I am tired of working for coin, anyway," Martine says. "It is time I let my mother teach me more of what she knows."

"And another pair of hands at the harvest will be welcome," Edward says. "Our little farm is growing quickly, in acreage and population."

"I helped my Pa pick apples last year," Wait says. "It was the first time he let me." The memory brings a smile to his face, but then he casts his eyes downward, the joy of reminiscence turning bitter as it is leavened with the recollection of his father's death. Ann pats him on the shoulder, and he rests his head on her bosom, shoulders heaving with sobs.

It is time to take our leave.

"I don't know what would have become of me without your help, Freegift," Matthew says as we go outside. The sun is up, and the world looks fresh and clean after the night's rain. I feel much the same way.

"It is what friends do," I say, rolling the precious words about my brain. "Rest well, and I will visit again in a few days. Do you need anything from your lodgings?"

"I have so little, it matters not," Matthew says. "I think this place has all the riches a man may need, don't you?" He smiles and looks to Martine, who has Wait by the hand, heading to the barn.

"Yes, I do. I think I shall wait no longer," I say, bringing us back to our conversation by the fire.

"Good. For if you do not, I shall seek to woo Martine myself. And I hate to be held in second regard by anyone," Matthew says, and we both laugh. I am fair warned to act now and will do so.

I see Topheny heading for the path to her wigwam and run to catch up.

"Topheny, wait please," I say. "What did you mean last night? About why Sally sent me here?"

"Sally was a smart girl," she says, not breaking her stride. "Benedict was clever. I am surprised you are neither, Freegift. Or maybe all those years a slave in the backwoods dulled what sense you had."

"She wanted me to hear of my youth from you," I say. "To learn something of my father. Right?"

"That is one reason," Topheny says, finally stopping short and facing me. "But do you not see the other? Sally knew I was with child before she left. I told her it would be a girl child. She sent you here to find Martine, so the two of you could unite. You are each two halves, boy. Only when you come together will you be whole."

"How could you know you would bear a girl? What if it would have been a boy child?"

"I had a vision. Before I was even sure I was with child. Visions are never wrong. Sometimes we misunderstand them, but they are never wrong. Now, stop being a dull boy and go with Martine. Now."

She walks away from me. I am stunned to think my future was decided by a vision some eighteen years ago. Did Maame know, all those years at Mr. Stoddard's? Perhaps.

I am glad I did not know. My heart has barely survived a week of knowing Martine, and I am anxious to tell her of my feelings for her. And frightened. No, so many years of foreknowledge would have been the end of me.

Wait is helping to harness Cricket to the wagon, proud to be doing most of the work himself. Except for the occasional wipe of a sleeve across his nose, the earlier tears are forgotten. I do not wish him to forget the parents who begot him, but I am sure he will grow strong and be loved here with the Hardwicks.

And free, I think. Not freedom from slavery, since he never knew that sort of cruel bondage. But a free man in his own free nation. Mr. Stoddard's patriot stance made little impression upon me at first. After all, he is an old man and prone to odd ideas. Nothing about this war had much to do with me, at first. But without Mr. Stoddard's notion of liberty for all, I would still be deprived of it. Now, seeing young Wait as an older brother or uncle might, I feel it important for him to grow up as unfettered as possible. Before being freed, my life as a slave was of a sameness, hemmed in by deep woods and the ownership of my master, no matter how kindly he rendered it. Today, it is as if all things have come apart, and that I may work this chaos into something new and bright, something to call my own, is a thing I never expected in this life.

Freedom. After all, is that not at the root of my name?

Yes, Topheny was right. I am of two halves, and in more ways than the shade of my skin. I am half for liberty and half for my father, who seeks to defeat it. But then again, he is half a patriot and half traitor himself, so we are both of a kind. Even the liberty I seek may be divided, the most precious to be taken by these new Americans in their white skins. Who can say how they will share it out among African and Indian?

I do not want to leave Martine.

I must seek my father. I am committed, a solemn promise made to Maame.

My two halves pull away and tear at each other, leaving me unsettled. How can I ever live in peace with them both? Either choice will be a traitor to the other.

"A word, Freegift," Edward says, handing me a letter with a wax seal. "Please deliver this to Colonel Harris, of the militia. His law office is across from the printer's shop, it won't take you long."

"Of course, Edward," I say, securing the missive in my waistcoat. "Official militia business?"

"Just so, and important as well. I am concerned that the supplies for the militia are stored in New London. Should the enemy attack, we may not be able to get to the gunpowder and musket balls we have there."

"Is that why you have some supplies here?" I ask.

"Indeed. I am asking Colonel Harris to distribute more supplies near New London, but away from the harbor. That's where the enemy will aim for if they attack. It will give us time to arm and organize instead of having to fight our way to the armory."

"What about Fort Griswold, across the river? Does that not protect New London as well?" I ask.

"Not enough cannon. Truth be told, Freegift, a determined attack upon our city may well succeed. Our only hope is a determined defense with militia quickly assembled and well-armed. The men at Fort Trumbull know to fire two cannon shots in quick succession if they sight enemy ships. That should give us enough time to gather our forces. I hope."

"But has not the war moved down south? To the Carolinas and Virginia, I hear."

"Yes, but there are still plenty of Redcoats in New York City and Long Island to bedevil us," Edward says. "We must be on our guard, and I fear Colonel Harris is more concerned with his position and influence than preparing to repel a real attack. Now do not speak of this to anyone. I say this in confidence, lad."

"I make it my practice to speak little," I say, and Edward claps me on the shoulder in agreement.

· Twenty Three ·

———

Martine and I sit close by on the wood seat of the farm wagon. It is small and narrow, but we fit comfortably next to each other. I have often been vexed in her presence, but on this fine morning, I feel at ease.

"You are glad to leave the tavern work?" I ask, even though she has said she is. I do not know how to start the conversation I wish to have, so I begin with whatever words are easily at hand.

"Yes, for the most part. It was interesting to see all the new faces whenever a ship came in and to hear stories of places far away. But it is not what I wish to do for any length of time. What about you, Freegift? Are you glad of your work?"

"I am glad of it, yes, but I cannot say it is what I sought when I came here," I say.

"From where did you come?" she asks.

"Has your mother said anything to you about me?" I ask, giving a gentle snap to the reins as Cricket slows her pace.

"Only that she and your mother were friends when they were young, and that you came to deliver news of her death," Martine says. "I know she gave you the tomahawk you wear at your belt, but she will not say why. I suppose because she and Sally were close. Still, it surprised me."

"Topheny is full of surprises," I say. If she has not told Martine anything about me, then I realize I am a great unknown to her. I pull on the reins and guide Cricket to the side of the road, where she has thick green grass to feed on.

"Why do we stop?" Martine asks, not seeming upset at all with the delay.

"I must tell you something," I say. So many things, I know not where to begin. "You know I have been a slave."

"Yes, that I know."

"I have known very few people, all told. I lived with Mr. Stoddard at his farm and cooperage, far from town and deep in the woods. He was not unkind but had little need of company after his wife died. Other than the people he spoke with at church."

"I had to go to church on the Sabbath when I was a child," Martine says. "The white man spends much time with a god who does so little in return, I think."

"As do I. But what I mean to say is that I have little experience speaking with new people. My days were spent alone in the forest, for the most part."

"Some would see that as good fortune, Freegift," Martine says. She twists her hands as they lay in her lap.

"Yes. But there are times I wish for a greater ability with words," I say.

"If you had any better familiarity with words, half the people in New London would not understand you, Freegift. You sound educated. Did your Mr. Stoddard teach you?"

"In a manner, he did. He taught me to read early on, then let me read the few books he had. Over and over. I do like the plays of William Shakespeare."

"I do not know him," Martine says. I want to say that she will, I will read his best plays to her, but I hold my tongue. I am breaking the command to speak little, but I do not wish to gush like a mountain spring after the thaw.

"What I wish to say, Martine, is that I have wanted to speak with you. Freely and easily, as we are now. But I have been too dull to see that I may."

"Why?"

"I did try," I say. "When Edward and I brought you back to the tavern. I tried, and then retreated. I returned later that night and saw Michael Gordon leaving your room. I thought he was there to make advances. You know."

"Oh, he is one for the ladies, that Michael. But he is a good man and came to give me fair warning. He might have stayed to offer more, if I had given him any signal. But I did not. Do you know why, Freegift?"

"No."

"You are very slow for all your learning," Martine says and takes my hand in hers. She tilts her head and presses her lips to mine. I have never felt such a thing before. The touch of her moist lips, the feel of her delicate fingers, the joy at what has come to pass between us. I run my fingers through her dark, silken hair and rejoice at the feel of great beauty.

We embrace after our long kiss. My arms engulf her, and she rests her head upon my shoulder. I could stay this way forever.

Cricket neighs. She has other ideas.

We laugh and stare into each other's eyes. Hers are moist with tears.

"Why do you cry?" I ask.

"Because I never thought I would find such a one as you, Freegift. And when I did, I hoped you felt the same. It was as if a thunderbolt came down from the sky on a sunny day and struck me square on the forehead."

"You were burned into my heart the first I saw you, Martine," I tell her. There is more I must say, and it pains me to be honest with her. But I must. "I did try to steel myself against you, and against everything I have found here."

"Why? What did you find so lacking, Freegift?" Martine pulls away, ever so slightly, distrust wrinkling the smooth surface of her face.

"Nothing," I say. "It is because of a promise made to Maame. There is someone I must seek out, and he is not here in New London. Not even close by."

"Who? Can I help you find him? My people are scattered wide, and perhaps some may know of him," Martine says.

"It is my father," I say. "A man I have never met. Maame charged me to find him and make my way in the world with his help, if he will provide it. I gave her my word to do so as she lay dying."

"Then you must," Martine says, nodding her head in the same sharp way her mother slices the air with her hand. "What is his name?"

"Will you promise not to tell anyone? It must be a secret. In the whole world, only you and Topheny will know."

"Topheny knows?" Martine rubs her hand along her jawline, and I see this news has sparked a thought. She stares into my eyes again, this time not with dreamy ecstasy, but with sharp observance. "I've never seen eyes of gray before. Last year, Topheny cursed a general who went over to the British. She said she knew him in Norwich and called him a gray-eyed bastard for what he'd done, both as a youth and as a man. That was Benedict Arnold."

"My father, the greatest traitor in history," I say.

"Do you know where he is now?" she asks.

"With the British General Clinton in New York City. Although the lad who died on the whaleboat said he was recently in Oysterponds, on Long Island," I say.

"That is not so far," Martine says. I see her study me again, stroking her jaw. She has a way of calculating me, I think. "Which pleases me."

"How?" I ask.

"Because it means you are not so foolish as to venture out in a mere whaleboat to get yourself killed for riches. You went to set foot on Long Island and make your way to your father."

"Yes, but there was no way to get close enough to make landfall. Even if there were, I could not leave those boys with one less oar. It was hard enough with Geer dead and Matthew wounded," I say. "I set off on that journey jealous of what I thought were Gordon's advances upon you. But that short-lived anger would not have sustained me if the Devil's Belt came between us."

"I am sorry you did not come straight to me that night and ask why Michael was there," Martine says, linking her arm in mine. "It would have saved you that mad expedition."

"How many fond fools serve mad jealousy?" I quote. "So asked the Bard in *The Comedy of Errors.*"

"The Bard?"

"Shakespeare. The playwright I mentioned."

"Ah. The fellow has a way with words, Freegift. I shall think of you as my own fond fool from now on. But you have no reason for jealousy. None at all." Her grip on my arm tightens. I feel the world an even fresher and sweeter place for it.

"I must ask, Martine. What of my father? Do you recoil at the thought of being with the son of such a hated man?"

"Remember, Freegift, I am Pequot, no matter how much French blood is in my veins. These English who now fight among themselves once massacred my tribe and sent us fleeing into the hills and swamps. Because I live among those who favor liberty over their king, I will be glad if they prevail. Edward is a fine man and fights for that cause, so I wish him well. But mistake me not. They are of a sameness. They will not grant liberty as readily to those who do not share their pale white skin. So what your father has done holds little meaning for me and has nothing to do with who you are."

"Thank you," is all I manage. Her words are more than I expected. She is not repelled by the blood of a traitor in my veins. She feels as I do— loyalty to the people who have befriended us. And suspicion of what their cause will mean for those of darker hues among them. "You are my other half."

She says nothing but leans into me as I snap the reins and pull Cricket back onto the lane. We are as one, heading for town and the uncertain future before us.

· Twenty Four ·

———

I am reluctant to leave Martine alone with Gill on the loose, so we remain together as I stop at the printer's shop to deliver the news of Matthew's injury. The proprietor is solicitous and begs me to give Matthew his best regards and hopes for a speedy recovery, given a large job of work due the next week. I promise to tell Matthew and then proceed across the street to Colonel Harris' law office, while Martine brushes Cricket's mane.

"Colonel Harris, sir," I say upon entering. He sits at a desk next to a large window which lets in the southern light. A clerk scribbles away at a small table in a dark corner.

"Yes?" He looks me up and down. I doubt he recalls me from the ranks when we drilled at Fort Trumbull. His nose wrinkles as if I have brought a foul odor into the room.

"A message from Lieutenant Hardwick, sir," I say, withdrawing the sealed paper from my pocket and handing it to him. "I was at his farm, and he asked me to deliver it."

Colonel Harris breaks the red wax seal and unfolds the letter, adjusting the spectacles he wears at the bridge of his nose. As he reads, his mouth turns down as if biting into a sour apple.

"What are you still doing here?" he demands, taking notice that I am still there.

"Awaiting a reply, if you have one, sir," I say. "I am returning to the North Parish and can deliver it today if you wish."

"No reply is warranted. Good day." Harris returns to his papers, shoving Edward's missive to the side. He is clearly not in favor of the recommendations made. That he is an educated man and put up for a colonelcy worries me some. Is this the best man for such an important position? Even I see the wisdom in Edward's ideas.

As does Martine. I tell her about the letter, not feeling I am breaking my vow to Edward to tell not another soul, since Martine and I are now as one. And after so much time of speaking less, I find that I cannot contain myself when I am with her, so I tell her joyfully.

"Everyone knows Colonel Harris thinks himself the cock of the walk," Martine says. "But he looks more like a chicken pecking the ground for seed, I think."

This is a most excellent woman I have found.

We pull up at the warehouse as Tink exits the door.

"Freegift, there you are," Tink says. "Greetings, Martine."

"Tink, I am sorry to have missed work. I meant to return sooner," I say. "Are you angry with me?"

"I would be, if there were heavy barrels to be brought ashore, but there's little work today," Tink says, then grins. "And after all, you are famous along the waterfront."

"What?" I say, wondering as to his meaning. The whaleboat venture was to have been kept secret.

"Why, you almost taking a cutter! And then being brought home by the ghost of poor Geer leading the way through the haze," he says. "I've heard the story in several versions, and by tomorrow they'll have the Poseidon himself guiding you home."

"Who told you this?" I ask.

"Everyone down by the wharf, Freegift. You are famous amongst the sailors," Tink says.

"Who else is famous with me?"

"Well, the poor departed Geer, according to the boy Gallop. He refuses to name the others, claims they are of no account, including himself, after Geer and you. Geer for storming the cutter and dying bravely, you for bringing them safely home, with the spirit of the dead lad helping, of course."

"There's barely truth to any of that," I say. "It was a foolish voyage." I am glad Gallop left out Matthew and the two brothers. If I judge him correctly, he is using the story to build his reputation in hopes of securing a berth on a real privateer. I cannot blame him and find myself wondering if I should exploit the growing narrative myself.

"Ah well, perhaps you'll tell me the real story someday," Tink says, eyebrows raised in eager anticipation. If everyone along the water is this curious, I shall be quite busy making my excuses as they ask to hear the tale. "Martine, shall I see you at supper?"

"No, Tink," she answers. "I have quit tavern work. Too many foul-mouthed sailors, if you understand me."

"Gill is it? I have heard him brag on what he plans for the two of you and the boy Wait, but I have not seen him take any action. All talk, I hope. But you are wise to remove yourself. And you, Freegift, watch who follows you," Tink says.

"That is fine advice," says Michael Gordon, who has crossed the street to join us outside the warehouse.

"Which?" Martine asks from her perch on the wagon seat.

"Both," Michael says. I watch his eyes. They do not linger over Martine, as I have feared they would. Before this morning, that is to say. How different a man looks when you no longer suspect him of foul deeds. "You have taken your leave of the tavern, then?"

"Yes," Martine says, with that sharp nod which reminds me of Topheny. "Freegift is to help me remove my belongings."

"Let me speak with Freegift for a moment, and then I will help as well," Michael says. It seems a fair bargain, a few words exchanged for help carrying whatever Martine owns down those steep stairs.

"Certainly," I say.

"Walk with me, Freegift," Michael says, taking me by the arm. I shake him off, not liking to be led anywhere now that I need not follow the pull of any man.

"Speak in front of my friends," I say. "I would tell them what you say in any event."

"Well, Tink is your employer, and unless I am a poor judge of men and women together, you and Martine are bound in some manner. But that is not my business," Michael says, putting his hands to his hips. "So hear my offer, and you cannot say I did not offer to propose it in confidence."

"By my leave, speak," I say.

"Captain Saltonstall has ordered me to recruit two men for the *Minerva*. We are outfitting for a voyage and have need of two stout fellows to replace a couple of drunkards who ran afoul of the magistrate. If half of what I heard about you and Gallop on your whaleboat adventure is true, you are the men for us."

"You find me an excellent choice to replace a drunkard?" I say, wary of what this entails.

"That is one way to put it," Michael says. "Especially since you are standing upright, which neither of these fellows can do."

"I am loath to leave Tink and my job, of a sudden," I say, but my thoughts are swirling, mostly around Martine and our new-found rapport. I cannot keep my gaze from seeking hers. True, I owe Tink for his help and friendship, but I am a free man and will do what I must.

"Do what you think best," Tink says with a smile, and I know he has seen my glance for what it is. "I would counsel you to consider long and well on this decision. But do not worry on my account. I can find another for the heavy labors here if need be. Now, I'll leave you to it.

Good day."

Tink doffs his cap and departs, leaving the three of us staring at each other. I am paralyzed. This is the chance I have been waiting for, presented to me as neat as I may wish, but I cannot say yea to the offer. I cannot leave Martine, not now.

"Michael," she says, stepping down from the wagon. "Perhaps Freegift could use some time to consider your proposal. It does come of a sudden."

"Of course, I did not mean to press you for an answer this moment. But if you will not oblige me, I must search elsewhere. Gallop has already signed on, if that helps you decide," Michael says. "I can give you one hour, no more."

"How does payment work?" Martine asks. "If you don't mind my asking. I've always been curious."

"The owners of the vessel get half of the value of what we take. They have borne the cost of all that goes into the Minerva, down to the salt pork and gunpowder we load today. The other half goes to the crew. Larger shares for the captain and mates, then equal shares of what remains to all crewmen. It depends on what we find and can capture. But I'll tell you, the *Minerva* has done well. I never thought to have so much money."

"Not Continental paper, but real money?" Martine asks.

"No, there's but little value in that. The Continental Congress just prints the stuff. Payment is in British pounds or gold coins. Real money it is," Michael says, addressing Martine directly, sensing she is the shrewder of the two of us. Also, seeing this is a matter between the two of us, he takes his leave. "One hour, then."

"Why did you ask all that?" I ask, as Martine leads Cricket town the street toward the tavern. "Do you not wish me to stay?"

"Freegift, I know you planned to cross over to Long Island to seek your father, but that is not what I want for you. Or us," she says, smiling. I am not quite used to the notion of us, but I do enjoy hearing her say the word.

"Then why ask Michael about the terms?"

"Because going over the side of a ship and making your way on foot through Loyalist Long Island is very dangerous," she says, shaking her head and reducing what I thought to be a fine plan to a shambles. "You would be abandoning your friends. Even if you made it back to New London alive, you would not be looked upon with favor. Life is hard enough for those of us not born English, Freegift. There is no reason to make it harder, if not impossible."

She stops at a water trough and lets Cricket lap at the water, while I drink in her words. She is right, and I tell her so.

"But I cannot give up on my promise to Maame," I say. "What other way is there?"

"The way the English understand. The way of coin," Martine says. "If you must do this, then you will need money. For a horse, for bribes to pay the militia between here and New York. I see no other way to obtain the amount you will need."

"Perhaps I should simply wait for the war to conclude," I say.

"Edward says the war is going well, now that the French are on our side," Martine says. "I trust him on this. If the Redcoats lose, where will your father go?"

"To England, of course. He would be hung as a traitor here."

"So if you are to keep the promise made to your mother, you must find him before the war ends. Otherwise her spirit will not rest," Martine says.

"You want me to go for a privateer?"

"No," she says with a slight shrug and pulls at Cricket's bridle. "But you must. Otherwise your spirit as well will not rest, and you will be uneasy forever. I do not want that, Freegift. I wish you to be at peace with yourself as we make our life together."

"What do you mean? We have not spoken of much beyond this very day, Martine."

"Do you not understand, Freegift? We are bound together. Topheny knows this, and so did your Maame. We are not like any of these English, but we are very much like each other. Of course we shall be together. Unless you wish otherwise." With that, she picks up her pace, so I must trot after her and Cricket.

"No, I do not wish otherwise," I say, taking her by the arm. "We are in accord. But you knew that, didn't you?" Her reply is a shy smile as we walk side by side. Cricket neighs, and I think she knows as well.

At the tavern, we go to the alley in the back, leaving Cricket to graze on the grass growing around a stack of firewood. Good solid oak and long-burning hickory. Everything is packed. The tavern keeper knows of her departure, and we are done in minutes. As I help Martine carry her trunk down, Jenny darts out from the kitchen, rubbing her hands clean on her apron. She gives Martine a long hug, burying her face in the folds of Martine's blue dress.

"You be good, Jenny," she tells the girl, stroking her hair. "I will visit you soon enough."

"Be careful," Jenny says, as Martine gives her a kiss on the forehead. "That skin and bones fellow Tom came by this morning, asking about you."

"Gill's man Thin Tom?" I ask.

"Yes, that's him. Someone told him you were leaving," Jenny says. "None of us, but a customer who knew no better. Keep her safe, Freegift!" With that command, Jenny runs back into the kitchen and to her duties.

"We should leave now," I tell Martine. "Do you have everything?"

"Not so fast," a shrill voice says. It is Thin Tom, still with a bluish bruise on his forehead from where Wait's stone took him. He carries a club, advancing from the alley. From behind a fence which hems us in, another crewman squeezes through two loose boards, knife in hand. Of Gill, there is no sight.

"We shall go as fast as we please," I say, advancing upon the man at the fence, since he has a bit of fear in his eyes. I draw the tomahawk from my belt and see him look wide-eyed to Tom. In two steps I am upon him, tomahawk raised above my head and a growl issuing from my throat. He scuttles back, retreating through the fence faster than he entered.

"Freegift!" Martine screams, and I turn to find Thin Tom at my back, his heavy club cleaving the air in the direction of my skull.

I duck and the club clears my head by inches. Tom wavers as he tries to recover his balance from the hearty swing, but before he can, Martine brings a length of hickory down on him, square on the shoulder.

I hear a crack. The hickory is intact. A dense, heavy, slow burning wood, hickory is.

Tom goes down, and I nearly feel sorry for the man and the injuries he has sustained in his attacks upon me. But only nearly so. I kick the club away from his grasp, since he still has one good arm left to him.

"Stay away from us," I say, my tomahawk slapping at my side, as if it wishes to be used.

"Owwwww," is Thin Tom's only response, clutching his shattered shoulder with his other arm.

"Did Gill send you?" Martine demands, a kick to his leg to focus his attention.

"He put up a reward," Thin Tom says, whimpering in pain. "A gold guinea."

"For me?" Martine says. "Over a crack of the whip?"

"No, for him and the boy," Thin Tom says, nodding in my direction, which causes him to wince. "I thought we might trade you for them two. Didn't expect him to be here with you. Gill is real put out over Wait runnin' off. Doesn't do to let folks know you can desert the *Badger*."

"Tom," I say, squatting to look him direct in the eye. "You have been gravely injured here, but you should live if you get yourself to the doctor. Next time, your luck may run out." Here I tap the tomahawk meaningfully on his knee. "I pray that doesn't happen."

"As I do myself," Thin Tom says, pushing himself up with a squeal of pain. "Wished to never have run into you on that damn river. I thank you for sparing me further injury. Fare thee well."

With that surprising courtesy, he shuffles off down the alleyway.

"I hope that is the last of him," Martine says. "For his own good, what there is of it. And more reason for you to sign on with the Minerva and be gone from New London for a time."

"I wish I had not put you in danger, Martine," I say. "I will never forgive myself if you come to harm."

"Then I shall not," Martine says. "You will stay safe and find riches on the high seas. I will stay in the North Parish and keep my musket and Wait close by always. Then we shall be together."

"That is a grand plan," I say, as we walk Cricket and the wagon with Martine's belongings to the wharf. "And I will find my father."

"One way or the other, you are destined to. Topheny told me so."

"Did she have a vision?" I ask.

"Yes. She said it was clouded, but you and General Arnold will meet. Visions are not always perfect, or at least how people remember them are not."

"Cloudy?" I say. "I wonder what that means?"

"It must be important, if it was in the vision. There is Michael," Martine says, pointing to Gordon as he walks along the wharf making for where the *Minerva* is berthed. He spies her wave and waits for us.

"I will sign on with you," I say. "Although you must know, my knowledge of the seas and sails is poor. At best."

"Excellent!" Michael says, shaking my hand to seal the arrangement before I can change my mind, I think. "Do not worry about sailing. You come on as an axe man. Ships cast netting down from their masts to keep boarders from getting on deck. With your courage and axe-work, you'll find yourself in the thick of things before long."

"Fine," I say, jutting out my chin to show how little this frightens me. "When do we set sail?"

"Why tomorrow morning, with the tide," Michael says. "Did I not tell you?"

· Twenty Five ·

—

"I is nearly dawn, Freegift," Martine says. "You must go." She curls up next to me under the quilt, which does not provide me with the motivation I need to arise and begin the long walk to town.

We are in the wigwam. Alone. Wait wanted to sleep out here with us, but Topheny promised to tell him stories of the trickster Chahnameed by the hearth, so he relented. Ann and Edward said nothing, Matthew smiled, and I blushed when Topheny insisted we sleep in her wigwam.

I blush now to think of it.

We have talked all night, it seems. Perhaps we slept, perhaps we dreamed, but always we were in each other's arms. For the first time, which would also not be the last, I fervently hope. I blink to take in the faint light framing the blanket which covers the door.

"Why is your hair like this?" Martine asks, as she threads her fingers through it. "It is like many strands of fine rope."

"Maame braided my hair since I was a child, so it grows like this," I say, lifting the long strands and tying them back with a piece of ribbon. "It is how our people in Africa wear their hair. The Akan people."

"Will you always keep it such?" Martine asks.

"I must. Maame said another Akan might recognize it and make himself known. We call it Mpese, although I do not remember why."

"We both come from a lost people, Freegift," Martine says. "Which is why the spirits led us to each other. To be found in each other. It is all we have."

"There is one more thing I must tell you before I go," I say, propping myself up on one elbow and drinking in her dark eyes. "My name. My Akan name. It is Kwasi, and it is a secret. No one else must know. No one else has known since Maame died."

"What does it mean?"

"It is my day name. I am Monday's child, destined to protect my family."

"Kwasi," Martine whispers.

It has always been a story of a faraway land to me. Maame protected me, and I never considered she might need my protection. Now for the first time, it is real. I am Kwasi, and this is my family. My future.

Which I must leave.

I arise, leaving the warmth of Martine behind. I stumble to the stream and throw water against my face, shivering at the chill, even as the sun peeks out from the horizon. I dunk my head, the water cascading from my Mpese onto my body like a waterfall. The air is crisp, clean, and beginning to warm. Martine appears beside me with my waistcoat, which I don and button, feeling like a knight girding for battle. Or leave-taking, which is battle enough.

We sit on a log, facing the gurgling stream, which Martine tells me feeds into the Okeshoksee River, as named by her people. We have a jug of beer and johnny cakes baked last night. Martine eats but little. I am hungry but stop, not wanting her to think our parting has not affected my appetite. I trust she will wrap the cakes in cloth and give them to me for the long walk back.

I offer her the jug, and she tips it to her mouth. She passes it to me, and I do the same. I feel it a ritual, like the act I have witnessed in church, where the English claim to drink and eat of their god. We are not gods, but we drink from the same vessel. At that moment, I know we shall for all our days.

"I will come back," I say, certain of it.

"I know you will," Martine says. "I had a vision."

"What did you see?" I ask.

"A man. Your father, I think. In his red coat."

"What was he doing?"

"Tempting you."

"With what?" I ask. She shrugs.

"Himself, perhaps."

"That is little enough," I say, laughing. This is a mistake, if the look on Martine's face tells me anything. Visions are not to be laughed at.

"A father's pull is strong. More so when the son has never felt it, Freegift. Remember that."

"I shall. I did not mean to make light of it," I say.

"You did, but you are forgiven," Martine says. "I will not vex you as you take your leave."

We kiss and there is very little vexing at hand. Finally, we stand and walk back on the path, bushes thick with blackberry blooms on either side. We stop at the wigwam. I put on my hunting shirt, arrange my knife and tomahawk at my belt and take my oilskin pouch from where I hung it.

"Next to you, Martine, this is the most important thing in my life. My emancipation paper," I say, handing her the oilskin. "It marks me as a freedman. Will you watch over it? I dare not take it to sea."

"I will," she says, taking it from my hand. "I know it is important to prove such things to the English, but know you are a free man. You have always been, even while unjustly enslaved. I hate that you must have this paper, but I will guard it." She spits out the word *paper* as if it is sour, and I admire her for it.

"The leather pouch holds money," I say. "Not a great deal, but something. And Tink owes me a bit more, but that can wait."

"Tink is a decent man," Martine says, hefting the pouch. She sighs, and I think this farewell has gone on long enough. She appears sad and preoccupied, even as she works to keep a smile upon her face.

"Good. Now, will you walk with me to the road?" I ask, stepping outside.

"No. You must go alone, Freegift," she says, her eyes filling with tears.

"Martine, we know this must be done. I only leave you to seek what fortune I need. Which we need. Walk with me, please."

"No. Please, go now." A tear spills out of one eye. She wipes it away and darts back into the wigwam, pulling the blanket closed behind her. I cannot chase after her, not wanting our parting to be marred with argument.

I walk alone to the road. I pass the farmhouse, where a light glows in the kitchen. But I said my farewells last night and have no wish to repeat them. Besides, I have much to think on.

Such as why Martine came to tears. And what she may have seen in her vision that she cannot bear revealing to me. I cannot know until I return, so I must put it out of my mind, which is difficult. Worry gnaws at me, and I work at not turning around and running back to her.

It would be unseemly. I am a soldier and now also a privateer. I shoulder my musket and march at a brisk pace. And eat johnny cake.

The wind is at my back, and I come to the wharf in time to see a crowd gathering. Privateers setting out in search of riches and victories is cause for celebration. It is a much better spectacle than was provided by my last voyage.

Tink is in the crowd, and he embraces me, wishing me good luck. I tell him I will return to his employ after the voyage. To be honest, I do not look forward to it. As Martine said, Tink is a good man, but I want something more for myself than carrying barrels.

What that may be, I have no idea.

I spy Michael Gordon, who directs me to assist with the loading of casks of fresh water and barrels of salt pork just delivered. I cannot escape the barrels, it seems.

Aboard, I find Gallop. I chide him for his stretching of the truth, but in a friendly manner.

"At first I thought it a good way for Geer to have a fine story and be remembered for it," Gallop says. "But then I saw the advantage, for myself and you as well, Freegift."

"Let us hope we both see the wisdom in that by the end of the voyage," I say.

"Best hope you live to see it," says a passing seaman, who laughs as he casts his gaze over us. I cannot but echo his wish.

"There are my brave axe men," Michael says, clapping us both on the shoulders. "It's a grand day to set off, isn't it?"

"Aye, sir," Gallop says, adopting a nautical tone.

Michael grins and shouts the order to weigh anchor. Crewmen work the windlass and draw up the anchor. Others climb rigging and do incompressible things with great agility. Wind ruffles the sails, and the ship begins to move away from the wharf, a cheer rising from the crowd. It is a grand moment, and I have no thought of danger or failure, only the exhilaration of adventure in the offing.

I hear a gasp, a shout, and then the crowd grows silent, all eyes on the water below the wharf. The *Minerva's* wake, small as it is at the outset, drags a body along with it. We lean over the side to get a closer look, and the cresting wake rolls the body over once, then again.

Thin Tom. Dead.

I search the crowd and quickly spot Gill, on the edge of the wharf. Hands on his hips, he looks directly at me. And smiles.

Tom failed him. Remembering his final words to me, I consider Tom may have refused to assail Martine and me again. And paid the price for it.

"My God," a crewman murmurs behind me.

"Get to your posts, dammit!" Michael yells, and shoves men to and fro. I look up to the quarterdeck and see Captain Saltonstall, hands behind his back and a grim look on his face. The festive moment is gone, and dread fills the eyes of the men around me.

"Bad luck," Gallop says, shaking his head. "A drowned man as we cast off. Very bad luck."

· Twenty Six ·

Captain Saltonstall takes to his quarters as soon as the ship clears the mouth of the river. Michael and the Second Mate storm about, bellowing orders and scattering crewman as they stalk the deck and watch the horizon. We are sent below to stow our gear and find our hammocks in a forward store room, strung over barrels of gunpowder.

"You don't favor a pipe, do you, Freegift?" Gallop asks.

"No, and I would not favor a candle either," I say, eyeing the barrels. The room is tiny, barely enough room for the two of us to turn around at the same time.

"Why have they put us here, instead of with the other crewmen?" Gallop asks.

"Likely because we are new and untested. These fellows are real seaman and probably think little of landsmen such as us," I say. We hang our belts and belongings from hooks set into the wall, or hull, I should say. With most of the men going barefoot, we shed our hose and shoes as well and make for the deck.

We do look like landsmen along for the ride, while the rest of the crew appears to be in their natural state at sea. Their duck trousers flared and loose at the feet, along with checked shirts, well-faded by water and sun, mark them as old salts. They ignore us until Michael Gordon opens a hatch and hands us the tools of our trade.

"Your boarding axes, gentlemen," our First Mate says, handing us the wide, curved blades. The handles are long, and I feel the heft of the deadly thing. It is well balanced, and the shaft will work for a two-handed cut as well and a one-handed swing. The downward curving spike opposite the blade makes for an excellent hook, for pulling rope or rigging away.

Sailors glance at us, some with a quick smile playing across their features. Not friendly, exactly, but relieved.

"I wonder what drove the two men we replaced to drink," I say, feeling the sharp edge of the axe with my thumb.

"Watching their three comrades slaughtered," a sunburned fellow leans in to whisper. He walks away in a rolling gait well suited to the low, cresting waves out on the open water.

"You are first aboard an enemy vessel," Michael says. "Your crewmates will be at your back, but you must go ahead and cut away any netting."

"How many of us are there?" Gallop asks.

"Two others," Michael says. "We had three wounded on our last voyage, and then lost those two others to the magistrate. But four stout lads are enough. A few slashes and then we all board. It's usually enough to force a surrender, especially if our quarry's a merchantman."

"Do they always drape netting?" I ask.

"Freegift, no two encounters have been the same," Michael says. "We've seen netting used twice. The first time we had to break off. The next time, we were prepared. We'll drill tomorrow, but for now, put your axes away and swab the deck."

Michael turns to shout an order at crewmen gathered on the starboard side, talking among themselves. They move sullenly, eyes averted. The image of the drowned Thin Tom is still with them, I think. As well as the dread of whatever bad luck clings to the *Minerva*.

"How long do you think he was floating there?" Gallop asks as we return from stowing our axes. "I heard a fellow say he was right up against the hull, and his ghost may have come inside."

"No," I say. "There is no ghost of Thin Tom to concern us. I believe he was killed by Gill, who grew tired of his failures. Did you not see him, smiling as he stood above the corpse?"

"I did. But remember, Freegift, Geer led us back when he was dead. Was that not his ghost at work?"

"More likely the current, Gallop," I say. "Best not to believe your own stories."

On deck, we are greeted by two sailors, dressed in the expected clothing of duck trousers and loose checked shirts. One is tall and dark-skinned, an Indian by his looks. The other is short and broad-chested, with long black hair and a bristle of beard. They stand with buckets and brushes.

"Abraham Stow," the shorter man says, extending his hand. "This here is Joe. He don't talk much." We give our names and shake hands.

"Joe Wansuc," the Indian says, giving a quick nod of acknowledgement.

"You are axe men as well?" I ask.

"I am the carpenter's mate," Stow says. "And I do wield a boarding axe. Joe helps in the galley and keeps the ship's blades in sharp condition. You two are the only men without other duties. If men you can be called." There is a challenge in his eyes. Joe betrays nothing.

"We have signed on at the last moment," I say. "Mainly for our skill at boarding and prowess with the axe."

"As it may be," Stow says. "But now the only skill required is to swab. And look sharp doing it. The First Mate and Captain are not happy with that business of the dead man in the harbor. The men are surly, and the officers will come down hard to take their minds off this haunting. If the men do not take matters into their own hands."

The second mate strolls by, eyeing our idleness. Stow quickly dumps a quantity of water onto the deck, and we commence to work. On hands and knees, we form a line and move slowly, scrubbing the seawater into the wood. We dump a bucket, swab, lower the bucket over the side to refill, dump, swab, crawl forward.

I ask what the purpose of scrubbing with nothing but seawater is. I learn that unlike fresh water, it keeps the wooden deck from rot. And that it keeps men busy, a prime preoccupation among the officers.

I also learn we are part of the starboard watch. Our responsibilities lie on the right side of the ship, called starboard by seamen. The larboard watch, naturally, is of the left side. We swab, stand watch, and are generally accountable with our fellow crewmen for this side of the vessel.

The larboard watch is swabbing their portion of the deck as well. We reach the end of the deck first and turn, scrubbing with all our might to keep ahead of them. I see that this arrangement of watches favors competition, as we hope the officer's ire will be directed at the more laggard swabs.

"What did you mean about the crew taking matters into their own hands?" I ask Stow as we lower our buckets over the side.

"You haven't heard?" Stow says, hoisting his sloshing bucket up. "The men blame you, Freegift. Gallop told the story of how you followed the ghost of Henry Geer into the harbor. He claimed the fog was so thick you could hardly see his spectral glow. Riled some of the crew into a state, I'll tell you. Some say you attract the spirits of the dead. Sailors are a superstitious lot, as you may know."

"What do you think?" I ask, suddenly aware of glances thrown in my direction.

"I don't think. I obey orders and hope to make my fortune so I must never leave the land behind again. Now scrub and be quick about it," Stow says. "And watch your back when at the gunwale."

I follow his injunction, wishing Gallop had not been so inventive with his story-telling. Now, not only is the mood of the crew sour, but I must worry about being cast overboard. We are only a few hours out of port, and already I miss dry land.

Captain Saltonstall emerges from his cabin and takes to the quarterdeck, paying us no mind at all, his features twisted in a grimace. Crewmen glance away, unwilling to meet his disapproving gaze. Thin Tom's ghost may be with us after all.

"Mr. Gordon," the captain bellows. "The wind is freshening, and we appear to be running before it."

"Aye, Captain," Michael Gordon responds. The sails which are set are full of the wind, so this must mean the wind is coming from behind us. Aft, I should say.

"Let us take advantage, then," he says, and nods to his First Mate, who seems to take his meaning. It is lost to me.

"Crack on sail!" Michael Gordon orders. "Get a move on, boys!"

Joe and Stow leap up from their scrubbing, as do the others. There is a mad scrambling up into the rigging.

"What should we do?" Gallop wonders aloud.

"Watch and learn," Michael says as he strides by. "Next time you'll go up with them."

"Let out the reefs," the second mate yells, hands cupped around his mouth. Men loosen lines that had shortened the sails, letting them out to their full billowy length.

"Square up the yards," Michael shouts, as halyards are tightened against the pull of the sails.

Seeing the swift movements of the crewmen, it makes a sort of sense: how the sails are rolled up, then let free. How the ropes must hold and contain them. Every man has his part in this effort, and I hope to be half as nimble as the slowest of them when it comes my turn to ascend into the rigging.

I move the buckets to the side, as men come down from the rigging, setting them by the gunwale to raise up water to complete our work once the crew disperses to their regular duties. The wind is sharp at our backs, and I look to Captain Saltonstall, who stands on the quarterdeck, a satisfied smile on his face as the white sails blossom against the blue skies.

The men take note of the change in the captain and that of the *Minerva* herself. The ship speeds now, cutting through waves and shooting seaspray off the bow. It is glorious, and I think perhaps it is a show put on for the benefit of the crew. For them to rejoice in the majesty of wood and canvas and our domination of the sea. I spot Michael giving a nod of acknowledgement to the captain. Yes, he agrees. A good idea.

The men are livelier now, the last of them down from the rigging and making for their posts. I hear laughter and hearty banter. Some lean over the gunwale on the forecastle, watching the ship's progress and delighting in the mist thrown up off the waves. Now this seems to be an adventure.

I lower a bucket, the hemp rope rough against my palms. Someone bumps against me, loosening my grip. I lean farther over the rail, not wishing to drop the bucket now heavy with water. More men brush against my back, and I feel the cold clasp of hands on my ankles.

I am in the air, my weight carrying me down as my heels rise and my assailant lets go. I gasp in shock and fear as the cold sea appears below me and I catch snatches of laughter from above. It happens slowly, as if in a dream, until my arm hits the barrel of a below-decks cannon and I grasp it madly, wrapping my legs around it, grateful for the hard iron that has caught me. I am astonished that the rope is still wound about one hand, the bucket trailing in the water and threatening to pull me off my perch.

"Here." It is Joe. His long arm stretches out, and I grab it. His grip is powerful, and he pulls until I can stand, wobbly enough, on the cannon. Other hands reach out, and I am quickly hoisted aboard.

"The usual method is to bring the bucket back up," Stow says, taking the rope from my hand. "Not to go down after it."

"Not a mistake I will make a second time," I say, barely able to get my breath back. I take in a gulp of air and scan the crowd of men around us, seeking meanness, disappointment, or both. But all I see is curiosity, along with concern from Gallop.

"Are you hurt?" he asks.

"No," I say, and glance at the captain. Had he seen from his perch on the high quarterdeck? Had it been his idea, to banish bad luck from his ship? Or was it some fearful fool and his friends, conspiring to rid the *Minerva* of a useless African who summons ghosts?

"Back to work, you swabs!" Michael Gordon barks, scattering the crew who gathered too close for my comfort. "And you, Freegift, take better care. We shall need you lively when we find our quarry. Now back to your duties."

"Thank you," I say to Joe, as we slosh water over the deck. He nods and begins to scrub, as if nothing untoward has occurred.

"Did you see anything?" I ask Gallop, as we stoop to begin our labors again.

"No, there were too many of the crew between us," says he. "What happened?"

"Nothing," I say. It will now be my practice once again to speak little.

And watch carefully.

· Twenty Seven ·

———

There is room in the crew's quarters," Gallop tells me as we settle into our hammocks. The crew is housed beneath the forecastle, in an ample space where the men also gather to smoke, speak, and carry on when off duty. It was boisterous as we passed by tonight on our way to our tiny room, crammed with gunpowder.

"We may be better off here," I say, wondering if Michael placed us away from the crew knowing that the story of our ghostly encounter might make us unpopular. Unpopular enough to be tossed overboard.

"It could have been an accident," Gallop says. I have not told him of the hands laid on my ankles, seeing no reason to worry him or have him feel guilty for his exaggerations.

"Perhaps," I say. "But bear in mind it may not have been. Be cautious and careful where you place your trust."

"I hope we find a ship soon," he says. "That will take everyone's mind off ghosts and spirits."

"Aye, it will," I say, but thinking that if we lose our quarry, or are defeated by it, the crew's attention may become even more focused on us. I say little, since I worry enough for the two of us. And fear for myself, I admit. No one has ever tried to kill me, and it leaves me with a knot in my belly that will not go away.

Sleep is a long time coming.

In the morning, we are fed oatmeal and beer, then begin to swab once again. The sea is calm, all clear horizon in every direction.

"We're out in the deep water," Stow says, as he kneels and works his scrub brush next to me. "We passed Block Island in the night. This is the Great Atlantic Ocean, lad. Enjoy the gentle seas while you can."

"It is peaceable," I say, then lower my voice. "Unlike some of the crew. Do you hear mutterings against Gallop and myself?"

"No one took Gallop and his stories seriously," he says. "Until that corpse bobbed up and followed us out of the harbor. You can't blame the men, being a superstitious lot."

"I knew the man. They called him Thin Tom, and he was one of the crew of the *Badger*," I say, wondering if this makes things worse, better, or a clean draw.

"The *Badger*? Those men are near pirates," Stow says. "Why did you not say?"

"What difference would it make?" I rise to take my bucket to the gunwale.

"Hold," Stow says, and takes it for me, returning shortly with a fresh bath of salt water for the deck. "The difference is, every man jack on this crew hates the *Badger*. They're known to take everything that floats, from a fishing skiff to a ferry boat crossing the river. Mooncussers, if you're familiar with the term."

"I am. I had an encounter or two with Gill, the first mate off the *Badger*. He ordered Tom to cause me a certain harm, which he failed to accomplish. I believe Gill killed him as a warning to his other men not to fall so short."

"I thought I spied that blackguard on the wharf," Stow says. "It makes sense, now that you lay it out. I will pass your tale on to the boys. You never know, it may make a difference. A few wondered if you were an African medicine man or some such."

"No," is all I say, deciding not to tell him that Maame had taught me to call upon my Akan ancestors if I am in need. Although I have never had the wit when faced with peril to think of it.

But perhaps, Joe was sent by my ancestors to pull me back into the ship. That is the problem with the spirit world—you never know what they will or will not do.

We finish swabbing as two bells ring out. Which, Stow informs me, means it is one of the clock. The ringing of bells will increase, until at five of the clock it will be two bells again, signaling the beginning of a new watch. The rules of shipboard life are unlike anything onshore. Simple, once they are explained, unfathomable until that is done. I hope the story of my conflict with the Mooncussers of the *Badger* will be as easily understood once Stow tells the crew of it. I greatly desire to stroll about the deck without fear of a dive into the deep Atlantic.

The first ringing of two bells also sounds the mid-day meal. Hard bread washed down with beer. What the food lacks in variety, it makes up for in quantity, although I may wish it reversed soon enough, I think, as the bread weighs heavy in my stomach.

Drill is next, for the axe men and boarders. This means most of the crew, less the gunners and what officers will remain on the *Minerva* to insure the ship remains in our hands. First, a dozen of us with muskets assemble on the foredeck, and practice, without firing, at following the commands of the second mate. The idea is to aim at gunners, if possible, to reduce cannon fire against us. We are cautioned not to shoot the captain, since his exchange or ransom is highly desirable. I think of Rebecca's husband, Jeremiah Moore, awaiting exchange last I heard from Mr. Stoddard. Well then, I will seek to capture a captain myself and hope for some say in how he is exchanged.

Next is the grappling hook. We stand on the main deck, well apart, since twirling and casting the iron hook takes some room. Michael Gordon demonstrates how to send the hook aloft, high enough to catch on the rigging, or at least on the gunwale. He casts into the sea, then retrieves the ghastly tool. I shudder to think of a man caught on the end of it, since we are told many hands will pull at the line once the hook is secure, to draw the vessels together.

Once together, then we launch ourselves into the rigging, or netting if the case may be, swinging our axes and trusting to the men at our backs. Of this, there can be no drill. We must simply wait and do our best.

"Once on the enemy's deck," Michael Gordon says, strutting before us. "Make for their cannon and cut the ropes securing them. Then watch out for the ninepins." This is greeted by laughter, as if heavy cannons rolling across the deck was an amusement for bowlers. He tells us our fellow crewmen will defend us as we proceed to render the enemy cannon useless. It seems simple enough. I am sure it will not be.

"That was better than swabbing the deck," Gallop says as we disperse.

"So is standing watch," Michael says, beckoning the two of us. "You have the first dog watch."

"Dog watch?" I ask, mystified once again but the odd words these sailors use. I am certain there are no dogs to watch for and wait for an explanation.

"From four of the clock until six," he says. So the dog watch is an hour before the second two bells. My head spins.

"Very well," I say. "Where shall we stand?" A two-hour watch does not seem overly demanding.

"Look above," Michael Gordon says, grinning. "It is a pleasant enough view."

"The crow's nest?" I ask, craning my neck and nearly falling dizzy.

"Aye. It's about time you both got used to the rigging. Gallop, you take the foremast, Freegift the main mast. Holler out if you see a sail. Look lively now, the last watch is coming down," he tells us sharply.

Gallop jumps to, for which I am glad, since I do not know one mast from the other. Gallop takes to the rigging to make his way up to the foremast, and I turn to the main mast behind me. As I begin my climb, I see it is taller by the length of a man.

I have climbed trees, but branches are much firmer than the swaying rope beneath the soles of my bare feet. I tell myself not to look down.

But I do. Breath leaves my lungs and sweat trickles down my back. The deck seems very far away. And hard. I look at the mast, almost close enough to touch, were I to dare and reach out my arm. I see it is white pine, and this comforts me, although I cannot think why.

"Keep going," Michael bellows. "You're half way there, don't stop!"

My grip is so tight that I fear I cannot let go. I raise one foot, then let go with one hand and hoist myself up. Then again, and again. I do not look down and keep my eyes on the hemp rope before me.

Soon I am beneath the crow's nest. I climb through the opening around the mast and haul myself up to the platform. It is only a few planks of pine, but it is firm beneath my feet, and I am thankful for that, as I grasp the thin wooden rail.

I look around me. I am at the highest point of the ship. It is magnificent. The white, billowing sails beneath me are like angel's wings. Our Continental ensign snaps in the breeze from a halyard on the quarterdeck, magnificent in bright red and white. My fear is forgotten, as I feel the wind on my face—clean, crisp and salty. There is nothing but blue sky, dark blue water, and the thin line of horizon encircling me.

I am in awe.

Gallop waves from his perch, looking as excited as I. I return the wave, feeling brave that I hang on with but one hand. Through shouts and gestures, we decide each of us will scan half the horizon, his forward and mine to the aft of the ship.

And so we settle in to the first dog watch. The climb up had its share of terrors. The summit has its own splendid glory. But by the time two bells are rung—halfway through our watch—things have settled into the familiar. The sky and sea look the same in every direction, and I feel dizzy as I turn this way and that, watching for anything that varies from the unending blue of sea and sky. Below me, the sails blossom white as the wind freshens and fills them. It stings my eyes as I shield them from the sun to focus on the far horizon. I face out of the wind to rub the tears away and see Gallop doing the same, leaning forward. He sees me and points out over the side.

A sail.

Small and distant, but a sail. He calls out, "Sail ho, on the larboard side!"

I turn to face the horizon at our backs. I cannot believe what I see.

Another sail, even smaller, has come into view as my back was turned.

"Sail ho, aft!" I shout.

I am a privateer, and I have sighted my quarry. It is what I have hoped for.

Then why do I feel such dread?

· Twenty Eight ·

———

Sailors crowd us as we come down from the rigging at the end of our watch. They are joyful, and I doubt a man jack of them wishes me over the side. Gallop and I have gone from unlucky Jonahs, bringing death in our wake, to the double heroes of the moment. Two sails spotted, and we are hailed to the heavens. I would say sailors are fickle beasts, but I know the draw of plunder outweighs many a fear, including that of witchcraft and ghosts.

My hair becomes a talisman, and men gather around to touch it, marveling at its softness, some saying they expected the hair of Africans to be like a hard bristle. I rub the head of a blond lad and tell him I thought it would feel like straw, and we all laugh. It is a silly thing, but I cannot help enjoying this sudden acceptance. I have never been part of such a grand endeavor of men, and I find it thrilling.

Now that none seem to want me dead. It is an odd thing, to be almost killed and then welcomed by the very same fellows. I must be careful about the joy I feel at their touch. It might turn back to fearful hate should things go awry. The sea is a very large place and this ship a small thing upon it.

I sigh with relief as I make my way with Gallop to the rail and watch the sails. The captain has come about, and we now sail on a course direct for them.

"Men o' war, do you think?" Gallop asks.

"All I can see is white sail," I say. "Guess we'll know soon enough." I strive to sound unconcerned, but I think we both wish for a nice slow merchantman, preferably crewed by Quakers.

"Well done, lads," Michael Gordon says, coming down from the quarterdeck. "The captain is pleased."

"Which one shall we take?" Gallop asks, as if the ships were ocean fruit ripe to pluck.

"See you there?" Michael Gordon says, pointing to the sail furthest off our starboard side. "She's heading southwest, probably making for the open sea and then on to New York from a southerly direction. Smart of the captain, since come nightfall he can change course and lose us if he goes dark."

"What about the other?" I ask.

"She's headed west, making for the Sound, I'd wager," he says, pointing almost dead ahead. "Going for the safety of Oysterponds, or straight on to New York, hugging the Long Island shore. Not a smart move, unless she has a light load and is under full sail."

"They are both headed to New York then?" I ask.

"That was their heading when you spotted them," Michael Gordon says, squinting and shielding his eyes to make out the ship ahead.

"They must not be warships," I say. "Otherwise they'd join together to fight, would they not?"

"Indeed they would, Freegift," he says, clapping me on the shoulder. "Smart lad. Let us hope she's not a fast schooner or packet. If she's a brig or larger carrying cargo, we're sure to run her down by morning."

"There are British ships in Oysterponds, so I hear. Along with Benedict Arnold," Gallop says, spitting over the side as if to wash the traitor's name from his mouth.

"If we had enough daylight, we'd catch her long before she reaches the North Fork. We shall keep a sharp watch tonight, gentlemen, you can count on that. When dawn comes, she'll find us closing fast. The wind is with us."

"And with her as well," Gallop says.

"Aye, but remember, that means any warship venturing out from Oysterponds must beat against the wind. The advantage is ours. Now, to your supper and rest yourselves. The morning may prove to be hot and heavy."

We go to the galley where our meal of meat and peas is doled out, with ample beer to wash it down.

"In here, boys, in here," shouts Stow from the crew's quarters. Others wave and gesture for us to enter. What a different ship this seems. A bit of luck and the thrill of the chase brings out the best natures of these men. Perhaps the chance of death in the morning also puts them in a forgiving mood.

Joe makes room on a bench, sliding silently to the end. He is so tall he must stoop over even when seated.

"Enjoy your salt-horse, fellows," Stow says, to the amusement of all.

"Horse?" I ask. "I have been on the back of a horse, before a horse, and even once been kicked by a horse. But I have never swallowed one." Gallop looks to me, and then at the meat with suspicion, which brings forth gales of laughter.

"No, we call both salted pork and beef salt-horse," Stow says. "Since it all looks alike after a while and may as well have one name."

I spear a piece of meat and eat. Chew, I should say, since it takes a while to complete the process of eating it. The men smile and relax, leaving us to our food.

"You boys ready for tomorrow?" Stow asks, leaning in so this is addressed to Gallop and me.

"We shall do our duty," Gallop answers.

"Good," Stow says. "Watch what Joe and I do. Cut the netting if it be there and be quick about it."

"And if there is no netting?" I ask.

"Then we still go first," Joe says, his voice low and calm. He looks me in the eye. "Show no fear. The Redcoats will swarm and kill you otherwise."

"Won't they aim to do that anyway?" Gallop asks. His question seems logical, but I am eager to hear what Joe says. After all, he has done this before.

"You must frighten your enemy. If he has a pistol, make his hand tremble in fear so he will miss. If he has a cutlass, advance on him with a terrible face, so he will take a step back and fall before you. Use your axe in mighty swings."

"Have you killed many men?" Gallop asks, his eyes wide as he takes in Joe's advice.

"I do not speak of that," Joe says. "Remember what I told you. I have boarded seven ships, and I am still here." With that he gets up, head bowed, and makes his way out of the room.

"I didn't mean anything by it," Gallop says. "Why'd he leave?"

"Don't mind Joe. He's a decent sort, for an Indian," Stow says, without a trace of animosity. Then he leans even closer and speaks in a whisper. "He's a Pequot. Not many of his kind left these days. He's spooked that the good folks ashore will not take kindly to a Pequot with white man's blood on his hands, Redcoats or no. He might have a point."

"So he has killed men?" Gallop asks, not giving up on his question.

"Mind you, don't get in his way when he's swinging that axe," Stow says. "And stop asking questions."

Which answers the question neatly.

Stow moves to another seat for a card game, and we work at our supper in silence. Gallop moves his food about but eats little.

"I don't know if I can do it, Freegift," Gallop whispers.

"Do what? Eat the salt-horse?"

"No. Kill a man. With an axe. Maybe a musket shot from some distance. But with a blade, up close? I can't imagine it."

"You do not have to imagine it," I say. "Leave the imagining for after it happens. Let us watch Stow and take Joe's counsel. I will make myself a terror."

"I'll try," Gallop says, uncertainty written across his furrowed brow.

"There is something you could imagine," I say, worried he will falter and seeking to buck him up.

"What?"

"Imagine the man you face killing you. Imagine your own death and seek to avoid it," I say, trying to sound like Joe, self-assured at the prospect of physical combat.

Gallop is silent, and I wonder if I have said the wrong thing. After all, what do I know of killing? Living is difficult enough.

"You know, I think that is precisely the way to think of it," Gallop says, nodding in agreement with himself. "Yes sir, that is how I shall imagine things." Satisfied, he tucks into his salt-horse and peas with a vengeance, his appetite restored.

I leave Gallop to the remains of his meal and make my way to the deck, where I seek out Joe. He leans by the gunwale, staring out over the darkened sea. Few men other than the watch are above deck, since the captain forbids any light from giving away our position. So, pipes are lit in quarters tonight.

"I haven't thanked you properly for saving me yesterday," I say, as I take a spot next to Joe. His hair is long and dark, tied back in the same fashion as the other men, but markedly different. It is thick and shiny and reminds me of Martine. As do his high cheek-bones.

"No," he says. I wait, but there is nothing else.

"Thank you," I say, realizing what he is waiting for. "You knew someone threw me over. It was not an accident."

"You are welcome. Yes, I knew." Joe, talkative enough moments ago, now is his silent self again. A man who can speak little indeed.

"Stow tells me you are Pequot," I say. To this he gives a small nod.

"Do you know Topheny? And her daughter Martine?"

"I know of Topheny," Joe says. "You?"

"I am acquainted with her," I say. "And Martine."

"She is the last of our elders. She carries the knowledge of the Pequot people. We have been scattered to the winds and will never come together again. How do you know her?"

"Because my people have been scattered to the winds as well. She knew my mother, back when I was born. We were slaves then."

"Ah, yes. You come from far away."

"Akan," I say. "Very far away. Tell me, do you have a name? I mean, other than Joe?"

"Yes," he says. I wait several minutes for him to continue. "Owaneko. Do you have a name from Akan?"

"Kwasi," I say, with no hesitation.

"Is it far to Akan, Kwasi?" he asks.

"It is a huge ocean away and far south," I say.

"It matters little," Owaneko says. "My land is close by but lost forever. These people, Redcoat or Continental, they steal everything. Remember that."

"Yes. Except now, it is our turn to rob them," I say.

Owaneko smiles.

· Twenty Nine ·

The deck is crowded at first light. Everyone is eager for the first glimpse of sail. I am eager that it appear close, for I have no desire to follow this vessel into the enemy harbor at Oysterponds. I do wish to find my father, but without enduring a naval battle to do so.

Gallop and I are in the forecastle near Michael Gordon, who, as first mate, has the best position, by the bowsprit, the long spar jutting out over the figurehead. He counsels us to silence, lest our voices carry out over the water and alert our quarry.

There is a sliver of light at our backs, but the sun has yet to dawn. Forward, it is still dark. Clouds cover the heavens, blurring the line between water and sky. Whitecaps dot the sea ahead for a few ship lengths, then vanish into the murk.

Part of me wishes for dawn to light an empty ocean, so I need not worry over living or dying, killing or cowardice. I am no longer a child, but I never thought I would throw myself into the martial world of blood and death quite so soon and leave childhood behind forever.

The Bard comes to mind, as he often does. I love the stirring scenes of *Henry V*, and in days past, alone in the woods, I would recite lines such as these, gesturing with my axe as if it were a broadsword:

Once more unto the breach, dear friends, once more;
Or close the wall up with our English dead.

But this morning, on the deck awaiting battle, I recall a different line and find the words whispering in my brain:

There are few die well that die in a battle.

"What did you say, Freegift?" Gallop asks me in a low voice. I must have spoken the line fully out loud.

"Nothing," I answer. Gallop lays a hand on my shoulder, as if to steady me. I am surprised that it does and clasp his shoulder as well. We smile, although there is little cheer on deck. My guts are in a knot and sweat breaks from my brow, even in the morning chill.

I am afraid of killing a man. That fear gnaws at me, more so than the dread of dying. I remember the first time I felled a tree myself. Not a sapling for firewood, but a large elm for Mr. Stoddard's cooperage. I was alone, with the tree huge, dark, and looming over me. I was afraid then. Afraid it might fall on me. Afraid I would be unable to finish and be defeated. Afraid of a slip of the axe and a cruel wound. Afraid of everything.

As I am now.

No word is spoken, but I sense a sudden alertness around me. Men crowd close together and lean out over the gunwale. The light has brightened, and all things are clearer. Whitecaps crest and disappear, the roll and lapping of the waves against the hull louder as the wind picks up.

Then she is there.

"By God, we have her," Michael Gordon says, raising his spyglass. The men murmur and point to the vessel, perhaps no more than half a mile ahead. There is little need for quiet now, with the dawn breaking at our backs and lighting the *Minerva* for all to see.

"A three-master," Stow says. "But no ship of the line by the looks of her."

"She's a fat merchantman," Michael Gordon says, pocketing his spyglass. "The *Hannah*, by name. Weighed down with cargo and wallowing low. Make yourselves ready, boys."

A cheer goes up, and we scatter to prepare for boarding. Gallop and I gather our muskets, powder, and ball, along with the axes. The grappling hooks are ready on deck, and we return to the forecastle and our firing positions. The second mate reminds us not to shoot the officers, since we will want them to make exchanges, not to mention for what information may be coerced from them.

So we are to kill only our own kind, lowly seamen. It does not seem right. If both sides targeted officers first, there would be much less bloodshed overall, but I must obey orders.

We kneel by the gunwale and make ready. The helmsman steers the ship to larboard, and I think the captain means to get our vessel between the *Hannah* and a possible escape to Oysterponds. We all shift to the starboard side of the forecastle, or the fo'c's'le, as the common sailor slurs the term.

My palms sweat.

We draw closer.

The *Hannah* opens her gun ports. Six to a side, although I cannot tell how large the cannon be. We have sixteen twelve pounders, and the gunners say they are true shots. We shall see. I am certain the gunners of the *Hannah* lay the same claim before their shipmates.

"Steady, lads," the second mate says from behind us. He is the steady one, standing tall while we kneel against the gunwale.

Closer.

Orders ring out from the quarterdeck, and I see we must slow, otherwise the *Minerva* will speed by the slower ship.

We are two ship lengths away.

One ship length. Gallop looks to me, perhaps to assure himself I am still here. I am rooted to the spot, afraid I will fail to stand and fire when the time comes.

A cannon booms, belching fire and smoke. A single shot from the rearmost gun on the *Hannah*. A signal across our bows that she will fight.

My mouth is dry. I cannot swallow.

Our bow comes close to that last gun, and I squeeze my eyes shut, as if that offers any protection against solid shot.

"Now!" shouts the second mate.

I rise. I fire my musket at the gunners at their cannons. I reload as the crack of musket fire ripples from both decks. An echo of hornets fills the air, and now I know what bullets sound like. I fire again with the four axe men, as directed by the second mate.

The world explodes.

Five of the enemy's cannons are discharged, followed within seconds by our eight. The sea between us is filled with smoke and fire, and I can see little of the effect on either side.

We draw closer now, and as the two ships move and leave the smoke behind, I see we still are properly afloat. The *Hannah's* guns are twelve-pounders also, terrible enough if they catch men in their flight, but not heavy enough to sink or cripple a vessel.

I also see men down on the deck, bleeding.

"Once more, boys!" the second mate tells us, pointing to a gun crew directly opposite. We fire, and one of the men goes down. I should care that it might have been my ball, but I am too happy at not seeing the cannon blast.

We reload and follow the second mate to the grappling hooks. The ships edge closer together, and I hear both captains shouting orders—one to avoid collision and the other seeking it. We fire our muskets a last time, then take the grappling hooks in hand, waiting for the order.

Another broadside is unleashed against us. Projectiles fly over our heads and into the sails. A section of rigging and spar comes down on the quarterdeck, hitting the helmsman and knocking him from the wheel.

"Chain-shot," Stow says. "To take down the sails. It'll slow us."

The ship veers.

"Freegift!" Michael Gordon beckons from the quarterdeck. I am the nearest to him of my party and make my way quickly to him. The captain has taken the helm, and he wipes blood from his face as he grips the wheel.

"The colors!" Michael says. "You must raise the ensign, or they'll think we've surrendered the fight."

I nod and run for the Continental colors now lying beneath the fallen spar, taken down by two small iron balls linked with a yard of chain. We cannot continue the fight if the enemy were to lessen their fire, thinking we've given up. It would be dishonorable. I find the halyard cut cleanly above the flag, and I pull and tug until I have enough of the line to reattach. I scramble up the rigging, high enough for the flag to be seen and tie it off.

I hear a cheer as I descend, then then another blast of cannon fire.

This time it is only ours.

"Well done, lad!" the captain himself shouts as I pass. Michael Gordon is already on deck, pistol in one hand and cutlass in the other. It is time to board.

We throw the grappling hooks as we practiced. Three take hold. As Gallop pulls his in for another try, crewmen grab the three lines and pull. With ten men on each, I can feel the ships coming together.

"Axes!" shouts the second mate as the lines are tied off.

It is time. We grasp our weapons.

A single cannon fires from the *Hannah*. Half a dozen of ours answer, firing grapeshot which sweeps men from their feet.

"Now!"

We vault over the gunwales, now cheek to cheek. There is no netting to impede us.

I yell, but cannot hear myself, as I am deafened by the gunfire and shouts of men all around me. I hoist my axe two-handed over my head as I leap to the enemy deck, aiming to look as ferocious as I can be.

I slip, the deck wet with blood. I roll and regain my feet, finding a wounded sailor clutching one arm and backing away from me.

"Mercy," he pleads, his face a horror of fear.

"Strike the colors!" This from the *Hannah's* quarterdeck. Her crewmen— those that remain above decks—lay down their weapons and edge away from us.

"Mercy," the man says again, and only then do I realize I still hold the axe as if to swing.

"Mercy," I say, and set it down.

The ship is ours.

· Thirty ·

┝━━━┥

The *Hannah* is ours, but we have paid a price.

Michael Gordon is dead. Struck down by the last cannon to fire as we began to board.

Two others are dead, several wounded.

It could have been worse. We learn from the enemy crew that the captain's tactic was to fire chain-shot at our sails and rigging, hoping to cause enough damage to affect an escape. That meant most of the fire went over us. Except for the last ball that took Michael Gordon, the man who so well befriended me.

I help to wrap Michael in a shroud, as the ship's carpenter begins his work to fashion three coffins. He works quickly, sawing and shaving the soft pine planks he had stored below. For this express purpose, I figure, since the lengths are right. As first mate, Michael Gordon may well have ordered them brought aboard himself, never thinking one might be built as his final resting place.

I cover Michael's face with canvas. His chest is smashed by a cannonball and looks nothing like the outward appearance of a man. I am glad to cover it and thankful he did not linger to suffer the agonies of a wound that would kill him before the day was done.

I mourn him. I wrongly thought him a competitor, but he was my ally and took a chance bringing an untried lad on this venture. He has forfeited his life, and I a friend. I look out to the sea and ask Maame if she will help Michael Gordon find his way to his ancestors. I cannot say I believe she will hear me, but it comforts me to think she might.

Food and drink are brought on deck, and I marvel how easily my thoughts turn from death and loss to the more immediate concerns of my stomach. A lesson of life, I think.

"Grape-shot is an awful thing," Stow says as we drink our beer, taking our morning meal and gazing out over the captured vessel. A prize ship, they call it.

"I don't think I will ever forget those bodies," Gallop says, his eyes downcast. "Enemy or no, it was frightful to behold."

"That volley saved us from wielding axes against enemy flesh and doing much the same," Owaneko says. "Be thankful."

"Joe is right," I say. I do not use his true name, since it is a secret given to few. "If they had kept up the fight, it would have been worse for them and for us. It put an end to things quickly."

"Still, it is terrible," Stow says, and we all agree. The small metal bits fired by cannon shear and shred flesh something horrible. So horrible, that the British captain gave up as soon as we swarmed onboard. Too many of his men retreated below deck after the first round of grapeshot, and once we came aboard in force, he had little choice.

Well, he did have a choice. I, for one, am glad he chose to live.

We gnaw on hardtack and drink beer as other crewmen supervise the prisoners in cleaning the ship. Which also means burying their dead at sea. While our dead will come home with us to be buried with their kin, these English sailors have no kin among us and must make do with the deep. I feel sorry for the dead cast into the sea. I hope they can find their ancestors.

After the funeral proceedings, Captain Saltonstall takes the British captain and a Redcoat major into his cabin. Guests for dinner, I suppose. The high and mighty of both sides like to hobnob with their own, I figure.

The ships still remain lashed together, as there is a great deal of back and forth, sorting out of wounded and securing the British prisoners below decks. The second mate and the purser go over to the *Hannah* to search her hold and take inventory of what she carries.

"How long before we get underway?" Gallop asks, standing to survey the horizon. "I wouldn't wish a warship to find us bound together so."

"I heard the captain is going to parole some of the crew and let them row their wounded to Long Island," Stow says.

"Then we lose the value of a good rowboat," Gallop says.

"But you gain the blessing of mercy," I say. "We all may need that someday."

Before we can debate the value of a stout rowboat against the quality of mercy, a shout rises from the *Hannah*. It is the purser and second mate. I think it an alarm, but as they vault across the gunwales, I see it is unrestrained joy.

"Riches, boys!" the purser shouts. "I've never seen such a cargo! Riches, I tell you!" He makes for the captain's quarters, clutching the papers upon which he's made his tally. The second mate is all grins and stops to impart his knowledge before following him.

"A heavy load of gunpowder, along with rum, sugar, and all manner of goods from the Indies and England," he says. "She's fat with 'em! And give a listen to this. There's crates and trunks all marked with the name of General Henry Clinton! The top damn Redcoat, and we've got his silver plate and more!"

We join in with the whoops and hollers, rejoicing in thoughts of the wealth this will bring us. How much, I cannot calculate, but if the celebration gives any indication, it is more than anyone dared hope for.

Soon Captain Saltonstall appears, graciously leading his captive officers back to the *Hannah* and giving orders for the ships to be separated. The British officers do not seem distraught, perhaps because they know they will be exchanged soon. It was not their blood that was shed, not even their goods and luggage taken.

"You, Freegift, is it not?" Captain Saltonstall says as he returns to his ship.

"Yes, Captain," I say, standing smartly.

"Good work with the flag, my boy," he says. "It would have been a disgrace to fight while the enemy thought we'd struck the colors. Well done."

"Thank you, sir," I say. "May I ask a question?"

"By all means but be quick about it. We shan't linger here long."

"Know you Jeremiah Moore, of Saybrook? He has a privateer vessel as well."

"Yes, I know him. Taken prisoner not long ago. The Tories burned his house and boat. A bad business all around," the captain says.

"Might he be exchanged for one of these officers?" I ask. "I do not know how such things are done, but perhaps you will have some influence in the matter."

"Some, young man, but the decision will not be mine alone. Tell me, how do you know Moore?" I can see him thinking, why does an African lad care about Jeremiah Moore?

"I am acquainted with his father in-law and wife. I hold the family in some esteem and hope to help them," I say. All true, and I see no need to tell any more of the story.

"I shall make the request, Freegift. It is a good notion, but the governor likely has a long list of men waiting for exchange. We shall see. Now, you and your comrades take your muskets and join the prize crew. Guard those prisoners well, and you may get your wish."

We join the second mate and his party to sail the *Hannah* back to New London, following in the wake of the *Minerva*. The common sailors are locked below decks, while the captain, first mate, and a Redcoat officer are crammed together in the captain's quarters. Gallop and I take the first watch, and I fervently hope they harbor no plan for rebellion.

For I would hate to shoot the officer who may free the man Rebecca and her children depend upon. I was Ira Stoddard's slave, yes. But I cannot forget the kindnesses he showed me. If I can repay that kindness, I shall.

Then I will no longer feel in his debt.

· Thirty One ·

┣━━━┫

As we round the western edge of Fisher's Island, the mouth of the Thames River beckons. We are nearly home. Ahead, the *Minerva* leads the way, as is proper. We follow in the *Hannah*, battered from cannon fire but still seaworthy and possessed of the bulk of her sail. We have secured prisoners for exchange, precious gunpowder, and a wealth of valuable cargo. That some of it belongs to the Redcoat General Clinton—or once did, I should say—makes us rejoice. It feels a blow struck direct at the head of the British army which oppresses us.

Us. I surprise myself with that. My father is of that army, and only a short time ago I was enslaved by these colonial English. Americans, they now wish to be called. So, life is full of surprises, I conclude. Felling trees every day for Mr. Stoddard held very few surprises, and now I must prepare myself for an onslaught of them.

General Clinton's luggage is not only a source of prideful boasting. It is a rich treasure. Silver plate, furniture, crates of wine, elegant uniforms, and all matter of clothing have been noted, along with a small box filled with gold coin.

'Tis a great victory indeed. For liberty, yes. And for myself. I cannot calculate my share, but by the reaction of the crew who have had portions from smaller, less valuable prizes, it must be substantial.

And substantial I will need. I must purchase a good horse and supplies to get me to New York. Coin for bribes. Perhaps a pistol to be kept close at hand.

We enter the river, and I see the church steeple of New London ahead. I think of Martine and how the money will help us once I return. Or send for her. Who knows what surprises the future holds?

I lean on the gunwale and watch as New London draws closer. Fort Trumbull comes into view. I jump as the *Minerva* lets loose with a cannon, sending smoke billowing out the larboard side. Then another, then a third.

"The signal that we're bringing in a prize," Gallop says, slapping me on the back. "The three-cannon salute."

"Of course," I say, and then we both laugh, since obviously it took me by surprise. Which I must acknowledge as my new acquaintance.

"See you there?" Stow says as he joins us, pointing to a thicket of masts in the harbor. "It's the *Badger*, still not left port. Watch yourself ashore, Freegift."

"Why has she not sailed?" I ask. The captain and crew of the *Badger* are evil men to be sure, but they are not known to be lazy evil.

"I heard they had trouble getting their Letter of Marque," Stow says. "The governor must issue one for every voyage and tales of their misdeeds may have reached him. Without it, they are little more than pirates."

Which is what they are, having tried to plunder me upon the water.

I put them out of my mind as we draw closer. The *Minerva* drops anchor not far from the wharf, leaving room for the *Hannah* to dock and begin the off-loading of cargo. A crowd is growing along the water, people waving and cheering.

Cheering the victors, of which I am one. I feel pride swell in my bosom.

I see Martine, in a green dress, waving. She is at the forefront of the crowd, and I wave back, as if I am Caesar at the gates of Rome. Everyone is waving and cheering, the taking of any prize cause for jubilation.

But something is wrong. Even at a distance, I see it in Martine's face.

Very wrong.

I have much time to fret as the helmsman maneuvers the ship to the dock. Lines are thrown, the anchor is dropped, and we are ordered to stand guard, muskets at the ready, as the prisoners are brought up from below deck. They shield their eyes as they emerge into the bright sunlight, the air filled with jeers and derision. I feel sorry for them, but it is a feeling tempered with relief that I am home and not marching to imprisonment as they are. The world is an odd place. These men are from the world's greatest empire, and I am but an upstart. Yet I hold the musket.

"Stay where you are, lads," the second mate tells us. "Let none step aboard. I'll see these people to the magistrate, and then we'll commence to unload. Hold fast."

The crowd's attention is now focused on the sorry line of prisoners, and I understand his point. In their enthusiasm, some might board us and make off with portions of the cargo. As souvenirs or loot, it matters not. The captain begins to make his away ashore in a rowboat, standing tall and waving his hat.

The crowd is diverted and Martine takes advantage to work her way closer.

"They've taken Wait!" she shouts from below, her hands cupped about her mouth.

"Who has?" I yell back, but there can only be one answer.

"Gill and his men," she shouts. "They have him on the *Badger*."

She says something else, but it is lost in the sound of the crowd as Captain Saltonstall comes ashore. He is cheered and applauded, and all else is drowned out. We lock eyes, and I see the worry in hers. I shout that I will come to her as soon as I can but cannot tell if she understands.

"What is the matter?" Gallop asks, Owaneko and Stow behind him.

I tell them all the story of Wait Jenkins, how he begged for rescue and how Martine helped both of us escape Gill's clutches. Of how his parents were cruelly taken from him and of the tender mercies he found at the Hardwick's farm.

"He is with Topheny then?" Owaneko asks.

"Yes. Martine's mother," I explain for the others. "Gill must have raided the farm to take him." I realize what this means and rush back to the gunwale, leaning out and hollering to Martine, asking if everyone else is alright.

"Well enough," comes the shouted answer. Well enough.

"I will help you get the boy back," Owaneko says.

"By God, I will stand by your side," Gallop proclaims.

"I won't hinder you fellows," Stow says. "But that crew on the *Badger* is a murderous bunch. And seeing as I am not acquainted with this boy, I can't see a reason to risk my throat to go after him. Not when I'm sitting on wealth for the first time in my life, no sir."

"Very well," I say. I had not expected two allies, and I cannot blame a third for declining his services. "I see the wisdom in what you say, but I am obliged to proceed. Since I rescued Wait once, so I must again. Joe, and you, Gallop, think carefully if you really wish to join me."

"Topheny and Martine are of my people," Owaneko says. "If a hand is raised against them, it is raised against me."

"Well, I'm just a damn fool," Gallop says with a grin. "What do we do?"

"That is an excellent question," I say. "We will make a plan, but first we need to speak with Martine and find out more." Stow looks down to the deck. Perhaps embarrassed by his refusal to join us. But I do understand him. He is older than us, probably over thirty years of age, when men grow into an abundance of caution. Gallop and I are of the same age, and Owaneko looks to be less than twenty. Still of an age to be a damn fool and join in a good cause.

"First we need to get off the ship," Gallop says. "How long will the second mate want us here do you think?"

"He'll want everything brought into the warehouse and tallied," Stow offers. "It is how we have done it before. It will take a while with this much loot."

"Then we will wait. If the *Badger* does not sail today, we will have time," I say, gazing out to the tall mast of Captain Cowburn's ship. I pray the governor will not choose today to grant the Letter of Marque, for I believe Wait to still be alive. If only because it will be easier to dispose of his body at sea, where the laws of the land do not hold, and there are no witnesses other than the guilty.

It takes an hour for the rest of the crew to row ashore, the crowd to disperse, and for the second mate—is he now the first mate?—to commence the unloading. A gangplank is raised from the wharf and we begin to carry off barrels of gunpowder. Most onlookers remaining decide they have business elsewhere once they see the prodigious amounts of explosive gunpowder we carry into Tink's warehouse.

Martine remains, among a few other curious or foolhardy folks. As I walk by her, she shakes her head ever so slightly. A warning. One of the bystanders may be from the *Badger*. I avert my eyes, pretending to focus only on my burden. Which, being gunpowder, is an excellent notion.

"Owaneko," I whisper, as we set down our casks of powder. "Will you speak to Martine in your native tongue?"

"Good idea," he says and gives me a curt nod. "There is at least one *Badger* man on the dock. But he will pay me little mind."

He is right. One thing I have learned about the English is that they make themselves blind and deaf when those they think less worthy converse among ourselves. They think we have so little to say that what we do utter is of little consequence.

We make several more trips, dozens of crewmen laboring under heavy loads of sugar, now that the gunpowder is safely stored away. Martine appears on the dock with a bucket of water and a ladle, kindly giving drinks of cold water to the men. Owaneko takes his time, standing to speak with her after his drink. Men with other business along the dock, whatever it may be, pass them by without notice.

"Well, Joe?" Gallop asks as soon as he is back on board.

"The boy is on the *Badger*. They received their Letter of Marque yesterday and took on supplies. They sail with the tide at first light," he says.

"Then we take Wait back tonight," I whisper, wanting not even Stow to have this knowledge.

"Aye," Gallop says. "My luck's improved since I met you, Freegift, so I will stay the course." Owaneko speaks in what must be Pequot, which neither of us know.

"What does that mean?" I ask.

"That I must be a damned fool," he says and cracks a rare grin.

· Thirty Two ·

———

Tink is in his office. As is Martine. All I wish to do is embrace her, but we are here on deadly business. I refrain from any display of emotion, even though I feel a great joy in my heart. I have become good friends with Gallop and Owaneko, and I do not wish them to see me as love-sick.

"What did they do when they came to take Wait?" I ask Martine. I take her gently by the hand, and she presses her fingers in my palm before speaking.

"They came last night, after everyone was asleep. Gill and four others," she says. "They pounded on the door and demanded Wait be returned to them."

"They did not break in?" I ask, wondering at the deference of a knock, or pounding, as she describes it.

"Edward later said their aim was to do nothing the magistrate could act upon," she says. "They had a piece of paper and claimed Wait was bonded to them for ten years. It was signed by Wait's father. So they claimed."

"Edward let them take Wait?" I say, unable to believe what I am hearing.

"They had torches and muskets. Their intent was clear, to burn us out if we refused."

"And blame it on Mooncussers, most likely," Tink adds. "They might have killed everyone. Edward had no choice."

"Did he seek redress with the magistrate?" I ask.

"He did," Tink says. "The paper was declared legal. For all I know, the ink was barely dry and the signature a forgery. But it has the look of the law about it."

"Why would they wait until now?" Gallop asks, as I wondered the same.

"I would guess they knew the Letter of Marque was coming, and they could soon take to sea safely," Tink said.

"Where they will kill Wait as a lesson for any who think of deserting their foul company," Martine says. "It leaves no time to discover if the signature was forged or not. They can easily claim Wait killed in battle or swept overboard."

"What shall we do?" Gallop asks, looking to Martine, and then to me.

"Wait is aboard the *Badger* now?" I ask.

"Yes," Martine says. "He told me where he was previously housed, in a small storeroom between the galley and the captain's quarters. I suspect they may have him there now. But what can the three of you do?"

"In daylight, very little," I say.

"In the darkness then," Owaneko says.

"Gill and a group of his men are at the tavern," Tink says. "Their supplies are already loaded. They will likely drink their fill tonight."

"And Captain Cowburn?" Martine asks.

"He won't arrive until the morrow," Tink says. "There will be crew aboard her, but I haven't seen them mount a proper guard the whole time they've been moored here. No need, really."

"Tonight, then," I say. "Before the tavern closes and they return."

"Tomahawks and knives," Owaneko says. Gallop nods. I swallow my fear and agree.

Tink leaves to fetch food for us. We agree to stay in my room adjacent to his office. Out of sight. It is cramped, and Martine sits on the bed next to me.

"How is Matthew?" I ask, uncertain what to say in front of my friends. Or how to act.

"Well," she says. "I brought him to his lodging today. It was only by that chance I saw your ships in the harbor."

"I'm glad to hear of it," Gallop says. "But we should give some thought about what to do when we have the boy in hand."

"What do you mean?" I ask.

"They will search here, for certain," Gallop says.

"And then to your farm, if they have time," Owaneko says. "Topheny must not be harmed."

"No one will be," I say. "Martine, once we are successful, will you go with all speed to the Hardwicks and warn them to be on guard?"

"Yes. I hope Gill will be too drunk or too worried about setting sail to think of taking men all the way to the North Parish. But it is a wise precaution," she says. "Where will you three go with Wait?"

"Matthew's," Gallop says. "I know his place behind the print shop. I doubt anyone of Gill's crew knows of our connection. I am certain he will have us until the Badger sets sail."

"He will, I am sure," Martine says. "He is a good fellow."

"I'll go and ask," Gallop says, laying down his weapons of war.

"I will come," Owaneko says. "To be sure no one follows you."

"Thanks to you, Joe," Gallop says.

"My real name is Owaneko," he says. "After my grandfather, a great sachem."

"Fits you better than Joe," Gallop says, after a moment's thought. Then they both slip out the door. Owaneko leaves his tomahawk but keeps the knife at his belt.

"Is it true?" Martine asks. "Michael was killed?"

"Yes," I say. "At the very last, when the ship was nearly ours. It is so unfair."

"I am sorry. There are so many bad men in this world, it saddens me when a good one dies."

"Until coming to New London, I have only known old people to die. My uncle and Maame. It was sad but to be expected sooner or later. This is so different." I see the terrible work the cannon shot did to him and shudder. Martine rests her hand on mine.

We stay that way for a long time.

"I am glad you are alive," she says finally.

"As am I. So glad that I rejoiced even as I stood over Michael's shattered body. I could not help myself. It felt wrong."

"War is wrong," Martine says. "And you are brave to face it, Freegift."

Her hand reaches for my cheek. It feels cool and hot at the same time. I feel the breath from her mouth close to mine.

The door opens. Tink with food and drink, Gallop, and Owaneko all tumble into the room.

"Hungry?" Tink asks.

Well, I am. Even as we speak of death and feelings of love swell within me. I cannot help it. So we eat.

Then we wait for the night.

As the sun sets and the room darkens, Tink takes his leave. "I will sit in the tavern and enjoy my cider," he says. "I will stay as long as Gill does. If he leaves too soon, I will return and fire my pistol out on the steps as a warning." He withdraws a small flintlock pistol from his pocket to show us. "Good luck."

"Thank you Tink, for all your help," Martine says, standing and giving him a kiss on the cheek. I do believe he blushes to receive it.

"Liberty for all!" he proclaims and departs.

"We shall need a boat," Gallop says.

"I know just the thing," I say.

Two hours later, we judge the time to be right. Or, we can wait no longer and decide the time must be right. I am not sure.

Martine gives Gallop an embrace, shares some words in Pequot with Owaneko, and then stands before me as they step outside. Her hand graces my cheek again, and this time we kiss. A kiss of sweetness and longing.

"Come back safe," she says.

"To you," I say. "As I will do all my days."

I leave her in the doorway, with the fervent wish that my days will not end tonight on a ship of miscreants.

Owaneko, Gallop and I run down the side of the warehouse, the same narrow alley where Gill first chased me and Wait begged to be helped. From there, we stoop low and go under the steps leading from the warehouse down to the wharf. Thence along the dock, until we come to where my raft is secured, tied to pilings where small craft might easily offload their wares.

"Untie it carefully," I whisper. "We must return it so no one thinks Tink to be involved."

The rope is wet and difficult to loosen. It takes time, but finally we free the raft, taking lengths of hemp with us. The very pole I used is still on the raft, and we are quickly adrift in the harbor, squatting low and propelling our own privateer raft toward the hull of the *Badger*, no more than a hundred yards away.

There is no moon tonight, which is in our favor. Darkness and quiet are our allies. We pass other ships, hearing snatches of conversation and laughter from within. We are invisible.

The *Badger* is within reach. A lantern glows on deck, toward the stern. A guard? Or a light for those who will come aboard later?

The raft bumps into the hull, and we steady her, glancing up to see if anyone has taken note. No one sounds the alarm. No one suspects.

Grasping the hull, we pull the raft along to the steps built into the side of the ship, between two cannon. Wooden steps about a foot wide and two inches deep, constructed for the very purpose of accommodating visitors in rowboats.

Friendly visitors.

Gallop ties off the rope on the raft, then takes the other end and ascends the steps. There is no sound but the lapping of lazy waves against the hull. He vanishes over the gunwale. Seconds later he gives the signal, and Owaneko and I climb the rope. Now we have our raft secured for the escape.

We crouch against a cannon. All is silent. The lantern we spied is set near the gangplank, a beacon for drunken sailors to find their way home. I move to the door under the quarterdeck. This leads to the officer's cabins. I open it slowly, waiting for the creak of hinges to give us away, but they are well-maintained. And silent.

Voices.

Low murmurs. The clink of coin and the slap of cards. A game is in progress. The noises come from a corridor to our right. Several steps lead down to a middle deck, where flickering candlelight dances upon the floor.

We go left and find the galley. Empty, but with a single candle in a sconce. A plate of ham sits on a cutting board, thin muslin tossed over it against flying insects. A carving knife is at the ready. The few crewman left on board have been feasting, and I pray none are hungry enough for another slice.

Owaneko backs into the galley, his knife in hand. I nod my understanding—he will guard against anyone coming up the stairs in search of more food. Gallop and I continue, moving barefoot quiet. We pass cabins most likely for the first mate and officers. No one is inside. Martine said Wait described a very small space, nearby the captain and these men, to serve them as needed. I decide to take a chance.

"Wait," I whisper.

Nothing.

Again, "Wait," this time a fair bit louder.

A thump. Then another.

Gallop beckons to a small door, more of a hatch, on the hull side.

I open it and there lies Wait, trussed up with rope, lying on a bare wooden bench. It is a storage compartment, barely large enough for a small boy.

One eye is bruised and swollen, but the other widens in joyous surprise.

I put my finger to my lips. He nods ready agreement. I cut his bonds away and Gallop unties the gag forced into his mouth. He clutches me, his small fingers digging into my skin. I do not let him go, but sheath my knife and carry him off, away from his dark prison. What foul men these are.

Wait does not make a sound. His legs and arms are firmly about me. He does not cry, but I think soon he must.

Perhaps not only him, but that is a matter for a time that has not yet come.

We pass the galley, and I take note again of the knife. I tap Gallop with my elbow and look to the knife, with a nod back to Wait's chamber. Gallop smiles and grabs the knife, padding back and placing it on the floor. Let them wonder what careless crewman left it for the boy to snatch and use to free himself.

A confused enemy is to be preferred, I wager.

Owaneko goes on deck first, opening the door slowly, casting his gaze
across the darkened and shadowed deck. It is quiet, no sound but the
faint murmurings of the card game below and distant revelers ashore.
We make our way to the stairs and the waiting raft.

A gunshot.

Wait gasps. I whisper it is nothing but Tink's signal, as if it means little,
and pat his head reassuringly. We hasten to the gunwale, ready to go
over.

"Who is there?" The voice is disembodied, coming from the shadows
cast by the lantern near the gangplank.

We freeze.

A guard. He rises from a pile of folded canvas at the far end of the deck,
where he took his sleep, thinking there no reason to stand watch in port.
He rubs at his eyes, as if not believing what he sees.

"By God, look at this!" Another, louder voice issues out from the
darkness.

It is Gill. Alone on the gangplank, swaying, drunk, and barely able to
stand.

The guard backs up, out of Gill's line of sight, perhaps fearful his first
mate has seen him sleeping.

"I'll gut the lot of you," Gill says, stumbling forward, a foot-long blade
in his hand. He grins and looks to each of us, sizing up the fight. He
half turns his head, to where the guard stands behind him, about to
summon the crewman to join in.

A loud crack snaps the night air, and Gill falls to his knees. Behind him,
the guard stands with a club. He gives Gill a shove with one foot and
the big man falls forward, his face flat on the deck.

"Thin Tom was a friend of mine," the guard says. "Now be off with you,
and you never saw a thing, mind you. Understand me?"

"Thin Tom had some goodness left in him, sir. As you do," I say. "Good night."

Owaneko goes over first. I carry Wait down, using the rope for balance. Gallop unties the rope and skitters down the stairs. We push away as a goodly splash kicks up by the gangplank.

Wait still clings to me.

· Thirty Three ·

——

We have him!" I say to Martine, even though the words are unnecessary. The proof of our success in my arms. Owaneko watches the alley at our back, while Gallop grins and strokes the face of Cricket, who is tied up outside Tink's office.

"Oh, Wait," Martine says, kissing his brow. For a moment she is full of tenderness, and then looks to me with a stern face. "You must be quiet, Freegift, or they may hear you. Is Gill in pursuit?"

"Gill is pursuing the fish in the harbor," I say. "I think no one will come after us, but it would be wise to follow our plan."

"Good," she says, and hands Gallop a sack with the bread and beer left over from our meal. "If anyone dares approach the farm, they will find four muskets facing them."

"I want to go home," Wait says. He looks to Martine, who takes his hand.

"You've been very brave, Wait," she says. "Right now, you and Freegift must visit Matthew. I shall come for you in the morning, and we will all go home."

"Matthew? He said he'd show me how to set type in the print shop," Wait says. He looks around, fear still lingering in his eyes. "I never thought I would. Gill said he was going to feed me to the sharks."

"Gill will hurt no one," I say. "Now we must go."

"Put me down, Freegift," Wait says, rubbing at his eyes with his sleeve and pretending it was all my idea to carry him. "I can walk on my own."

"Certainly, Wait," I say, as he releases his grip and drops to the ground. "I only thought the rope you were bound with might have hurt your ankles."

"No," he says, but allows, "At least not much. Are these your friends?"

"Yes, and yours as well," I say. "Now, let's hurry to Matthew and see how he is. Are you hungry?"

Wait nods fervently. Gallop breaks off a piece of bread and gives it to him.

"Thank you," Wait says, the bread almost to his mouth. "For coming to get me."

"We came as soon as we heard," I say. "You would do the same."

"I would," Wait says and bites into the crusty bread. He is over the first wave of fear and shock, and now is all pride and certainty, as only a ten-year-old boy can be.

Martine leans in and kisses me. A peck on the cheek is all, but it feels like the blessing of a princess. "In the morning," she says.

In the morning. I have so much to tell her.

She takes to the saddle and rides off on Cricket, the horse hooves loud on the dried-out ground. We make our way to Matthew's, watching for any who might note our progress. The street is deserted, but light glows from within several houses as we pass. We slip behind buildings and soon come upon the printer's shop from the rear. Matthew's lodging is built off the back of the main building. Its two windows are dark, and Gallop approaches the door as we hold back, hiding by a nearby woodpile.

He knocks, once. Then again.

The door opens, and he waves us in. We file in quietly, not wishing anyone to hear and take note of our commotion.

"Matthew!" Wait exclaims, unable to bear the silence. They embrace, and even in the darkened room I see the tenderness with which Matthew caresses Wait's brow. He knows the terror of a child mistreated. Wait does not know of Matthew's scars and how he came by them, but I see that they are bound together in ways beyond my understanding.

"You are all unharmed?" Matthew asks, lighting a candle as Wait lets him go. He sets it on a table, and we gather around, barely fitting on two chairs and a rickety bench.

"Yes, unless Wait is injured," I say. "He was bound and gagged."

"They were going to feed me to the sharks," Wait says, with a matter-of-factness I would find hard to muster. "And they gave me nothing to eat or drink."

"Of course not," Matthew says. "That would only mean more food for the sharks."

This amuses Wait, and Matthew fetches a jug of cider and a plate of cornbread to supplement the feast of bread and beer we have brought. I note again that food and drink possess a special taste when it comes directly after avoiding a nasty death.

"I forget my manners," I say, and introduce Wait to Gallop and Owaneko, who states he does not mind his true name used with such company as ours. But when with the common English, he prefers Joe.

"I have another name as well," I say. The table goes quiet, and I hope Maame does not disapprove, for I wish those with me to know my true self. "Freegift is a good name for this world I find myself in. But my Akan name is Kwasi. It is a secret name, and means I am Monday's child, the protector of my family."

"A real secret name?" Wait asks, his mouth stuffed with cornbread.

"Yes. The only other person alive who knows is Martine," I say.

"I wish I had a secret name," Wait says. "But I'm glad yours is Kwasi. Otherwise you might not have been able to protect me."

He drinks his beer, and I smile. I have wondered at why I was given this name and left with no family but a distant and turncoat father. Now I see why, in the form of this yellow-haired boy. There is such a thing as destiny, after all.

It is not long before Wait begins to fall asleep, filled with food and feeling safe among friends. Matthew puts him to bed and returns to the table. We fill him in on the details of our raid upon the *Badger*.

"Gill is dead, you are sure?" he asks.

"Unless he can breathe face down in the water, with a crack in his skull," Gallop answers. "A fitting end, I say."

No one disagrees.

"Are the rumors true then?" Matthew asks. "Of the prize you took?"

"I know not of rumors, but she carried a heavy load of gunpowder, sugar, and other goods. Not to forget General Clinton's baggage. I never knew a Redcoat general needed so much folderol to wage a war," Gallop says with a laugh.

"Let us hope he does not want his breeches back," Owaneko says.

"He has more than breeches to worry about," Matthew says. "They say the war is going poorly for the British."

"Forget the Redcoats, Matthew," I say. "How is your wound? You seem spry enough."

"It is well healed already. Topheny said not to lift anything heavy for a while, and the collarbone should knit nicely in a few weeks. It has not inconvenienced me much. I told Edward I will join the militia once I am fully recovered. We can march together, Freegift."

"Digging ditches is more likely," I say. "Up at Fort Nonsense."

"A waste of time," Gallop says. "Ever since the French marched from Rhode Island through Connecticut on their way south, the war has passed us by. Except for privateering, that is."

We debate the progress of the war, then attempt to calculate how much our share of the prize shall be. Matthew is determined to go out on the *Minerva* if there is an opening. We tell him there will be at least three, since none of us will go out again and risk losing all after gaining so much.

We grow weary and fall asleep where we may. As I close my eyes, I see a vision of riches, but they give way to Martine, my real treasure. Then sharply remember I must journey to my father in New York, and joy is replaced by concern, if not dread, at the prospect of leaving her and all that I have come to treasure in this town.

Sleep does not come as easily as I wish.

· Thirty Four ·

⊢——⊣

What day is today?" I ask Tink, as I begin my work. The day is warming, the early morning sun blazing low in the sky.

"It is Thursday, September the 6th, in the year of our Lord 1781," he answers, letting out a long sigh. "One day later than when you last asked, Freegift."

"It has been weeks," I say. "Why does it take so long?"

"You ask why the government does not act quickly enough to suit you? You may as well as why the sun never hurries to high noon," he says. "I promise, if a message comes from the governor, you will be the first person I tell. You have my word, Freegift."

"I am sorry, Tink," I say. "It has me at sixes and sevens with myself. I'll leave you in peace."

He nods wearily as I make for the wharf, my head indeed in a state of confusion. It has been nearly a month since we took the *Hannah* and effected the rescue of Wait. For the latter, all is well. The *Badger* did set sail, and no one has heard of her since. Gill's body—what was left after the fishes feasted on his ample frame—washed up near Fort Trumbull. No one cared to make much of a funeral, and he ended up in a shallow trench with a few stones to mark it. All's well that ends well. So the Bard tells us.

As for the prize goods stored in Tink's warehouse, the governor has yet to approve the final disposition. No one doubts it will happen, but as of now, the official paperwork is in the hands of clerks and accountants, as Captain Saltonstall informed the crew. There are taxes and fees to calculate, duties to be paid, and the auctioning of the goods themselves. The inventory of the ship and cargo alone took nearly two weeks.

That this is the largest and most valuable prize taken is beyond doubt.

Eighty thousand English pounds, Tink guesses.

These circumstances favor him, since he is to be paid for storage out of the proceeds. Which is one reason I stay on to work for him, since I have resigned as axe man on the *Minerva*. One such outing is quite enough. And Tink needs someone he can trust to work around such riches, without threat of pilfering. For myself, I like keeping an eye on this prize and will do so until it is sold off.

Then, to New York.

Today, I have barrels of salt pork to unload. Later, I will visit with Martine and Edward as they bring in their load of produce to sell. It is not a bad way to pass the time while awaiting a fortune. It is a hazy day, and flies buzz me as I work. The docks are busy, and the waterfront prospers even while the war rages to our south. General Washington and our French allies are now south in Virginia, and the news is good. How much longer before the Redcoats give up and sail back to their homes? My father must go with them. There is no hope for him here. So I wish for my share to come quickly, or wish for the war to go on. Which gives me no joy.

I carry the first barrel of salt pork from a barge which has come across the river, setting it down at the top of the stairs to the warehouse. It is as heavy as the day is hot.

A cannon shot. Another quickly follows. A warning of an attack? Then, a third. No, another prize ship has been taken! I run to the far end of the dock, shielding my eyes against the sun as I see the white smoke from the guns at Fort Griswold drifting on the breeze.

I search the river for the ships that the men at Fort Griswold have spied from the heights in Groton town. Others join me, voices raised in excitement at the prospect of another privateer victory, not to mention the spoils it will bring.

"Nothing?" Tink inquires as appears next to me.

"No. Perhaps the ships are damaged and coming up river slowly," I say. "But they do have the tide, so it should not be long."

"Ah, well, back to work," Tink says. "They'll be here soon enough."

So I work, rolling heavy barrels up the ramp and into the warehouse. It is not long before Martine hails me from Bank Street, where she sits on the wagon with Edward. I run up to them, happy to see Martine after an absence of several days.

"What news is there?" she asks. "A prize ship?"

"Not yet," I say. "Fort Griswold fired their cannon, but nothing has come into view."

"Three shots, it sounded like," Edward says. "Or did I hear an echoing?"

"No, it was three for certain," I say. Two would be the signal for an enemy attack, but I am sure of what I heard. "It could be the ships are slowed from damage. Since the tide works for them, they should be in sight soon enough."

"The tide comes in?" Martine asks, her brows knitted in worry.

"As it does," I say. "What is the matter?"

"Look there," she says, pointing to where Town Hill Road empties into Bank Street, at my back. A line of women and children emerges and draws close. They carry bags over their shoulders, driving cows before them. A cart appears, laden with furniture. The poor souls coming our way have the look of shock and fear writ over their faces.

Distant musket fire sends faint pops into the heated air. That is where their menfolk are. The tide has carried the enemy to our shores.

"A trick!" Edward exclaims. He leaps from the cart and stops the first woman in this sad parade, her young girl beside her. "What has happened?"

"Redcoats," she says. "Landed off Brown's farm. They came in on rowboats. Hundreds of them. Pray God, let us pass. They will be here soon."

Brown's farm is only three miles south. It fronts a sandy stretch of beach. Perfect for longboats to bring in soldiers.

"Dear God," says Tink. "What is this?"

"War," Martine says. "It has come to us after all."

"Freegift, help us unload," Edward orders. "Tink, run to the church and sound the alarm. The Redcoats must have added a third cannon of their own to sow confusion." Which they have.

Tink dashes off, and I join Edward and Martine in dumping bushels of corn and squash onto the ground as the stream of people, young and old, pass us by. Beyond them, in the direction of their homes, smoke rises in the sky as volleys of musketry increase.

War. The very dogs of war of which the Bard speaks so blithely.

"Martine, race back to the farm and fetch the powder and ball I have stored there," Edward says, as the church bell begins its insistent tolling. "We shall need it before the day is done. There is little enough at Fort Trumbull. Bring it to this very spot. Go no further, do you understand?"

"I do. I will return within the hour," she says, her hand on my arm. A squeeze, and she is on the wagon, turning Cricket about with a sharp command.

"Freegift, go to Fort Trumbull," Edward tells me. "I must find Colonel Harris. It falls to him to organize the defense."

"What shall I do there?" I ask, watching Martine as she snaps the reins.

Taking me by the arms and turning me so I face him, eye to eye, Edward says, "You shall do your best. Now go, there is not a moment to lose."

The church bell continues to toll as I run to my room and don my hunting shirt. Ammunition and knife are at my belt, along with my tomahawk. I pat my chest for the reassuring feel of my pouch. I take my musket and leave, wondering if I shall ever see this room again. Or be with Martine within it.

I run to Fort Trumbull, seeing only a few militiamen making their way. The procession moves entirely in the other direction, mainly older boys leading farm animals or carrying boxes with what must be family treasures. One lad cries as he struggles with a small chest. These must be the last of the refugees, older sons instructed to bring what valuables they can and follow their mothers to the safety of town. If safety might be found there. If none, perhaps to the forest beyond.

Closer to Fort Trumbull, I see that the smoke in the sky is not from gunfire. It is the thick, black smoke of houses and barns afire. Dark columns rise in swirls, like tornados advancing upon the town. Brown's farm and the other homesteads along the road are being put to the torch.

I am nearly winded as I come to Fort Trumbull and hear the clatter of horse hooves from behind. I expect Colonel Harris, but it is Colonel William Ledyard, commander of the militia, who only last week attended our drill and commended Edward on our appearance. This morning, there are no such niceties. Jordan Freeman and another rider are hard upon his heels, their mounts slathered with sweat.

"Captain Shapely," Colonel Ledyard barks as he pulls his horse to a sudden stop, the creature himself as winded as I am. "How many men do you have?"

"Twenty-three at last count, Colonel," the fort's commander says. "Not enough to hold for long, sir." He gestures to his useless cannon, three of them situated to fire at ships in the river. Only one fieldpiece faces the road on which the British are advancing. With Fort Trumbull so open at the rear, it will fall easily.

"Spike those cannon," Ledyard orders, pointing to the battery of three.

A steel spike driven into the touchhole will render the cannon useless to the enemy. "Fire one volley for the sake of honor, then take to your boats and cross to Fort Griswold. Join me there. Am I clear, sir?"

"We'll give them a proper salute, Colonel," Shapely says, and his men cheer. Perhaps at the prospect of beating a hasty retreat after a single cannon blast, which seems prudent.

"Have you seen Colonel Harris?" Ledyard asks.

"No sir, I have not," Shapely says.

"Lieutenant Hardwick has gone in search of him, sir," I say. "Not ten minutes past, up on Bank Street."

"You are in his company, are you not?" Ledyard says, suddenly taking notice of me.

"Aye. Freegift Cooper, sir. The lieutenant told me to report to Fort Nonsense," I say, offering up this lie so I will not be forced across the river with Shapely and his men, putting wide water between myself and Martine returning with her dangerous cargo.

"Then off with you, Freegift, and Godspeed," Colonel Ledyard says. "If Colonel Harris can be found, I shall tell him to organize the defense south of the harbor. Which means you fellows up that hill will need to hold the Redcoats for as long as you can."

"I will do my best, Colonel," I vow, remembering Edward's words. With that, he digs in his spurs and gallops off with his party. More musket fire ripples in the distance, and I notice the road is now empty. The next to come along will be advancing with bayonets.

I run up the hill to Fort Nonsense, not waiting a moment in case Captain Shapely has any thought of pressing me into his service. I see other men running low through fields, chased by the crack of scattered muskets, making for what safety Fort Nonsense offers.

One man pitches forward, falling into a patch of vining vegetables. He does not rise, nor do his companions slow. I hasten my steps, vaulting over the crude earthworks on which I have long labored, never truly thinking I would need them as a shield against lead shot.

There are a few lads of my company here, along with cannoneers for the four 12-pounders which are arrayed to fire along the road, down upon the Redcoats as they advance. Smaller field pieces than what Fort Trumbull has, but they do possess the virtue of pointing directly at the enemy.

"Freegift, have you seen Lieutenant Hardwick?" asks a fellow named Miller, who I have come to know. "Or Colonel Harris? We have no orders here."

"Yes, the lieutenant has gone off in search of Colonel Harris," I say.

"Good luck finding him," another fellow says. "He lives two houses from me, just up the road. Took off at the first volley the Redcoats let off. I never saw a horse whipped so."

"Perhaps he went to bring reinforcements," I say, trying to sound hopeful. But the only response is bitter laughter. They are farmers from along this road who know Colonel Harris and hold him in no higher estimation than I do.

"Between us and the boys down in Fort Trumbull, we'll give 'em something to worry about," Miller says. I am sorry to disillusion him.

"Colonel Ledyard ordered the men at the fort to fire one volley and retire across the river to reinforce Fort Griswold," I say.

"Leaving us alone?" Miller asks.

"He wishes Colonel Harris to form a defense south of the harbor and says we must delay the Redcoats as long as possible," I say. The men are silent. I grip my musket and gaze out over the scene below. The twenty-odd men at Fort Trumbull are gathered around their cannon. The road is visible for fifty yards or so and then blocked by a dense thicket of trees, where the land slopes to the river's edge. To our rear, the hill climbs until it forms a ridgeline. Behind that stands a farmhouse and field of ripening corn.

We wait.

"Look there!" Miller says. "Down the hill."

Soldiers in green jackets filter through the woods, not acting like Redcoats in neat rows and columns. Not a scarlet coat to be seen.

"Hessians," one of the farmers says. "Saw them at Saratoga. Skirmishers. It means the main body is close."

The Hessian skirmishers fire at Fort Trumbull and fade back into the woods. It is a diversion. As the defenders return fire, more shots are fired at them from the road. The volleys increase, and the single cannon defending Fort Trumbull fires.

As the smoke clears, the defenders take to their boats, as ordered. Several Hessians lie in the road, caught in that round fired for the honor of the defenders. Others of the enemy gather around the Fort and inspect the spiked guns, uselessly pointing out to the river.

"Fire!"

Our own cannon blast and belch smoke at the enemy. They are caught by surprise, two of the balls exploding in the open fort, felling a good number of the recent victors. I cheer and spare not a moment to mourn the rending of flesh, since it is that of the enemy and most importantly, not mine. This is a selfish thought, but war brings on such base instincts I find I do not care.

The Hessians return to the woods below and fire from behind trees, like Indians instead of proper British, who are known to obligingly line up on the field of battle. We fire back, with musket and cannon, ball and grapeshot. It is a great advantage being behind stout logs and packed earth, even as there are many of them and few of us.

We keep up our share of the firing, but by the sounds of lead hitting the trees and ground around us, we are at a disadvantage. The Hessians are everywhere. We are crammed together. And running low on powder.

"Behind us!" Miller shouts. It is not the enemy. A dozen or so men come from the direction of the farmhouse. None I recognize, likely local citizens ready to defend the town. Straight through the cornfield crashes a horse and rider, coming from a different direction and making for the cover provided by the ridgeline. The new arrivals gather around him.

"By God, Colonel Harris shows his face," one of the farmers says. "I thought he'd be to Norwich by now."

"Colonel, we are at your service," one of the reinforcements proclaims. "What shall we do?"

"Defend this place. Now you must excuse me, gentlemen, as I have a violent sick headache this morning and can hardly sit on my horse," Harris says. With that, he gives his horse a sharp stab of spurs and does an excellent job of sitting upon it as it gallops off the field of battle.

The men curse his departing form, and one raises and cocks his musket.

"Don't waste the shot," Miller says and directs them into the fortification.

"Who is in charge?" someone asks.

No one answers.

The fire from the Hessians has lessened, and as I scan the woods I cannot see a single one. Quiet descends over the field, and we exchange nervous glances. Have we driven them off? Or are they working their way around us?

The tramp of feet rumbles from the road below. Now we see Redcoats.

Many Redcoats.

They form up with drums playing and bugles sounding. Three ranks deep and with the green-coated Hessians at their side. Our cannons let loose, but the shots are high, and the lines of British regulars begin to advance upon us. The cannons fire again, some balls hitting the lines and sending bodies spinning. A tall British officer sits upon his horse, calmly ordering his men forward.

They obey.

A crackle of fire comes from the woods, close by. One man falls, his skull shattered with shot. Another is hit in the arm. We fire back, but the Hessians have vanished into the greenery. Soon they will be behind us.

"One more volley," the lead gunner orders. "Then we must go or be slaughtered."

No one argues with such a sensible order, even though he has no authority to issue it.

The cannons roar, and we all fire our muskets. Immediately we spill out of the fort, up over the ridge to our rear. Then it is a race through the cornfield. We leave Fort Nonsense to the Redcoats.

I glance back as Hessians pour from the woods, not twenty yards from our last position. The gunner was right. They were about to assault us from two sides. And they are not done with us. Shots whizz through the cornfield, seeking targets where the stalks are disturbed by our flight. Next to me, Miller exclaims and falls, blood spreading across his back. I stop, but his eyes tell me all I need to know. He is gone, and the balls clip corn stalks all around me.

I run.

I make the safety of the far side of the farmhouse, where a group of men are reloading and firing back to discourage the Hessians from pursuit.

"Damn him all to Hell, did you see who that was?" says the man next to me. "I fought under him at Saratoga."

"Who?" I ask.

"The damned traitor Benedict Arnold, that's who. It was him, sitting on that horse, pretty as you please." With that, he moves to the side of the farmhouse, fires, and runs off.

Benedict Arnold is here.

My father.

I have no time to think. I cannot take this news in and figure what to do with it.

Because Martine is at the harbor by now with a load of gunpowder and ball, and there is nothing between the British and her.

Except me.

I run, thinking not of Hessians or even my father, the damned traitor.

I think of Martine.

· Thirty Five ·

⊢——⊣

I have seen my father. The man I seek has come to me, hurling death and destruction my way. It is not how I imagined things. When I did think upon it, I saw an office or perhaps a drawing room, with myself standing at attention, and my father listening, considering, and finally offering an embrace.

A fantasy, I know. But it gave me comfort, which I have little of this morning. For my father is now hurrying his troops up the road to town and the harbor, where he surely means to wreak havoc. Martine is perhaps waiting there, alone, thinking a stout fight is being waged at our forts.

All appears lost. I run through fields and gardens, making the straightest line I can to Tink's warehouse. Armed men run in every direction, some with purpose, others betraying a bewilderment at the rattle of musketry growing at my heels. The sky is dark with smoke.

I dart between a barn and a house, coming again to Town Hill Road. I glance to the south and think I see the green coats of the Hessian light troops again. The regulars cannot be far behind.

A shot cracks out, and I hear the whistle of a ball close to my head.

"Hold your fire!" The cry comes from behind a stone wall, where the road curves away, and the formation of rocks gives cover to a dozen or so men. "Freegift, hurry!"

It is Edward, and I run to the wall and jump over.

"What news?" Edward asks. I am again winded, in body and spirit, and can barely answer.

"Fort Trumbull, gone. We fought at Fort Nonsense. Long as we could. Too many."

"Damn," Edward mutters. "We can't do more but hold them up as well. Have you seen Colonel Harris?"

"Run off," I say. "Complaining of a head ache."

"The town is lost," one man says.

"It is Benedict Arnold in command," I say, rubbing my eyes as if I am so greatly exhausted, when in fact I seek to hide the tears I cannot stop from flowing. I know not if the sight of my father brings forth this unmanliness, or fear for Martine as she is in his path.

"What? Are you sure?" Edward and the others ask at the same time.

"A fellow who fought with him at Saratoga swore it was Arnold," I say. "I saw him myself, sitting on his horse and giving orders. I believe it to be him." In my recollection, there was something familiar about the man, even at a distance. The pull of blood?

"He knows the town and the people," Edward says. "He will have no trouble marking the homes of Patriots."

"From the smoke, they are burning everything in sight," I say. The buildings along the road by the river are far apart, and I cannot imagine what the blaze will be like in the close-packed quarters along the harbor.

"Here they come," one of the men says, as the horde of Hessians spreading across the roadway halts all talk of turncoats and fires. Groups of them fire and advance, some reloading, while others repeat the process, forcing us to keep our heads low. I fire at a line of men running for the cover of the barn I have recently passed. I see a man drop.

It is the first time today I see I have scored a hit. Meaning I have killed a man, for he lies still, a crumpled heap of flesh clothed in green.

Forgive me, but I feel no pity. This is my duty, this is my home. Martine is close by, at my back. This is what I must do.

I reload and take aim again.

Fire comes from our left, and one man falls. They are on two sides of us. We are close to being surrounded. I turn and fire at the flash of green across the road, as does Edward.

Edward is hit. He falls against me, blood flowing from his side.

"Retreat," he gasps, our position now hopeless. Shots come from the front, lead balls pinging off the stone and snapping branches behind us. I grasp Edward, pulling his arm over my shoulder and half-carry, half-drag him away.

"Leave me," he says, his face twisted in a grimace of pain. I look behind and see four Hessians in pursuit. Two chase down a militia man running with a limp, blood soaking his thigh. They overcome him and kill him with bayonets, amidst much screaming and curses.

"You must leave me," Edward says, as the other two gain on us.

I set him down on the ground and draw my tomahawk. The Hessians charge me, close by each other, which is a mistake. I swing my left arm, which holds my empty musket, and knock the bayonet thrust before it can strike home, sending one man into the other. With my other hand I swing the tomahawk quickly, chopping into one skull and the other while they are off balance.

They are not dead, since dead men do not writhe upon the ground and bleed profusely. I find it matters not to me, given their deadly intent. I hoist Edward up, secure his arm across my shoulder, and we proceed to the harbor, making our way as best we can. He seems barely sensible, and his blood soaks my hunting shirt so heavily I think I must be bleeding myself.

We stumble out onto Bank Street, and there, hard by the warehouse, I see Martine.

And what a sight surrounds her.

The wounded and dying are scattered about at her feet. She, Topheny, and Tink load as many as they can onto the cart as Cricket whinnies, the smell of so much blood strange to this peaceable creature.

"Freegift!" Martine screams and runs to me. Our eyes meet, but there is no time for words, only action. "Are you hurt?"

"No, I think not. But Edward was struck in the side," I say. Edward is barely conscious, his eyes fluttering open then closing with the effort. Tink rushes to us, taking Edward by the feet, and between the three of us we lay him in the wagon, next to a militia man with a shattered leg.

"Freegift," Edward mutters. I lean in and take his hand. "Go to Colonel Ledyard. Tell him we cannot hold. Bring the ammunition and tell him..." His speech becomes jumbled, and Topheny pulls me away.

"We will take them north on the Norwich Road, to a safe place," she says. "Then return for the others."

"No," I say, whispering to Martine and drawing her closer. "Do not return. By the time you do, the Redcoats will be here. In force. They are right behind us." A crackle of musket fire, sounding very close, enforces my point. "Promise me."

"That is a simple promise," Topheny says. "We cannot care for the wounded if the Redcoats take us. Come find us, Freegift, after you deliver your message. Hurry."

"It is Benedict Arnold himself who leads these troops," I say. Tink is busy with the remaining wounded, helping them across the street and away from the docks which will likely be in flames before long.

"These troops?" Topheny says, pointing to the smoke rising above the buildings.

"He may be less than a half mile distant," I say, nodding.

"Go across the river, Freegift!" Martine says, pounding on my chest. "This is not the day to meet your father. You will be killed as all these others have been. You make that promise to me, now!" She is ferocious in her zeal for me to have a wide river and a stout fortification between my father and me.

"I can make no such promise," I say. "Although I see no way through it, I cannot promise to abstain from what I must do. There has been a previous promise made, as you know."

Martine says nothing. Moans from the wounded men in the wagon rise, gunfire echoes from behind, and spires of smoke make mid-day appear as dusk. It is Hell on Earth.

She grasps my neck and kisses me, leaning against me for a precious moment, then turning away and mounting the wagon, her light blue dress splattered with blood.

The pull of blood carries in all directions. Part of me wishes to chase after her and protect her. Another part urges me south, to find General Arnold and fulfill my pledge to Maame, no matter the cost.

But blood draws me elsewhere. The blood spilled today calls for me to do my duty and carry what message and munitions I may to Colonel Ledyard. I see Fort Griswold from where I stand. Our flag flies over it, and no British troops have appeared. We may not have won the day on this side of the river, but perhaps the eastern shore will be different.

Tink helps me carry the casks of powder and shot Martine delivered to his rowboat at the dock. He offers to accompany me.

"No, Tink, you must get those wounded men as far away as possible. You yourself, as well," I tell him.

"I shall do my best, although there's one lad who doesn't have long to live. I cannot leave him alone in his last moments," Tink says as he pushes the rowboat off. "Bring back my boat!" With a forced laugh and a wave, he heads back to Bank Street.

I strain at the oars, wishing to be out of musket range as soon as possible. New plumes of fire and smoke show themselves along the shoreline, creeping closer to town. The occasional cannon sounds, and muskets discharge constantly. A battle rages, but it is very one-sided.

My father has the advantage. Should I be proud? I know not.

I see the British ships clearly now, their many masts rising like a forest on the water. They are clustered along either shore at the mouth of the river, where they landed their troops on sandy beaches. If the Redcoats on the New London side are almost to the harbor, then the enemy on this side should be drawing close as well.

They are. I spy the red of the British regulars along the shore, marching on a road flanked by houses and shops. They set no fires, not yet. They are intent upon Fort Griswold.

As I reach the shore, four men dash to the embankment to help me unload. There is no time to speak, as the Redcoats march out into the sloping fields below the fort and form up. There are hundreds of them. Carrying the casks of munitions, we run up to the side of the fort, keeping a hillock between ourselves and the assembling enemy.

The fort itself is a square with bastions at each angle. Its walls are of stone, ten or more feet high, and surrounded by a ditch. On the wall is a parapet with shooting positions, as well as a platform for cannon. In a bastion at the rear is a flagstaff with the flag of white and red stripes and thirteen stars on a blue field flapping in the breeze. Opposite is a gated tunnel which leads from the field into the fort. Before it lies a triangular breastwork to defend the gate against breaching.

It would be a fine fort if there were more men to defend it.

"Freegift, is it not?" Colonel Ledyard inquires. "Have you news as well as powder and ball?"

"Sorry to say, Colonel, but New London is lost. Colonel Harris claimed illness and rode off. Lieutenant Hardwick is wounded. There is no organized defense."

"Then we shall defend where we can," he says. He is firm in what he says, his gaze confident as he surveys his men on the parapets, his hand resting on the hilt of the sword at his belt. It is a large fort, and I figure there to be little more than a hundred men to defend it. I see Jordan Freeman at his position, and we nod a brief greeting. I wonder if it might be our last.

"Are there more men coming, Colonel?" I ask, before departing to take my place on the wall.

"There are others nearby," he says, which tells me little. Or much, since nearby is not as close as five hundred or more British are.

A white flag approaches. Two Redcoat officers wait some distance from the fort, their comrades aligned behind two hills so all we can see are their gleaming bayonets. Colonel Ledyard sends Captain Shapely out to parley, and I wonder why they do not simply commence to attack. What is there to discuss? My father is in the process of burning New London town without speaking a word to any Patriot officer.

"Colonel Eyre sends his compliments, sir," Captain Shapely reports as he returns from the parley. "He demands the immediate unconditional surrender of the fort."

"And if we do not comply?" Colonel Ledyard asks, his voice loud so it will carry to all the men.

"It is Colonel Eyre's position that if obliged to storm the works, martial law will be in effect. No quarter will be given to the defenders," Shapely answers. Meaning we will all be put to death.

Colonel Ledyard eyes his men, looking to the parapets and all those arrayed on them. Not a one flinches. "We shall not surrender," he says. "Let the consequences be what they may."

Captain Shapely hastens to deliver that response to the waiting British officers.

"There's more militia out there," the man next to me says. "Captain Stanton of the Groton militia left this morning to round up more men." Everyone within earshot agrees, reinforcements are close by.

I would prefer they make their presence known, but the only thing which occurs is that Captain Shapely returns, the British officers depart, tossing aside their white flag, and columns of Redcoats begin to maneuver around us, closing in on three sides. Within moments, they move forward, drums, bugles, and fifes playing. I feel awe at their power and precision.

We have one cannon of any size, an eighteen-pounder which lets loose a charge of grapeshot, and one Redcoat column has a gap blasted through its lines. This scatters the well-trimmed lines of scarlet, and suddenly the Redcoats are crouching low, some bending to fire, others falling to the ground, then rising as their officers push them forward. I think they are in disarray, but still the hordes of them press forward, firing, reloading, cursing, and surging into the ditches below the wall.

They are spread out before us, and since we face an attack on three sides, with perhaps forty men on each wall, we cannot stop them. But in a moment, something odd occurs. Many of the British stand and begin walking straight for the fort, no furtive movement, or hasty crouching. Our fire knocks several of them down, and I hear a shout to my rear.

It is the flag.

The lanyard shot away, just as aboard the *Minerva*. A young boy, an African who I have not seen before, runs for the banner and lashes it to a pike, a long pole used for repelling attackers if they storm our walls. He waves it at the parapet, but I fear some damage has already been done. If there was any hope of avoiding the no quarter edict, it has now vanished. We have killed men who thought we struck the colors. For the first time today, I feel regret.

But I cannot linger over this notion. The British keep coming. They gather at the eastern wall, and although we pour fire into them, it cannot be sustained without sacrificing the defense of other points along the wall. Colonel Ledyard orders men with pikes forward as a British officer and his men climb up from the ditch and gain the top of a wall to my side. More Redcoats come straight at me, and the man to my side who was certain of reinforcements is felled with a ball between his eyes.

We are about to be defeated.

I reload and watch as Jordan Freeman races to the far wall, a long pike in hand. The British officer waves his men forward, about to descend into the fort, when Jordan bravely steps forward and thrusts his pike upward. He impales the Redcoat, who dies in an instant, his heart pierced. Soldiers jump over his fallen body and take their bayoneted revenge on Jordan, the steel blades flashing in the sun as they are coated with his blood.

Then the gate is forced, and although several British fall as they pour through, the battle is lost as the enemy breaches us at two points, with more still advancing on the field. The Redcoats form up and deliver a volley against those opposing them. Captain Shapely, among others, falls.

"Throw down your arms!" Colonel Ledyard commands, although a number already have, seeing how useless it is to prolong the fighting. But now all do, including myself. I lay my musket down and stand still, unwilling to make a sudden move that might provoke violence.

Colonel Ledyard stands before the Redcoats who advance with bayonets leveled, some red with blood.

"Who commands this fort?" A British officer demands, his voice enraged.

"I did, sir, but you do now," Colonel Ledyard responds, raising his sword in salute and then lowering it. He advances to where the conquering officer stands and presents it to him.

The Redcoat officer takes it and plunges it fully to the hilt through Colonel Ledyard's chest. The young African lad who'd saved the flag rushes forward, a bayonet in hand, and stabs the officer who so ruthlessly attacked the colonel. He is killed, along with others who try to attend to Ledyard, who lies dying. More British soldiers rush into the fort and begin firing at the assembled men who have just surrendered. It is an orgy of blood and violence.

I cannot think or form a plan, I simply leap over the parapet and roll down the sloped wall into the ditch, as do several others. We are fired upon from above and from soldiers still in the field. Two men are shot dead, and another apprehended. But even as shouted commands tell me to halt or be killed, I know that to halt is to be killed.

I run downhill, hearing the stomp of men following, hearing the discharge of muskets and the sound of buzzing hornets, which I know to be shot flying close to my head. I do not stop or dare to look back, until I am lost in a maze of low buildings along the river.

I gasp for air and ready my tomahawk in case I am still chased. But no one has followed me. Shots and screams echo from within the fort, and I wonder if they shall ever cease ringing within my mind.

This is not war, this is wanton slaughter.

And now, I must find the man responsible. For this carnage. And for my own existence.

If any harm has come to Martine, I will kill him, father of mine or no.

· Thirty Six ·

⊢——⊣

I push off in the rowboat, my pursuers nowhere in sight. Redcoats form up around the fort, busy with their bugle calls and drums. What glory they find in such wanton murder, I cannot fathom. This side of the river has seen its cruelties, but the western shore has its own evil inferno raging. Ships anchored in Shaw's Cove are ablaze, their masts sending flames aloft. The air is thick with smoke which billows out over the water in a choking haze.

Martine is there, somewhere. I strain at the oars, my mind a tumble of worry and fear. How far will the British go? Will they march north and discover where she and Topheny have taken the wounded? Will my father countenance a massacre?

I try to stop the thoughts racing through my brain and work only to row straight, quick, and strong.

A shattering explosion deafens me. Burning debris drops around me. Smoke and haze is blown clean away by the force of this blast. I look to the harbor. Tink's warehouse is gone, replaced by a fiery, gutted hole above the wharf.

The gunpowder.

The treasure from the *Hannah*.

Gone. The ship itself is now aflame, the explosion scattering fire everywhere, doing the work of the British raiders. Embers float on air, dropping where they may, igniting new fires. Steering for a dock not yet burning, I secure the rowboat, then climb the ladder. The heat from the fire rolls over me in waves, a scorching, clawing presence. I run up the embankment, away from the inferno and hide myself between two buildings not yet destroyed.

The scene before me is horrific. The courthouse, the jail, the tavern, the church, already char and ash. The warehouse burning itself to nothing on the deadly fuel stored within. The baker, Matthew's print shop, other stores and dwellings, all in the process of being consumed.

Of Redcoats, I see none.

I run to the print shop where the cedar shingles burn brightly, hoping Matthew has already left. But he has not. I hear him inside, coughing and hacking in the smoky air. He has the side doors wide open to the room where the printing press sits. As I near him, I see the body of his employer, Mr. Gates, lying on his back, his eyes and mouth open. A look of surprise lingers on his face. There appears to be not a mark upon him.

"Matthew!" I shout.

"Freegift, thank God," Matthew says, stumbling out. "Help me."

"What happened to Mr. Gates?" I ask.

"I think his heart failed him," Matthew says. "Trying to move the press. Come help."

"Matthew, the whole building may give way," I say, as flames work their way down from the roof.

"Exactly, let's hurry!" With that, he dashes back into the building. I follow, and we are instantly wreathed in smoke. He hands me a rope, and I see what he and Mr. Gates were trying to do—drag the heavy press outside and save it from the flames before the roof collapses.

We begin to pull, and I also see why it was the death of poor, gray-haired Mr. Gates. We strain and labor to move it barely a foot when we must catch our breath. I slap at my neck, as if an insect has bitten me, but it is an ember. The roof is beginning to fall in.

We put the ropes over our shoulders and pull like pack horses. The floor is not level, sloping toward the sliding doors. We are outside, and as the press clears the threshold, the ceiling gives way, showering the room with fire.

"That must do," Matthew says, as the press settles into the soft ground. He takes a spade from a pile of tools and pushes away burning wood from the machine. "I'll fetch water and keep her doused. Mr. Gates would be pleased."

I think he would also be pleased to live but stop myself before uttering such words. The events of the day have coarsened me to suffering, and I must mind my tongue.

"Any news of Martine? Have you seen her?" I ask.

"She and Topheny took the wounded back to the farm. They said they doubted the British would go that far north," Matthew says. "Edward looked poorly, but Topheny said the ball went straight through him, which was good. Still, he bled a dreadful amount of blood."

"You should leave," I say. "They still may come."

"No, I will not leave. I think they must be satisfied that the fires have done their work. I've not seen a Redcoat for the past hour. There was an officer and dozen or so men trading shots with some militia, but nothing since then."

"An officer? General Arnold?" I ask.

"No, some young fellow on a fine horse. What of Fort Griswold? Has it fallen?"

"Fallen and worse," I say. "Colonel Ledyard run through with his own sword as he surrendered. Men with their hands raised butchered with the bayonet. I barely escaped with my life."

"How many dead?" Matthew asks, a look of stricken horror on his face.

"I know not. Dozens, perhaps more. It was a horror."

"What shall you do now? Go to the farm?"

"No," I say. "There is something I must do first."

"Take care, Freegift. The Redcoats are roaming the streets south of here." As if to punctuate his warning, two shots echo nearby.

"We should both take our care," I say, clasping his hand. "I will return this way when I am done." I leave Matthew kicking away embers from his printing press. Well, I do not know if it is now his, but Mr. Gates, of a certainty, has no further need of it.

I make my way along the backstreets which run near Bank Street. There, the fires are so heavy, it would be impossible to walk in the center of the road and not be licked by flames from both sides. A man would be a target so placed, as well. Instead, I venture from one alley and garden to another.

What am I seeking? I cannot even put it into words. My father? Vengeance? The truth? I do not know, but I press on through the smoke.

I climb a fence and come face to face with a young woman standing by an aged man, who sits on a chair in the midst of a rose garden. It is unexpected, to say the least. She does not react, as if nothing can now surprise her.

"Excuse me, Ma'am," I say. "Should you not go inside?"

"No, I think not. A kind British officer said I should stay out here in case anyone put the torch to our house. Father is too infirm to move quickly, so here we wait."

"You will forgive me, but kindness is not a virtue I have encountered this day from the Redcoats," I say.

"This young officer did show kindness, although perhaps he is trying to balance out cruelty from earlier acts. I do not know. What I do know is that he ordered his men to leave us alone and suggested this course of action, to which I agreed. I wish you well, sir."

"And I you," I say, then look to her father. His eyes are watery and filled with confusion. I give him an obedient bow, which I do not think he observes.

I continue making my way through lanes and alleys, looking to come close to Town Hill Road and observe the movement of the British forces. And to spot my father upon his horse. I have no plan beyond that ill-formed thought. I circle around a house engulfed in flames and see a gang of Redcoats tossing torches into an adjacent barn. They take off laughing, and I run into the barn as soon as they are out of sight. I grab the three burning torches and throw them outside. With a pitchfork, I remove burning hay until the threat of fire is gone. One small victory on the day.

I move on, tomahawk at the ready. Muskets fire to my right, and I duck behind a stand of blackberry bushes. The firing continues but moves some distance. Militia being chased away, perhaps.

"Good day to you," a voice says. I stare through the blackberries and see another elderly gentleman. This fellow is more alert than the last, standing on the far side of the bushes, a few yards from the back door of a clapboard house. He doffs his tri-cornered hat. I remain on my haunches, not wanting to display myself quite yet.

"Is that your house, sir?" I ask.

"Yes, and I hope to keep it in one piece," he says, leaning on a cane.

"Did a pleasant British officer spare your residence and suggest you wait outside?" I ask.

"Indeed he did," the old man says. "I asked him to not burn me out since there's little I can do against the King these days. He agreed. Has he done so elsewhere?"

"Yes. He seems to be the only decent Redcoat in the vicinity," I say.

"Didn't catch his name. Young fellow, shiny blond hair. Air of the aristocrat about him. I'd stay low if I were you, young man," he says. "Here come a pair of them down the lane. Don't know if these are his men or not."

I duck further and watch as he doffs his cap once again, in the direction of the lane. Two shots follow, and he drops to the ground. Both have found their mark upon his chest. I stifle a gasp and feel a rush of sorrow for the kindly man who nearly waited out this terrible battle. Perhaps they thought him of the militia. Perhaps they were simply cruel. I listen to their footsteps fade, as they walk in the direction of Town Hill Road. I follow, unable to look again at the man who lies dead in his garden.

As I enter the lane, a horseman approaches. I reach for my tomahawk at the sight of his red coat but quickly see he is not a threat. He is slumped over, one arm dangling and dripping blood. He is alone.

I try to calm the horse. The creature steps back, as nervous as I am. But I gain his bridle and walk him to the front of the house. Then the officer stirs. He moans and asks for water.

He has fair, blond hair. The kindly aristocrat. Alive, but barely.

I ease him off the horse and see he has taken a shot close to his heart. It has not exited, which according to Topheny, is a bad thing. I am surprised he still lives. I mean to take him inside, thinking the recently deceased fellow would wish it so. I lay him on the ground carefully. He has a flintlock pistol at his belt, which I remove and place beneath my shirt. Then I lead the horse to the back of the house and tether him, not wanting him to run off. I may need to escape quickly.

Then back to the officer. His eyes open and look into mine.

"Water," he asks.

"I shall help you," I say. "Let me carry you inside."

"No," he gasps. "It is pleasant in the sun. Let me die here. But please, water."

I tell him I shall be back in an instant. I take the steps and open the door, then discard my fringed hunting shirt and weapons. Except for the pistol, which I keep hidden beneath my waistcoat. I find a jug of water and clean cloth in the kitchen and go out front. If Redcoats pass by, perhaps they will think me a servant giving succor to their dying officer and not kill me. Or so I hope.

I raise his head and dip the water to his lips. He drinks and coughs. I lay down his head and unbutton his shirt, pressing the cloth over the wound. There is considerable blood.

"I won't tell," he says.

"What, sir?"

"That you are of the militia," he gasps and then manages a smile. "Or were, a moment ago."

"You acted with kindness today, sir," I say. "It is only proper that I repay it so."

"The old gentleman?" he asks.

"Fine, sir. In good spirits," I lie, for why should another death burden him so close to his own?

The wind shifts and sends a flurry of smoke over us from the buildings burning on the heights above. I close my eyes, then open them. He is dead, his blue eyes staring at nothing but emptiness. I feel pity for my enemy, dying so far from home.

Pity is a deadly distraction, since I have not taken note of the horsemen riding in from the smoke, descending from the hill above on their way to the river.

Redcoats, a half dozen.

I dare not run or show fear. Instead, I kneel as I am, next to the body of their brother officer and hope for the best.

"Dear Lord Sandys, there he lies," the lead officer says. I look up, after a respectful moment of downcast eyes, as a servant or slave might do.

I am looking straight into gray eyes, which look so familiar and yet so strange.

I look at my father.

As Topheny saw in her vision. Except he came to me in smoke, not fog as she had foreseen.

"He spared this house, General," I say, for I know not what else to utter.

"He was a gentleman, and I see you have cared for him in his last moments. No one will bother you. His horse?"

"He fell from it, General, and then it ran off. Down there," I point to the river.

"Very well," he says and instructs his men to take Lord Sandys' body on horseback. As they do so, I stand, and the General looks at me. "You called me general. Know you who I am?"

"I do," I tell him. "You are General Benedict Arnold. From these parts, originally."

"That I am, and I thank you for all you have left out of my biography," he says, smiling. He has a face I would not call handsome, but strong. Commanding. His men begin to ride away, with Lord Sandys draped over a saddle. "Thank you for your kindness."

"There has been little enough of that today," I say, and he halts himself, turning his horse back to me.

"Do not overstep yourself," he says. "This is still a field of battle."

"May I show you something, General?" I ask. "It will take but a moment, and as the field is yours, I hope you will grant me that much."

He looks at me, his forehead furrowed and eyes narrow, in the way someone might when trying to recollect how they know another person. It is a risk to accost him so, but I must press my advantage. Maame will never rest if I let this pass. I know I never will.

"Why should I?" he asks but does not leave.

"My name is Freegift Cooper," I say. His eyes widen for a second. The name has hit a mark and aroused his curiosity. Which sends my heart pounding. There is something between us now, a link which had once been broken.

"General!" one of his officers calls to him.

"Wait upon me," he tells him, not taking his eyes off me. "So, Freegift Cooper, what is it you wish me to see?"

"This, sir," I say, pulling the pouch from around my neck. I open it and withdraw the yellowed newsprint. I hand it to him. "For no fault but being saucy."

"What is this?" he says. I see in those gray eyes, a dawning awareness. The idea has yet to penetrate fully, but it has been planted.

"You sold my mother," I say, not willing to speak the full truth of the matter.

"Not I," he says. "This was my father's work. I was but a lad. How do you come by this?"

"Do you recall her name, sir?" I ask. Silence stretches between us. He nudges his horse closer, leaning down to study me.

"Of course I do," says he, in a whisper. "Sally."

"She named me after your grand-father," I say, as calm as I can manage. There, I have laid claim to his line.

"I do not believe this," he says, a flash of anger knotting up his face. "Anyone could have a scrap of paper." He throws the newsprint to the ground. But he does not leave me.

"She said to tell you she remembers the shade of the locust tree. Behind the barn," I say. More silence, followed by a sigh. I think of Maame, telling me that secret as she lay dying, and nearly weep. My father's face weakens, the rage gone, a distant memory turning his gaze wistful.

"Ahhh... you are my son, are you not?" There is a sadness in his voice. Or resignation, I cannot tell.

"I am, sir. My mother told me to find you. I never thought you would come to me. And in such a dire fashion."

"Sally, is she alive?" he asks, his voice betraying a tremor of hope.

"No, sir. She died in July. She told me all on her deathbed."

"I never knew. My father sent me away, then sold everything. I am sorry. I never knew," he says. The infamous traitor, the great arsonist, Benedict

Arnold, is near to tears as he sits upon his horse before me. "Freegift, come with me. Come with me now. I shall help you."

He smiles, certain his invitation will be taken up.

What forgotten son would not weep to hear those words? Perhaps I shall. But not today.

"I cannot, sir."

"Then why have you sought me out? What purpose does it serve you?"

"Maame told me to find you. That by doing so, I would find my place in the world. She was right. I was a slave, and now I am free. I have a home and a cause. Why have you come here, sir?"

"Damn impertinent of you to ask, but since you do, it was at the invitation of General Clinton. Sir Henry took offense at having his personal baggage taken by pirates cruising out of this harbor. That, sir, is why I am here!"

"Privateers, I believe, General," I say, stunned that I had a part in bringing this invasion down upon our heads. I wonder what my father would think of that and remember the injunction. Speak little.

"Brigands, all the same. Now come with me, Freegift. I can find you a place, some position close to me. Let me help you," he says. His aide calls out to him again.

"No, sir. You are my father but also a turncoat. I could not bear the betrayal."

"Mind you, Freegift Cooper, we all turn coats now and then. These people once enslaved you, and now you serve their cause. I doubt you ever fancied that when a man owned you."

Now it is Martine's vision that is fulfilled. He cajoles me, tempts me with position and revenge. But it is not to be.

"Never, sir. Not after what you did here. And across the river. I was there."

"You are not a servant here at all, are you? I could take you prisoner and let you rot for the remainder of the war." His voice is cold, and any softness in his face has vanished. A traitor he is, but also a strong-willed man, I see.

"I am no man's servant," I say. "And yes, I was at Fort Griswold and saw what your men did. The slaughter."

"I sent a message to stop the attack," he says. "It arrived too late." He looks chagrined, and I think he speaks the truth. My father likely does not wish another scandal attached to his name.

"Very well then," I say. "There is enough on this side of the river to hold against you. The burning and killing." I begin to shake, the rage at what I have seen coming to the surface. Visions of the slain at Fort Griswold, the old man killed in his garden, the shameful retreat from Fort Nonsense, all these scenes flitting across my mind. Has the battle affected me so? Or is it the temptation he offers which riles me more than I wish it would. For I know, if not for Martine, this son might well follow his father to Hell itself.

"You are a man, Freegift, and this is war. There is nothing else to say, but for me to ask one more time. Will you come with me?"

"Never," I say, remembering Maame and wanting to hurt him as much as possible.

He stares at me for a long minute. Then he turns his horse and trots away, without a word. Not a word, not a goodbye, not a single glance, nor sign of affection. As if I am nothing but a servant met by the side of the road.

He has ignored me all my life, perhaps unwittingly, if in truth he did not know he fathered me. But today, now, upon this lane, he knows who I am and how I came into this world. And he turns his back on me.

I am all calmness now. The rage has flown away, leaving me clear-eyed. There is only one thing to do. It is so simple. Perhaps, I even think, this is what Maame intended. That I find my father and free myself of him.

I take the flintlock from my waistband. I aim it at my father, his red jacket a bright target in the middle of the road.

I fire.

He pulls up the reins on his horse, as his aides ride to him, pistols in hand. He holds up a hand to stop them and turns to face me. He pokes his finger at a furrow in his sleeve where the ball nearly hit him.

Then he grins and salutes me, his hand held to his hat.

I lower the pistol, and with my other hand, I wave to him.

As a young boy might, reluctantly, when a father leaves before he is ready to see him go. Love and anger. The pull of blood. He releases his salute, kicks his horse into a gallop, and disappears into the swirling smoke from whence he came.

I have fulfilled the charge given to me by Maame. I have found my father and made myself known to him.

· Thirty Seven ·

━

I ride a dead lord's horse through the lanes of New London, ash and soot falling on my shoulders. There are no more Redcoats to be seen, except for those glimpsed at a distance, marching in good order south on Town Hill Road. They head back to the beaches where scores of rowboats wait to ferry them back aboard their men o' war.

I wonder if my father will be the last to board, and if he will give a longing look to the road, wishing to see me making my way to him. But I think he knows we have made our way to each other as best we can, and that promises and honor have been served.

I will never forget those few minutes with him.

I flatter myself he thought me a decent man, even as I ruined the sleeve of his coat. Perhaps more so for it, since he is a man of action, regardless of risk or consequence.

I hold the newsprint he threw to the ground in a flash of anger. It is brittle and yellow, as old as I am. I thank Maame for keeping it and passing it on, but it no longer has a purpose. It has done its work, and now it is nothing but a reminder of my bartered past.

For no fault but being saucy.

I lift my hand and let it flutter away, borne by hot currents and swirls of smoke.

I ease the horse, a handsome chestnut mare, through a deserted yard, the house already falling in on itself, charred timbers collapsing in a shower of sparks. The past is at my back. In the next street, people are at work trying to extinguish flames licking the side of a house. They have it well managed, and truth be told, I have no passion for anything but Martine's arms.

I ride on.

In the harbor, burned out hulks of vessels float on water covered in charred debris. It is impossible to tell where the warehouse once stood. Where riches were held. Now burned and blown to kingdom come.

Matthew stands by his printing press. He has trays of lead type saved from the flames, along with an array of tools. "All you need is a roof," I say to him, pulling in the reins.

"Roofs can be rebuilt," he says. By the look on his face, there is a deeper meaning to his words. "Tink is dead, Freegift."

"Are you certain?" I ask, looking around, as if he might appear and tell us it was all a mistake.

"Too certain," Matthew says. "He was across the street from the warehouse, helping to move some wounded to safety, when it blew up. I found his remains, along with those poor fellows."

"Tink," I say, wishing for no more terrible news today. My first friend in New London and such a good man. "I cannot believe it. Where is he now?"

"The magistrate organized a burial party to collect the bodies and take them to the burying ground," Matthew says. "It must be done quickly, before disease takes hold. They took away Mr. Gates as well."

"There will be many graves dug tonight," I say, still trying to get used to the idea of Tink's tragic death. "What will you do, Matthew?"

"Search for a roof, I guess," he says with a shrug. "Or at least some canvas to keep the press from the weather." I sense a careful cheerfulness in Matthew. A lad with such a hard start in life now has a chance to make his own beginning here. The town will need a good printer. "Where did you come by that fine horse, by the way?" he then asks.

"He belonged to Lord Sandys, who died in my arms," I say. "He spared a few houses from the torch before he was shot in a skirmish." Perhaps one day I will confess to my friend what happened next, but the events are too raw and harsh in my mind to recount. Both meeting my father and receiving the news that my privateering venture brought this inferno down upon us. Perhaps one day, but this is not that day.

"Farewell, Matthew, and good luck," I say. He waves, hardly hearing me as he cleans soot from his precious printing press.

People begin to fill the road, heading back from hiding places in the woods or nearby farms. The Redcoats did not come this far north of the harbor, and it strikes me as odd to smell the smoke from their fires, while I see houses and barns standing whole. I have a good view of the river. I see a cluster of sails to the north, where those ships which escaped the harbor in time have gathered. A few have begun the trip back to the ruined city.

"Freegift," a voice shouts from a jumble of boulders by the side of the road. It is Owaneko, his musket cradled in his arms. "Are the Redcoats leaving?"

"Swarming back to their boats now, down by the mouth of the river," I say. "How have you fared today, Owaneko?"

"As poorly as all of us who have lost our shares in the prize," he says. "But not as badly as Gallop."

"Dead?" I ask and pray not.

"Near as bad," he says. "Taken prisoner. We fought down by Shaw's Cove, until there were too many of those Hessians all around us. I saw Gallop being led away."

"Tink is dead," I say, hoping that the night will not bring more exchanges of who is killed, taken, or wounded.

"I did not know," he says, shaking his head. "I was glad to see Matthew well, at least. And you, upon a fine horse."

I tell him the story of Lord Sandys, and Owaneko tells me of standing guard, ready to run back to Hardwick's farm and give warning if the British marched north. I dismount, and we walk together to the farm. It is close to dusk, and the western sky is filled with color, the sun gracing the clouds of ash with brilliant rosy hues.

It seems wrong.

As we near the farm, I see the yard is filled with people, many of whom fled New London, along with neighbors who have come to help. Tables are set up outdoors, laden with food. But it is not a festive scene.

"Freegift!" Wait shouts and runs to us. He grabs me about the waist and hugs tight, and I admit to such a feeling of warmth and devotion that I am nearly overcome.

"Wait, will you take the reins?" Owaneko asks, seeing my distress. He knows Wait will not be able to resist this excellent horse.

"Whose horse is this?" Wait asks, taking ahold of the reins, and studying the animal. "What's her name?"

"She is mine. But once she belonged to a good man, though he was a Redcoat," I say. "I think I shall call her Sandy. In tribute to him."

"Why?" Wait asks.

"I will tell you the story later," I say. "Will you care for her and make a place in the barn? She's been through terrors today."

"As have we all," Owaneko says, Wait scampering off with Sandy in tow. His gaze moves to Martine, who draws close. He nods to her and walks away, leaving us alone on the path to the farmhouse.

There are no words, not at first. We embrace and stand together, almost as one person. I feel the heart beating in her breast. Or ours together, I cannot tell.

"I thought you dead, across the river, when I heard what happened there," she says. Her fist pounds my shoulder, scolding me for the fright she took.

"Have you heard the news of Tink?" I ask, after I can no longer bear the weight of this news.

"Oh, no," she murmurs, understanding instantly. "Oh no." She buries her face against my chest and cries. After a while, she lifts her face to mine. "He was a most gentle man."

"Freegift, come inside," Ann calls from the door. She wipes her hand on a cloth spotted with blood. "Edward must speak with you."

"I want to hear everything," Martine says. "But first speak with Edward. He is desperate to see you." She links her arm in mine and takes me to the house, where two men lie bandaged on the floor, with Topheny tending to them. Another sits in a chair, his leg in a splint.

"Will Edward live?" I ask, worried that he waits with his final words for me.

"Yes, but it will take time. He was eager to see you. Come." Ann opens the bedroom door and goes to Edward's bed. He is asleep, but his face does not look at rest.

"Freegift is here, Edward," she says, her hand caressing his cheek to awaken him. She rises and bids me to take her seat. She and Martine leave us alone.

"You live," he says, his mouth in a grimace as he speaks.

"Still," I say. "How do you fare?"

"Busted ribs. Two holes in my side. Hurts to breath. Other than that, dandy," he says, forcing a smile.

"I have a present for you," I tell him, and take the flintlock pistol from under my hunting shirt.

"This is well made, Freegift. Expensive by the looks of it," he says, turning it this way and that to admire the workmanship. "You should keep it. Spoils of war."

"I shall keep the horse," I tell him. "You take the pistol."

"I thank you, Freegift. Listen, I must speak with you. My mind is unsettled."

"What can I do, Edward?"

"There's little labor I can do in the coming weeks. It will take me time to mend, and there's much work to be done. If you will, stay with us. Help us get through the winter. I know you and Martine are close, and I thought you would wish to be near her."

"Of course I will help you, Edward. I do need a place to live in any case, since my workplace and abode is nothing but ashes."

"Freegift, I need a firm answer. My family depends upon it. Ann, Wait, Topheny and Martine. Do this for me, help me plant in the spring, and I'll grant you a deed to fifty acres on the north side of my property."

"Fifty acres?"

"I know it's not much, but there's good timber there," Edward says.

"Are you certain, Edward? It is a large tract to give away," I say, overcome by his offer, and frankly, stunned at the thought of my own land. My own trees.

"I am not giving it away, I am exchanging it for your work and your help as I recover. I won't rest easy if you don't have a reward at the end of your labors. I bought those acres a year ago and haven't done anything with that land. I'll be glad to see you have it, and thankful for your work in the coming months. Are we agreed?"

"We are," I say, shaking his hand. I see the wisdom in his approach. I am now committed to this land with him, in joint effort. If I fail him, I fail myself.

"Thank God, now I can rest," he says.

I sit with Edward until he sleeps. Then I tell Ann I have agreed to his terms.

"It's all he talked about once we had him bandaged up," she says. "Thank you, Freegift."

She kisses me on the cheek, and I am flustered. She leaves the kitchen to sit with Edward as Martine comes in.

"Well?" she says.

"It is agreed to," I tell her. "I will live here and work."

"Good," Martine says, as if she knew what I would do. After all, she does have visions. "Come, walk with me."

Outside, we take the path to Topheny's wigwam. We take a turnoff which leads to a wider spot in the river, where the water flows and tumbles over rocks in a great ferment. There is only a thin line of brightness left in the sky, but it is enough with the sliver of rising moon to light the scene.

"There is something we must do," she says.

"What?" I ask, unsure of our purpose here.

"Look," she says, pointing to the reddish stains on her dress. Edward's blood and the blood of others. "And you." Her hand traces the dried blood on my shirt and brushes my sleeve, her hand coming away covered in gray ash.

"What do you mean?" I ask.

"We must put the past behind us. It clings to us like death. Can you not smell the smoke? And the odor of blood and battle?"

"I fear I will never smell anything else," I say. The blood is like iron in my nostrils and the smoke clings and reeks of acrid ash and gunpowder.

"Then follow me," she says, offering her hand. I take it, and she leads me into the water.

"But we are fully clothed," I say as we step into the river. I do not understand her purpose.

"Everything old and dead must be washed away. Everything."

She is intent upon this, so I shall be as well. I leave on my leather belt, knife, and tomahawk, glad to have the clean waters wash them of their sins.

Up to our knees, and though the night is warm, the water chills me, but Martine keeps on.

"I know this river well," she says. "I played here often as a child." She leads me to a rock where the water gushes and roils around it. We sit in the lee of it, up to our necks in a pool of placid water, loose gravel at our feet. I reach out my hand and the rush of water sprays against it.

Martine's dress billows around her, the color pale in the darkness. She is smiling, lifting her hands in and out of the water, letting it caress and sooth her. I dunk my head, once, then again, and taste the sweetness of the water. I look to Martine. She is smiling, her long black hair floating like a necklace about her throat.

"You sat here as a child and watched the sky, did you not?"

"Yes," she says. "I always knew one day you would be here too."

I tell her of my favorite spot in the forest when I was a boy, a moss-covered granite rock with a cedar tree growing out of a giant crack. I would hide there and dream of fantastic things, but nothing ever so wonderful as this moment. We relax into silence, the stars above our only company.

"What of you, Freegift?" Martine finally says. "Did you find him? Your father?" This last, in a whisper.

"I did," I say. "He appeared nearly as Topheny said in her vision. And, as in yours, he tempted me. But I declined his offers. I would not give you up for the world, Martine."

"He acknowledged you?"

"Yes. He told me he had never known of my birth and spoke of my mother with remembrance. As I said, he bade me go with him. For a turncoat, he behaved with honor."

"Then that is all you need of him, Freegift. You are free of your obligation, to both your mother and your father," she says. It is so simple. I have been a slave twice over, once to Mr. Stoddard and to this quest to seek my father. Now, today, I am finally my own man.

"Yes," I say. "The past is behind us. The future is ours."

Historical Note

Slavery existed in Connecticut since the Pequot War in 1630. The first slaves were Pequots taken as a result of their defeat at the hands of the colonists. A survey in 1678 showed no more than thirty slaves in the state, some African and the others Native American. By 1756, census records showed 3,019 African Americans and 617 Native Americans living in Connecticut, although it did not distinguish between those enslaved and those living free.

In 1774, just before the start of the American Revolution, there are just over 5,000 African Americans in the state. In that same year, the importation of "Indian, Negro or Mulatto Slaves" to Connecticut is banned. In 1784, the "Gradual Emancipation Act" declared that the children of enslaved African Americans born after March 1 of that year were to be granted freedom upon reaching the age of twenty-five. By 1790, free African Americans outnumbered slaves, 2,801 to 2,759. In 1840, there were still seventeen slaves listed in Connecticut. It was not until 1848 that Connecticut became the last New England state to outlaw slavery.

While Freegift Cooper is fictional, it is an established fact that the Arnold family, originally from Norwich, Connecticut, did own slaves. The elder Benedict did sell off his slaves due to financial reversals partially brought on by alcoholism. An advertisement from a New London, Connecticut newspaper in 1760 survives. Benedict Arnold the senior (who died one year later) put up "A likely Negro Boy" of eleven, "to be sold cheap".

A likely NEGRO BOY Eleven years old, understands house work to be sold cheap for ready cash or short credit, by Benedict Arnold, of Norwich,

In the same year, another ad appeared in that newspaper. This one offered three slaves to be sold "for no Fault but being Saucy." While not connected to the Arnold family, this advertisement gave me the idea for the story behind Freegift and his father. As I was writing, I often wondered how this family survived, and if they were sold together or broken apart.

TO BE SOLD, for no Fault but being Saucy, A Likely Negro Man and Woman, with their Female Child of five Weeks old—The Fellow is a good Sailor, able Bodied, and can do all forts of Labour and Farming work : The Wench is good at any fort of Kitchen-work——They are both Young ; Enquire of the Printer.

The decision by Ira Stoddard to emancipate Freegift was one taken by some New England slaveowners who and were inspired by the rhetoric of liberty. The exact numbers are unknown, but it did point to a change in public support for the practice of slavery. For narrative purposes, I have created Freegift's owner as one of these men. However, there were slaveowners of all types in Connecticut and New England, and the treatment of slaves varied greatly.

It was not unknown for northern slaveowners to free elderly or ill slaves, only to avoid supporting them when they were no longer economically productive. This was so widespread that a 1717 law had to be passed in Connecticut forbidding the practice. While different from slavery as practiced on the plantations of the South, enslavement is never "better" in one place than another.

For the background to life in Revolutionary New England, particularly regarding slavery, I am indebted to Allegra di Bonaventura's excellent book, *For Adam's Sake: A Family Saga in Colonial New England*. Using the diaries kept over four decades in the pre-Revolutionary 1700s, she analyzes the inter-twined relationship of two families, bound together by ownership and intimate proximity. It is a remarkable and revealing work.

New London was a haven for privateers during the Revolution. A British ship carrying the personal effects of British General Henry Clinton was taken by a crew of privateers. The actual degree to which this led to Benedict Arnold's deadly raid on New London and Fort Griswold is unknown. Clinton was looking to distract General Washington from the campaign in the South, which was to culminate in the Continental victory at Yorktown.

It was a terrible blow to the area on both sides of the Thames River. Approximately 150 militia and civilians were killed, over one hundred families were left homeless, and all the waterfront buildings in New London were destroyed, along with the goods taken by privateers.

The raid had no material effect on the outcome of the war, and was the last major battle fought in the north.

This book was designed, edited and set by Storyknife Press in Vancouver, WA and printed by CreateSpace in the USA.

The text face is Minion Pro, designed by Robert Slimbach. An enlargement and revision of Slimbach's original Minion type (Adobe,1989), it was inspired by the elegant faces of the late Renaissance.

The interior titles are set in Neris, designed by Eimantas Paškonis. It takes its name from the river Neris that flows through the designer's hometown of Vilnius, Lithuania.

Made in the USA
Columbia, SC
03 November 2022

70418763R00174